Praise for Vicki Del

"Charming, entertaining, and smart."
—*Library Journal* (Starred Review)

"Bestselling crime writer Vicki Delany has penned more than forty hair-raising whodunits—and her latest tale follows suit!" —*Woman's World* (Book Club Selection)

"Find a comfy chair, raise a cup of fragrant, freshly brewed tea to your lips, and settle down for murder and mayhem in a mystery novel set in a tearoom for a delightful form of armchair travel." —*TeaTime Magazine*

"Delany's down-to-earth heroine wraps up this investigation with even more than her customary panache."
—*Kirkus Reviews*

"[A] well-crafted series launch from Delany . . . Fans of culinary cozies will be sure to come back for more."
—*Publishers Weekly*

"Sympathetic characters, a charming setting, the baking frame, and appended recipes distinguish this cozy, which will appeal to fans of Laura Childs' Theodosia Browning tea-shop mysteries and Cleo Coyle's coffeehouse-set series." —*Booklist*

"Delany's latest work can hold its own against anything in the genre being published today."
—*Deadly Diversions*

"It's a crime not to read Delany."
—*London Free Press*

Kensington Books by Vicki Delany

The Tea by the Sea mystery series

Tea & Treachery

Murder in a Teacup

Murder Spills the Tea

Steeped in Malice

Trouble Is Brewing

Steeped in Malice

VICKI DELANY

Kensington Publishing Corp.
www.kensingtonbooks.com

KENSINGTON BOOKS are published by

Kensington Publishing Corp.
900 Third Avenue
New York, NY 10022

All Kensington titles, imprints, and distributed lines are available at special quantity discounts for bulk purchases for sales promotion, premiums, fund-raising, educational, or institutional use.

This book is a work of fiction. Names, characters, businesses, organizations, places, events, and incidents either are the product of the author's imagination or are used fictitiously. Any resemblance to actual persons, living or dead, events, or locales is entirely coincidental.

To the extent that the image or images on the cover of this book depict a person or persons, such person or persons are merely models, and are not intended to portray any character or characters featured in the book.

Special book excerpts or customized printings can also be created to fit specific needs. For details, write or phone the office of the Kensington Sales Manager: Kensington Publishing Corp., 900 Third Avenue, New York, NY 10022. Attn. Sales Department. Phone: 1-800-221-2647.

ISBN: 978-1-4967-3774-8 (ebook)

ISBN: 978-1-4967-3773-1

First Kensington Hardcover Printing: August 2023

First Kensington Trade Paperback Printing: July 2024

10 9 8 7 6 5 4 3 2 1

Printed in the United States of America

To the Hall sisters, always an inspiration

Acknowledgments

As I write this in fall of 2022, it's been a long time since I last enjoyed a traditional afternoon tea. Everything from a global pandemic to family illnesses to a broken foot (not mine!) have prevented me from that treat. Here's hoping Alexandra Delany and I can rectify that soon.

I'd like to particularly thank my good friend Cheryl Freedman for providing early recommendations and suggestions to help make this book better; my agent, Kim Lionetti, for believing in Lily and Tea by the Sea; and the good people at Kensington for turning my imaginary little tearoom into an imaginary reality.

Steeped in Malice

Chapter 1

At Tea by the Sea we take tea seriously. It is, after all, the entire reason for the business. As far as I'm concerned, mugs are for coffee and cups with saucers are for drinking tea, and I do not—shudder—serve tea in mugs. Presentation is a vitally important part of the image of a traditional afternoon tea.

The reason I mention this is that at the moment I was going through the Great Teacup Shortage. Every restaurant has a substantial turnover in crockery. Things get damaged: dropped by staff, chipped in the sink or dishwasher, sometimes even stolen or deliberately broken by customers. Only yesterday a gentlemen picked up his entire tea service—teapot, cup, saucer, side plate—and hurled it against the wall. Point made, anger abated, he paid handsomely for the damage before storming out and leaving his embarrassed family behind to enjoy their own tea selection, as well as the (fortunately) untouched arrangements of scones, sandwiches, and sweets.

"You can't use mugs from the B and B?" Cheryl asked.

"I'm not serving oolong or Darjeeling in coffee mugs!" I replied.

"You might have to," Marybeth said.

"Not gonna happen," I said firmly. Then I added, less firmly, "I hope."

As well as the aforementioned gentleman with a temper, it had been a bad week damage-wise. This is a tearoom, and we set every place with fine china, including when serving from the children's menu. Slightly damaged cups are often relocated to the ancient oak in the center of the garden patio, where they hang from colorful ribbons and make a cheerful display, as well as a pleasant sound on a windy day.

"We'll have to wash faster," I said to MaryBeth and Cheryl, the mother-and-daughter team who were my assistants. The supply of fine china had been getting low over the past couple of busy weeks. I'd put off noticing until now, when I couldn't not notice any longer. Marybeth had run up to Victoria-on-Sea, the B & B owned by my grandmother, Rose Campbell, to get extra cups and plates. She'd returned with not only teacups but coffee mugs. Mugs I refused to use on principle.

I folded and patted scone dough and glanced at the clock on the oven. Four o'clock. Unless we had a rush of customers without reservations, we'd make it to the end of the day.

Marybeth finished arranging food on a three-tiered stand in the traditional arrangement of scones in the middle, sandwiches on the bottom, and desserts on top and carried it into the dining room, while Cheryl scooped tea leaves out of canisters, added them to teapots, poured in hot water from the airpots, and set the individual timers. Different teas require different water temperatures and steeping times, and we adhere closely to their requirements. My English grandmother taught me not to bother making a cup of tea if you aren't going to prepare it as it deserves.

The kitchen smelt of heaven itself—good tea, sugared

pastries, warm spices, and fresh baking straight out of the oven.

"Once these scones are in the oven," I said, "I'll take over washing-up duty. I'll do the cups and saucers that can go into the dishwasher by hand rather than wait for it to finish its cycle. We'll be okay until closing, and I have a plan."

"A plan." Cheryl clapped her hands. "What plan?" I detected a note of sarcasm but decided to ignore it.

"Tomorrow's Wednesday. Usually the quietest day of the week in here. If I stay late tonight and call in reinforcements, I can get enough baking done so I can take the morning off. By fortuitous coincidence a big antique show's starting tomorrow in town. What do you find at antique shows?"

"Teacups?"

"Bingo," I said.

I have to confess that I wasn't making any sort of great sacrifice by going to the North Augusta Antique Fair in search of vintage tea sets. There isn't much I love more in life than fine china, and browsing antique shows is my happy place.

Working alone in my kitchen after everyone has left for the day, making fragrant, delicious things, is also my happy place, and I didn't mind working long into the night, preparing sandwich ingredients and baking cookies, pastries, and scones to have ready to serve tomorrow. I decided not to call in reinforcements, meaning the B & B gardener Simon McCracken, who knows his way around a kitchen, and my friend Bernadette Murphy, who does not. Better, I thought, to save the calling-for-help part for a genuine emergency.

It was coming up to midnight when at last I took off my apron and hairnet, shook out my hair, gave my shoulders and neck a good stretch, checked the stoves were off, turned out the lights, and locked the door of Tea by the Sea, highly satisfied with my night's work.

The antique fair opened at ten o'clock, which suited me perfectly because although I was taking the morning off from the tearoom, I still had my other job to go to.

I was in the B & B kitchen at six, putting the coffee on and getting the breakfasts under way. Luck was on my side this week: we had no overly demanding guests, and everyone came down for breakfast in good time. I was finished by nine and left Edna, the breakfast waitress and kitchen assistant, to clean up. I had enough time to take a mug (not a cup!) of coffee and a slice of coffee cake with me to enjoy an all-too-brief period of relaxation before plunging into the next round of the day's activities.

I live in a small cottage on Victoria-on-Sea property. My front porch overlooks the sparkling waters of Cape Cod Bay. It was a beautiful summer day, full of the promise of heat to come, and I made myself comfortable on the porch, sipping my coffee, munching on my own baking, and watching the activity on the bay, while my labradoodle, Éclair, explored the patch of yard she'd explored a thousand times before. At twenty to ten, I drained my coffee mug, licked my index finger to scoop up the last of the cake crumbs, pushed myself to my feet, and called Éclair to come inside.

Last night, I'd phoned Bernie and asked her if she wanted to join me today. She was waiting on the veranda when I rounded the big old Victorian house the B & B's named after. My grandmother was with her. I hadn't invited Rose to accompany us, as she's anything but an early riser, but I should have known. I'm Rose's granddaughter, but she and Bernie are as thick as the currants in my fruit scones. I might physically take after Rose, fine-boned with blue eyes, pale blond hair, and a complexion that's sometimes called "English Rose," but our personalities are totally opposite. She and Bernie, however—*hotheaded* and *impulsive* are the words that spring to mind. Whereas Rose doesn't look the part, being tiny and demure, Bernie, at near six feet tall with wild red curls and flashing green eyes, does. We've been friends since grade school, and I've always called her The Warrior Princess.

"Are you joining us this morning, Rose?" I asked.

She tapped her way down the veranda steps, needing only a minor amount of help from her pink cane. "I thought a day of antiquing might be pleasant."

"Hope it's okay that I invited her," Bernie said.

I smiled at them both. "Of course it's okay. Now, remember, the purpose of going to this thing is to buy china for the tearoom. If you see me getting out of control, it's your job to stop me."

"As if," Rose muttered. She was dressed for the outing in wide-legged purple pants, a bright yellow T-shirt, and a huge red hat topped with an orange flower. My grandmother is a woman who likes color. Her lips and cheeks were a slash of red and her eyes rimmed by thick black liner.

I went to the garage for Rose's Ford Focus. Bernie helped Rose into the passenger seat, and then she jumped in the back and we set off. Tea by the Sea sits at the top of the B & B driveway, and as we passed I could see Marybeth raising the sun umbrellas prior to setting the patio tables. She turned at the sound of the car engine and gave us a cheerful wave.

"How's the book coming along?" I asked Bernie as I turned onto the main road. Bernie was working on a historical mystery novel. Her progress was, shall we say, sporadic.

"Don't ask," she said.

"That well, eh?"

"That well. Which is why I agreed to come with you today. A change of scenery will do me good. Get the creative juices reenergized and flowing."

"You must be in serious trouble if you think the North Augusta Community Center is a change of scenery."

"I'm thinking more of antiques. Grandfather clocks going *tick tick*, silver tea services, wooden children's toys, dolls with creepy faces. The sort of things my characters would have had around them in their daily lives."

As I'd planned, we arrived as the doors to the community center were opening. I was a woman on a mission, and I wanted to be one of the first to get my choice of what good china was available.

The cavernous room was crammed full of vendors and their wares. People chatted and laughed, called greetings to acquaintances. The air was full of the scent of aging wood and silver polish and dust rising from old fabric, and the bright overhead lights sparkled on crystal glassware, ornate candlesticks, and colorful Tiffany lamps. For the next hour I wandered happily up and down the aisles, trailed by Rose and Bernie, exploring the booths, checking everything out before deciding what I wanted to buy. I was delighted to see a wide range of china, ranging from what would have once been everyday stuff in a middle-class home to some truly lovely pieces. Once I saw what was on offer, I eagerly plunged in. More than tea sets caught my eye, and it took all of my self-control, plus Bernie's strong arm and Rose's disapproving stare, to drag me away from the purchase of a rocking chair; a porcelain chamber pot; a set of silver salt and pepper cellars in a mouse-chewed, velvet-lined box; an antique log-cabin pattern quilt; and two china dolls with painted faces and hand-sewn clothes.

Many of the vendors had tea service items among their wares, but one in particular specialized in fine china, and that's where I spent most of my money. The sign over the booth said D. MCINTOSH, FINE ANTIQUES, CHATHAM, MA. While I checked prices and quality and struggled to decide which pieces to get (I wanted them all), Bernie asked the vendor where she found her stock.

"Estate sales and the like mostly. I drive all over New England in the spring seeking out garage sales. Not many people want this stuff anymore. Used to be when Grandma kicked the bucket"—she peeked at Rose out of the corner of her eyes, realizing that comment was a mite indiscreet, "I mean, when the older generations passed on to their eternal reward, their silver and china would be cherished by their descendants. People these days want modern stuff." She herself was probably in her midthirties, same as Bernie and me. "Unlike your friend," she added, meaning me.

"I own a tearoom in North Augusta." I dug in my purse for my business card and handed it to her. "We serve traditional afternoon tea, and I'm always needing china. Fine china, as you know, is fragile."

She accepted the card and read it. "Tea by the Sea. Nice name. I might pop in while I'm here." She slipped it into her apron pocket.

"How long's this show going to last?" Bernie asked.

"Through the weekend. We break down on Sunday afternoon."

I continued selecting china and putting aside the pieces I liked. There were few full sets, meaning matching teapot, cups, and side plates, but I didn't worry overly much about that. I like to mix and match china to present an interesting and varied tablescape. *When did I start using words like* tablescape? I selected a good variety of things, adding some modern brightly colored or black and white geometrical patterns to the traditional flower designs and pastel colors.

"This is charming." My attention had been drawn to a brown wicker box, cracked and worn with age. The lid was open, displaying a lining of faded blue cloth and a children's tea set. Six teacups with matching saucers and side plates, teapot, milk jug, and sugar bowl. The china was half regular size, white with a thin gold rim, each piece illustrated with a scene from the Peter Rabbit books by Beatrix Potter. I examined it all carefully and found no chips or cracks.

Bernie and Rose came to stand beside me. "Reminds me of my youth," Rose said. "A similar set was in the nursery at Thornecroft Castle." She was referring to the English stately home where she'd been a kitchen maid before (literally) running into my grandfather, Eric Campbell, outside a Halifax tea shop, marrying him, and moving to America. "It also had illustrations from Beatrix Potter, although a different image."

I read the price tag. Two hundred dollars for the set, including the box. "It's a bit on the expensive side for the tearoom."

"Moving right along," Bernie called cheerfully. "Now that you're finished, pay the lady and I'll help you take this lot to the car."

I ignored her. "I do like it, though. Children will love it. American children don't often get to use lovely things designed especially for them."

"Sure they do," Bernie said. "My sister's twins have their own dishes. Nice bright cartoon illustrations."

"Your sister's twins are barely weaned and are still throwing their food at each other. Their dishes are plastic, not fine china."

"Lady Frockmorton," Rose said, "was justifiably proud of her afternoon tea service. She had several sets of china. I wonder what happened to them all."

I balanced one of the teacups in my hand. It was truly lovely, but it was expensive and impractical for children, for whom fine china has a high casualty rate.

"My job here today," Bernie reminded me, "is to supervise your spending, Lily. That's a lot for six teacups."

I reluctantly put the cup down. Sensing she was about to lose the sale, the vendor swooped in. "Because you're buying so much, and because I hope we can do business again, twenty percent off."

"Sold!" I said.

Rose chuckled, and Bernie sighed.

My wallet was light but my car was heavy as we bounced down the road heading back to Tea by the Sea.

Chapter 2

"A lady wants to talk to you, Lily," Cheryl said.

"Did she say what about? I'm busy. If she has a complaint about her food, tell her to write a letter."

"She's not a guest. She hasn't taken a seat, and she asked for you by name."

"A salesperson, then. Take her card." I continued piping swirls of pale-pink buttercream onto miniature vanilla cupcakes. It was one o'clock on Saturday. When the tearoom opened at eleven, people had already been waiting in the garden, and we had a full reservations book for today, including a bus tour of twenty people coming in one hour.

"She didn't look like a salesperson," Cheryl said. "But I'll check."

The rooster timer I use to measure the cooking time of my scones crowed, and I put aside my piping bag, wiped my hands on my apron, and opened the oven door. A wave of heat, along with the delicious scent of perfectly made teatime scones, washed over me. I put the hot tray on the cooling rack and peeked into the second oven to check the condition of the pistachio macaron shells. They were coming along nicely, so I returned my attention to the cupcakes. Once I had them iced, I needed to get to work on the next batch of sandwiches. Cheryl and Marybeth were hopping in the dining room, and I wouldn't be able to rope them into helping in the kitchen.

Cheryl returned. "She says it's a personal matter and it won't take long. To be honest, Lily, she's quite insistent. I think if you don't go out there, she'll—"

"Hi, there. Hope you don't mind my barging in like this." A woman came through the swinging doors. She was in her midthirties, short and slim and quite pretty, with large dark eyes and dyed blond hair cut in a blunt line at her chin, dressed in white capris and a sleeveless blue shirt, with flat white sandals. Her makeup was heavy but well applied, gold hoops were in her ears, and a thin gold necklace disappeared into the gap at the top of her shirt.

"I'm sorry, but this isn't a good time," I said. "We're very busy."

She waved her hand in the air. "Won't be long. I got your name from Darlene McIntosh."

"Who?"

"McIntosh Antiques? You bought some items from her a couple of days ago."

Cheryl was standing next to the fridge, watching. I gave her a nod, telling her I'd take care of this. She slipped past the woman.

"Yes, I did."

"You bought something of mine. I'd like it back."

"Something of yours? You mean it had been stolen?"

"Not exactly."

"I didn't get your name."

"Sorry. I'm Kimberly Smithfield." She gave me a dazzling toothy smile that didn't reach her eyes. "I'm happy to give you what you paid for it."

"This isn't a good time," I said once again. "As I said, we're very busy."

"No problem. I'll take it and leave. A Beatrix Potter tea set in a wicker box."

"I remember the one. If you come back at closing time, I'll see what I can do."

The smile on her face died, and her black-rimmed eyes narrowed. "I don't see why you can't give it to me now."

"I can't give it to you now because I have guests using it."

A large group had arrived not more than fifteen minutes ago. Four adults and five children. The adults had ordered the royal tea, which comes with a glass of prosecco, and for the children I'd been delighted to have the chance to use the Peter Rabbit tea service. Marybeth told me the children had been charmed by it, as had their parents.

"You can explain to them there's been a mistake," my unwelcome visitor said.

I put down the piping bag. "I cannot and I will not. My customers are enjoying their tea. I'm not whipping their cups out from under them."

"Give me the box, then."

"I'm sorry, but I'm not giving you anything. Not right now. I'm not even sure where the box is." That wasn't entirely true: the box was in the pantry. I'd decided to store the Peter Rabbit set in the wicker container it had come in. The pieces would be safe there, and the charm of it appealed to me. "It'll take time to look for the box, and I don't have the time right now."

She took a step toward me. I took a step toward her, not to get closer, but to be in reach of the long, slim, wooden French-style rolling pin on the butcher block in the center of the room where I'd earlier been rolling out pastry. I didn't care for the look in this woman's eyes.

What, I thought, *is her problem?*

She must have read something in my face, and she made an attempt to wipe the hostility off her own face. She made the attempt—but it failed completely. Her smile was forced and her eyes full of anger. "Okay. I'll come back in a little while. Say an hour?"

"I shouldn't have to keep saying this, but it appears I do. I'm busy, and I will be busy all day. I paid a fair price for the tea set. If McIntosh Antiques acquired it illegally, I'm happy to discuss returning it. Did they?"

"Did they what?"

"Acquire the tea set illegally?"

"It was sold to them by a person who had no right to do that."

I thought I understood. A grandparent or great aunt had died, the will was being disputed, and one party had taken the deceased's possessions without waiting for the court's decision. The Peter Rabbit tea set had been important to Kimberly, and she wanted it back.

Fair enough. All she had to do was ask politely, and I'd give it to her without question. But politely didn't seem to be part of her vocabulary. "If you come back at closing time, I'll talk to you about it then."

"I'm not hanging around until five o'clock."

"Sorry, but it's seven tonight." We usually close at five, but Susan Powers, the mayor of North Augusta, had made arrangements for a visit by a special group from a major tour company. They had a fully packed day and couldn't get here until five. I'd been happy to accommodate them. Getting a spot on their tour schedule would be a major boost for the tearoom. Marybeth and Cheryl were happy to stay late and earn the overtime.

"Seven!" Kimberly protested. "The sign on the gate says five."

"Special event tonight."

Her lips tightened and her brows moved even closer together. "Look, I'm not here to make trouble."

"Glad to hear it, because I don't want trouble. I'd like you to leave now, please."

"I want that tea set. I don't even need the dishes, just give me the box."

"As I said, I'll discuss it with you later. When I'm not so busy. Better phone before coming back. My schedule can be erratic."

"I'll give you—"

"Everything okay here?" Cheryl stood in the doorway, her arms laden with a tray piled high with used dishes.

"Can you give Simon a quick call, please, and ask him to come over."

"Got it. We've just seated two tables of four."

"Call Simon first and then get their orders ready."

Cheryl slipped away, heading, I hoped, for the phone in the front vestibule.

The easiest thing to do, by far, would be for me to go into the pantry, get the blasted box, shove it at Kimberly, and tell her I'd leave the dishes on a patio table after closing for her to pick up. That would take far less time than standing here arguing, but my back was up now, and I wasn't going to be bullied by this woman in my own place.

"Does this Simon have the box?" Kimberly asked.

"No."

"Look, I don't want any trouble, but I want what's mine and I want it now."

"It's not yours. It's mine."

She kept her eyes fixed on me and reached into her

purse. I swallowed. Okay, this had gone far enough. I didn't know what she was after in that purse, but I wasn't going to die for a Peter Rabbit tea set.

I picked up my rolling pin and balanced its weight in my hands.

"Everything okay here?" Simon came into the kitchen. Cheryl stood in the doorway behind him, watching. Dressed in his gardening overalls, short sleeved T-shirt, hands coated with good Cape Cod soil, he dominated the space. He was six feet tall, tanned, fair hair streaked by the sun. Broad chested, arms heavily muscled as a result of days spent working in the garden. A pair of gardening sheers was shoved into a chest pocket of his overalls, and heavy, soil-encrusted boots were on his feet. Obviously Cheryl had told him why I needed him, as he'd changed his usual soft, upper middle class English accent into something straight out of a Jack the Ripper movie. He made the three simple words drip with menace.

Kimberly gave me one last long look and then broke eye contact. "Everything's fine, thanks. I'll be back at seven and we can talk then."

My eyes flicked to Simon.

"You can talk to me," he said. "At seven."

"If I'm going to have to stay in this town overnight, do you know a nice hotel?"

"The Seabreeze Motel usually has rooms free." I didn't bother to mention that that was because the Seabreeze Motel was often shut down by the town health department due to their rodent problem.

Kimberly headed for the door. Simon stepped to one side to let her pass, but then she stopped abruptly and slowly turned to face me. "I won't forget how . . . helpful . . . you've been."

There isn't room for a stool in this kitchen, but if there

had been I would have collapsed into it. Cheryl ran after Kimberly, to make sure she left without making a fuss.

"What was that about?" Simon asked.

I put my rolling pin down. My hands were shaking, and I rubbed them rapidly together. I gave Simon a smile of thanks.

I hated having to call on the strong male for help, but as long as I had a big, tough-looking, tough-talking gardener on the premises, I thought I should use him. And it had worked. Rolling pin or not, Kimberly Smithfield was never going to be frightened off by anyone who looks like me.

"I have absolutely no idea," I said. "I bought a tea set at the antique fair the other day, and she stormed in here saying it's hers and demanding I give it back. Estate dispute, I suspect. I don't know why she had to get so hostile, though. I'm happy to sell it to her, but she refused to wait until I had time."

"She's gone," Cheryl said. "You okay, Lily?"

"Yeah, I'm fine. Let's get back to work. What orders do you have?"

"Full afternoon tea for four. Light tea for two and dessert plate for two. Creamy Earl Grey, English Breakfast, and Darjeeling."

"Make that another full afternoon tea for four." Marybeth came through the swinging door. "Mom, can you do me a big pot of English Breakfast while you're at it?"

As if the incident had never happened, Marybeth, Cheryl, and I swung into our rhythm. I took the macaron shells out of the oven, Cheryl prepared the tea, and Marybeth arranged the food trays.

My kitchen is crowded when I'm the only one in it. Simon ducked and dodged and tried, unsuccessfully, to stay out of our way.

"Fridge," Marybeth said.

"Sorry." Simon stepped aside to allow her into the fridge. "Can I see this tea set?" he asked me.

I cleared a space for the macarons to cool. "It cost more than I probably should have spent, but it isn't anything exceptional. The pieces are in use right now, but we should be able to have a peek." I ran my hands under the sink and took off my apron and hairnet.

Tea by the Sea occupies an old stone cottage on the B & B property. Built circa mideighteenth century, about a hundred years before the main house, it had been abandoned and allowed to fall into genteel ruin over the years. The moment I saw it, I knew it would be the perfect setting for the restaurant I wanted to open. I'm a culinary school–trained pastry chef; I've worked in Manhattan bakeries and Michelin-starred restaurants. I came to Cape Cod over the winter to try to help Rose run the B & B she'd bought on a ridiculous whim and to open my dream of a tearoom. I'd repaired the cottage, modernized the kitchen and restrooms, furnished and decorated the dining rooms, and installed a garden oasis on the patio.

I'd taken great care in decorating the restaurant so it resembled a drawing room in an English castle or a grand country home. The walls were a pale peach; the paintings showed English pastoral scenes or horses at the hunt. The chairs were upholstered in peach and sage green, the tables laid with starched and ironed white cloths. An antique bookcase stood against one wall, filled with old volumes, and a chest of drawers painted white displayed many of the tea sets we used. A display area near the hallway to the restrooms showed items we offered for sale: canisters of tea, teapots and cups, and locally made jams and preserves.

The tables were all adorned with fresh flowers. The smaller ones held a single rose in a crystal vase and the larger a full glorious arrangement. All the flowers came from the B & B gardens. I gave Simon kitchen scraps, coffee grounds, and used tea leaves for compost; he and his plants gave me beautiful flowers in return.

The guests who'd been served with the Peter Rabbit tea set had been seated in a small private alcove, large enough for one good-size table. As it was midsummer, the working stone fireplace was occupied by a chipped and faded terracotta pot overflowing with purple lobelia.

"Whale watching," a woman was saying as Simon and I popped our heads around the corner. "Alison Monroe said it was the highlight of their trip."

The sparkling wine was finished, the glasses whisked away, and a few crumbs of food remained. The adults were sipping the last of their tea out of the blue china we use for the royal tea; the children had pushed the Peter Rabbit cups to one side and were getting bored and restless.

"Hi," Simon said. "Checking to see if you need fresh flowers in here."

The woman who'd been talking about whale watching twisted in her seat and gave him a broad smile. "You must be the gardener. Your flowers are absolutely gorgeous, as are the grounds. Thank you so much, everything's been perfect."

"That's what I like to hear," he said, and we backed out of the alcove.

"Don't know what I was expecting," Simon said as we walked back to the kitchen. "But those look like ordinary cups and saucers to me."

"Which they are. That woman didn't seem entirely . . . well-balanced. I suspect the set has some emotional significance she's blown up all out of proportion in her head. I told her to come back at seven. We're open late tonight for the mayor's party. Would you mind . . ."

"Putting in an appearance? Doing my bouncer act? Happy to. Are you going to give her what she's after?"

"Immediately. I should have done so earlier, but she was so annoying she got my hackles up. I could haggle over the price and try to get more than I paid for it, but I can't be bothered. I just want to be rid of her and Peter Rabbit."

Chapter 3

Kimberly Smithfield returned well before seven o'clock. She didn't barge into my kitchen, fortunately for her, but Cheryl told me she'd taken a seat in the garden, where she sat scrolling through her phone, occasionally glancing up from the screen to scowl at the mayor and her party.

"Do you want me to tell her to leave and come back when the guests are gone?" Cheryl asked.

"No. If she's not creating a scene," I said, "let it go."

"Simon's lurking around the corner, watching, waiting to pounce."

"That I'd like to see," Bernie said.

"Let us hope fisticuffs will not be necessary," I said. "Otherwise, how's it going out there?"

"Well," Cheryl said. "Everyone seems happy."

Bernie had called me shortly before five to invite me around to her place for pizza and a bad movie when I finished work. I'd explained about the mayor's group and because we'd had such a busy day, I needed to stay and do some baking after closing. So she brought the pizza for us to eat here when the last of the guests had left. In the meantime, I set her to making sandwiches. As long as she followed my carefully laid out instructions, complete with illustrations, she couldn't go too far wrong. While we worked, I filled her in on the excitement of the afternoon.

"Sounds like the woman has a screw loose," Bernie said.

"Which is why I want Simon as backup."

Bernie'd laughed while Marybeth carefully hand washed the Peter Rabbit dishes and tucked them into their box.

I'd gone all out for the mayor and her guests. It was a lovely evening and we'd set a table on the patio with blue and white china, blue linens, and a fresh Simon-provided arrangement of peach roses and trailing ivy. We served glasses of prosecco in crystal flutes, orange scones with marmalade made by Edna Hartwell, who helps in the B & B in the mornings, roast beef on crostini, salmon on thinly sliced white bread, and curried cucumber pinwheels. The desserts were pistachio macarons, mini coconut cupcakes, lemon squares, and slices of delicate buttery shortbread.

At ten to seven, Cheryl dumped a tray load of dishes onto the counter. "Susan would like you to come out and say hi, Lily."

"She's not going to complain, I hope."

"Nothing like that. As you can see, they ate every scrap and drank all the tea and seemed to be enjoying themselves."

I started to take off my apron, but Bernie said, "Leave it. The hairnet, too. Makes it look like you've been hard at work."

"Which I have."

"Do they want to meet me, too, Cheryl? The hardworking kitchen helper?"

"No," Cheryl said.

The mayor's guests thanked me profusely and said

they'd be recommending Tea by the Sea as a stop on organized tours. Susan looked pleased, and I assumed the rest of the day had gone equally well.

Praise accepted, I headed for the kitchen. Kimberly Smithfield, who'd been sitting at a table near the gate, stood up. "Okay, I'm here now. Give it to me." She didn't bother to keep her voice down, or keep the hostility out of it, and I was conscious of conversation at the table behind me dropping off.

I heard the scrape of Susan's chair. "Is everything all right, Lily?"

"Perfectly fine." I reminded myself that all I wanted was for Kimberly to go away. About the last thing I needed was to get into a brawl, verbal or otherwise, in front of scouts for New England tour companies.

Simon marched through the gate. He'd cleaned himself up after work, shaken the sand out of his hair, and changed into jeans and a close-fitting dark T-shirt. He stopped in front of Kimberly and looked down at her. "Why don't we go inside?"

I led the way into the restaurant. The lights were low, the rooms empty, the tables set for tomorrow.

Kimberly opened her purse. I stepped back, regretting not having my rolling pin on me. Simon straightened his shoulders, but all Kimberly produced was a plain envelope. "I'll give you what you paid for it. One hundred dollars."

I'd paid a hundred and sixty but I wasn't going to argue. It was worth the loss of sixty dollars to be rid of her.

"Marybeth," I said, "will you get the box, please?"

Simon, Kimberly, and I waited in the dining room. From outside, I could hear the sounds of people getting ready to leave, and Cheryl inviting them to come again.

Marybeth was soon back, cradling the wicker box, followed by Bernie. Kimberly threw the envelope at me and snatched the box from Marybeth. To my considerable surprise, she didn't march out of the restaurant with it; she dropped it onto a table and opened it.

"I can assure you," I said, "it's all there."

Even more to my surprise, she grabbed a knife from a place setting and began slashing at the box's lining.

"What are you doing?" Simon asked.

The only knives we lay our tables with are butter knives. Nice for spreading butter and jam or slicing the last lemon square in half to share, not so good for ripping fabric apart. After a couple of useless attempts, Kimberly looked at me, her eyes narrow with anger. She brandished the butter knife in her fist. "Get me a proper knife."

"What? No, I'm not getting you a knife. Take what you want and get out of here."

"You," she said to Bernie. "Get me a decent knife."

"Not likely," Bernie said.

Simon took a penknife out of his pocket. "I've got one, but I'm not handing it over to you. Tell me what you're after and I'll do it."

Kimberly pointed to the inner lid of the box. "What I want is in there."

I stepped closer and peered into the box. The lining was a lovely soft blue silk, the shade of Mother Rabbit's dress and Peter's coat, the color faded with age but otherwise in good condition. The fabric was attached to the box with machine-made stitches of blue thread, except for a couple of inches of white thread sewn in a rough hand.

I ran my fingers across the fabric, and I could feel a slight bulge of paper beneath. "I think what she's after is in here."

Simon threw a question at me. I nodded, telling him to go ahead. He'd also seen the fresher stiches and instead of simply ripping the silk, he cut the thread and folded back a section of the lining.

Kimberly leapt forward and thrust her hand into the hole he'd made. When she pulled it back, she was gripping an unaddressed white envelope. "Got it. Thanks. You can keep the rest. And the money."

"What's that?" I asked.

"None of your business." She ran out of the restaurant.

"Uh," Bernie said. "What just happened here?"

"I have absolutely no idea," I said. "It would appear she isn't as emotionally attached to this children's tea set as I'd thought."

"What do you suppose she was after? A treasure map? Deeds to a long-abandoned gold mine in the jungles of Borneo or a disputed family estate?"

"Maybe we should go after her," Simon said.

I walked to the window and looked out. Kimberly was walking rapidly up the driveway, toward Victoria-on-Sea, not down to the road as I would have expected, but I paid that no mind, assuming she'd left her car in the B & B parking area.

"I've had enough of her," I said, turning away from the window. "Obviously whatever she was after was where she expected it to be, so the box must have been her property at some time. Or that of someone she knows. I have a lovely children's tea set and I'm a hundred dollars richer. Let's leave it. That pizza's calling to me. Simon, staying for pizza?"

"Never need to be asked twice."

Chapter 4

As much as I might have wanted to, I couldn't leave it. Or rather it couldn't leave me. I found myself far more involved in Kimberly Smithfield's affairs than I wanted to be.

Sunday afternoon around one o'clock, Cheryl announced, "A woman's asking to see you."

I looked up from the tart shells I was filling with pastry cream prior to adding fresh raspberries. "You are kidding me, right? Is this a joke?"

"Nope. You'll be happy to hear it's not that strange woman again. This one says you know her. She gave her name as Rachel Morrison."

"Fortyish? Looks like a racehorse?"

Cheryl laughed. "Good description."

"Okay, show her in. First, how're things out front?"

"Marybeth's showing a party of six to a table. They don't have a reservation, but it's so nice outside, most people want to sit on the patio, so we have room to seat the new arrivals inside."

"Thank heavens for nice days."

"You got that right," she said. "While I'm getting your

visitor, can you start a pot of Creamy Earl Grey and one of oolong, please."

I took down the tea canisters and added the leaves to the pots and by the time the fragrant steam was rising, Cheryl was showing my visitor into the kitchen. Rachel crossed the floor in two long strides and wrapped me in a ferocious hug. I hugged her back, less ferociously. I hadn't been aware we were on hugging terms.

Eventually, she let me go, stepped back, and beamed at me. "Lily Roberts! Look at you. And look at this marvelous place. Aren't you the clever one? No one could believe it when we heard you'd run off to small-town Massachusetts, but you've done wonders here. You should have consulted with me, of course. I would have given you my friends' rate, but I'll admit you've done a fine job. Can't go wrong sticking with tradition."

Rachel Morrison was an interior designer specializing in restaurants, and her services were in high demand in the constantly turning-over Manhattan culinary world. Our paths had crossed several times, but I mainly knew her from when she'd done the décor for a new place where I'd been hired as a pastry chef. When I said to Cheryl that Rachel looked like a racehorse I wasn't kidding. And I don't mean that in a bad way. She was tall and thin with long, long legs, a graceful neck, sharp cheekbones, tawny skin, and enormous dark eyes framed by thick lashes. Her black hair hung almost to her waist in a smooth sleek river. She was dressed in pale-blue distressed jeans so tight they showed those legs to perfection and a crisply ironed white shirt under a red linen jacket. Her red sandals had two-inch heels, ensuring that she towered over me, and at five feet eight I'm not short.

"It's nice to see you, Rachel," I said. "I'd love to chat, but as you can see we're in the middle of service."

"It's rather . . . tight . . . in here."

"We manage."

"A tearoom. How charming is that? I saw your hours posted outside. Eleven to five. What a great way to ensure you don't have to work nights." She gave me a broad wink. "Dare I hope you've found some incredibly handsome fisherman to take care of those nonworking nights?"

"This isn't a hobby business, Rachel. I work incredibly hard."

She waved her right hand in the air. The small diamond on her pinky finger caught the light. "I'm sure you do, sweetie."

While we'd been talking, Cheryl and Marybeth slipped in and out of the kitchen. Arranging food on stands, bringing in used dishes, making tea.

The rooster timer crowed and I slipped on my mitts to take a tray of golden scones out of the oven and place it on the counter. Rachel squealed. "Those are absolute perfection. Can I try one?"

Without waiting for me to give her permission, or not, she slid around me and helped herself. She broke the scone in half and examined the flaky interior. "Looks yummy." She popped a piece into her mouth. "Tastes yummy, too." She tossed the rest of the scone into the trash bin. "Do you see Wesley much?"

"Never. You know we broke up, right?"

"So I heard. Such a shame. I thought you two were a good match." Her face twisted. "You were better for him than the horrid woman he's with now."

"No concern of mine." Wesley Schumann was the owner and head chef at the last restaurant I'd worked at, the one designed and decorated by Rachel. Some top chefs can be notoriously temperamental, and Wesley was one of the best. He was starting to move into the celebrity chef category, and the attention was going directly to his head. He came at me one night with a butcher knife. No harm done as his sous chef pulled him off, but at that moment, I decided I'd had enough of both Wesley and the Manhattan restaurant world. I took off my apron, threw it on the counter, and walked out on the spot, leaving cakes in the oven.

"Did you hear he got married?" Rachel asked.

"Married. No, I hadn't heard. My . . . condolences to the lucky woman."

She laughed heartily. "It was a quickie affair, mere weeks, if not days, from meeting to engagement to wedding. Not likely to last long. Never mind that. As much as I'd love to get caught up, I have a reason for stopping by. My sister was here yesterday."

"Your sister? She came for tea?"

"Not for tea. She was after a set of teacups in a wicker box."

"That was your sister? Kimberly Smithfield?"

The expression on Rachel's lovely face turned so sour, it wasn't lovely anymore. "Sadly, yes."

"You don't look much alike."

"Half sister. Same mother. My father was Mom's first husband. He died when I was three, and she married again not long after. The product of that marriage was, I've had reason to regret ever since, Kimberly."

I wiped my hands on my apron and then ran them under the tap. "She was asking about a Peter Rabbit tea set in a wicker box."

"Yup. I've been looking for that box, and so it would appear was my dear sister. I got word she was in North Augusta, and when I heard an antique fair was in town, I figured I should check it out. Bingo."

"I assume someone at McIntosh Antiques gave you this address."

"She did. Did you give Kimmy the box?"

"No."

Rachel grinned. "Great. I'll buy it off you. Five hundred dollars for your trouble."

"She didn't want the box. She only wanted what was sewn inside the lining."

The smile disappeared. "Did she get it?"

"An envelope? Yes."

"You mean to tell me you gave it to her."

"I had no reason not to. It was obviously what she was looking for. She grabbed the envelope and ran. I have to say, she wasn't very nice about it."

Rachel threw up her hands, barely missing clipping Cheryl, attempting to edge around her to get to the tea canisters, across the face. "She's never been very nice. I cannot believe I came this close and you gave it to her."

"Don't blame me. This has nothing to do with me. Now, I'm sorry, but I am very busy and you're in the way." Marybeth was trying to squeeze past Rachel on the other side to grab a stand I'd prepared for her to take into the dining room.

"Did she open it? The envelope?" Rachel asked.

"Not when she was here."

"Did she tell you where she was going next?"

"No."

"Did she plan to stay in town overnight, do you know?"

"She asked me for the name of a nice hotel. I suggested the Seabreeze Motel."

"Is that nice?"

"No, it's a rat-infested dump."

"Cheap, though," Marybeth said.

"She won't stay there, then. My dear sister has no money of her own, but she likes to pretend she does. She might have gone there first, though, to check it out." She whipped her phone out of her pocket. "I'll give you my number, Lily. Call me right away if she comes here again."

I sighed and took out my own phone. We exchanged numbers before Rachel finally left.

Rachel went in search of her sister. I didn't plan to search, yet I found Kimberly first.

She'd taken a room at Victoria-on-Sea Bed and Breakfast.

I finished work that evening at a reasonable time and went home to my dog while it was still daylight. I pay the housekeepers a small amount extra to check on Éclair during the day, refresh her water bowl, and take her for a short walk. Tonight I was home in time to give her dinner and to heat a frozen meal in the microwave for myself. I enjoy cooking, but after a day spent in the tearoom, and having only myself to feed, I don't usually go to much effort.

I took a glass of wine and my unappetizing meal out to my small porch and ate as I watched charter boats returning to harbor after a day fishing or whale watching. A few B & B guests passed, enjoying a stroll along the edge of the bluffs or through our justifiably famous gardens as the sun dipped into the calm waters of the bay.

Dinner finished, I leaned back, stretched out my legs, and sipped my wine, content with my lot. I work hard here, but no harder than I did in Manhattan, trying to build a career in the tough, competitive cooking world. In the city I didn't ever get the opportunity to take a deep breath and the time to simply enjoy being surrounded by peace, quiet, and fabulous views.

As always, I took Éclair for a walk before turning in. She's well enough behaved to be allowed to run free on the property, although I keep the leash with me in case we encounter a guest who's afraid of dogs, and a sharp eye on her if she decides to leave anything on the lawn or in the flower beds. We walked up the driveway to the road, enjoying the warm night air, the gentle sounds of surf rushing to shore, the scent of the gardens, and the glow of the countless stars in the clear skies above. The interior lights of Tea by the Sea were off, but security lights shone over both doors. I turned at the road, called Éclair to come, and we retraced our steps.

We were almost at the house when I heard a car engine approaching, and headlights lit up the path ahead of me. Éclair was sniffing at a rosebush, and I half turned to ensure the driver had seen us. The car was an Audi, with one person inside, going too fast for the narrow driveway. It came to a halt in the guest lot at the side of the house; the driver got out and headed for the stairs leading to the veranda and the front doors.

Kimberly Smithfield herself. I wouldn't have thought a car like that—expensive but not flashy—was her type.

"Good evening," I called. "I'm surprised to see you here."

Her lips tightened and she gave me a poisonous look. "That motel you sent me to is a dump."

"I didn't know your budget."

"Whatever. This place is a B & B, and I had to come back, anyway, to get those papers, so I called and got a room. Do you own it, too?"

"My grandmother does. Are you planning to stay long?"

"What business is that of yours?"

"None personally, but I help my grandmother run the B & B and I need to know about room availability." I make the breakfasts, but that's all I have to do with the day-to-day running of Victoria-on-Sea. I lied to Kimberly, but she didn't deserve anything better from me. If I had my way, I'd kick her out. I doubled that would go down well with the North Augusta Tourist Association, so I held my tongue.

"If you must know, I've taken the room for four nights. The old lady said there's a two-night minimum on weekends, and then I decided why not. It would be fun to stay on. My husband"—she rolled the word around in her mouth and clearly liked the feel of it there—"was supposed to get here this afternoon, but he's been delayed in New York. He has business to do in this area; he's opening a couple of fancy new restaurants nearby. I'm helping him with that. It's going to be so much fun. I figured we might as well stay here as go back to my place. Have a sort of a honeymoon. This place is nice enough. I guess." Éclair sniffed at Kimberly's shoes, but she ignored the dog completely. I believe you can tell a lot about people by the way they interact with friendly animals. Kimberly not only didn't interact, she didn't even seem to notice the happy little pooch.

I hesitated, wondering if I should tell Kimberly her half sister was looking for her. My internal debate died without being resolved when Kimberly turned around and climbed the steps to the veranda without another word. Kimberly had finished talking about herself, so she had nothing more to say. She let herself into the house and the door slammed shut behind her.

"Have it your way," I said to the closed door.

I was unsure whether or not to tell Rachel that Kimberly was staying here. B & B guests do have a reasonable expectation of privacy. If Kimberly wanted her sister to know where she was, she would have told her. As I always do when I have a moral dilemma, I called Bernie as I crawled into bed.

"What's up?" she said when she answered.

"Not much. I hope I'm not disturbing you." Éclair leapt onto the bed and circled several times to make herself comfortable. I stroked the wiry curls. Her fur is mostly a light brown, except for a mocha streak across her belly. Thus her name, in honor of the pastry.

"You are, but that's okay," Bernie said. "I'm working flat out on a vitally important scene between Rose and Tessa that will test the bounds of their friendship to the breaking point." Rose, named for my grandmother, and Tessa were the main characters in the historical mystery novel Bernie had come to the Cape to write. She'd quit her job as a forensic accountant at a major Manhattan law firm, cashed in her savings, and rented a leaking, falling down shack for the summer to give her the time and the space to write. The progress of the book was, to say the least, not going as well as she might have expected. Bernie had trouble settling on one idea and was constantly haring off in all directions.

"Sorry. It's not important. We can talk in the morning."

"You're on the line now. Tessa and Rose can wait. I might be having trouble with the testing friendship scene, as your and my friendship never has been truly tested, has it?"

"There was the time you set your sights on Kyle Burken, but he liked me better."

"That's not the way I remember it, Lily, but we were in fourth grade. Fourth grade doesn't count."

"How about when Madison Greer invited me to her birthday party, but not you."

"Third grade. She didn't like me since I'd scored that goal against her." Bernie's deep laugh came down the line. "One of the highlights of my soccer career as I remember. The only highlight of my short-lived soccer career."

I told Bernie about Rachel's visit to the tearoom, what she'd told me, and that Kimberly had taken a room at my grandmother's B & B. "So, here's the dilemma. Rachel asked me to let her know if Kimberly came back. I'm not sure it's entirely ethical for me to reveal the whereabouts of a B & B guest."

"Sounds like a no-brainer to me. That Kimberly's a piece of work. She made you feel so endangered in your own place, you thought it prudent to call Simon to be on hand in case she tried something. She was rude and didn't even thank you for your time and effort or for giving her what she wanted without making a fuss or overcharging her. This Rachel, on the other hand, is she a friend of yours?"

"I wouldn't say a friend, more an acquaintance or a colleague. We've gone out for drinks a couple of times, but only as part of a business group."

"She didn't tell you what she's after? What's in the envelope?"

"No."

"As much as I'd like to advise you to tell Rachel because we don't like Kimberly, leave it, Lily. You don't want anything to do with them or their problems."

"You're right. None of our business. Good night. I'll let you get back to Rose and Tessa. Oh, if you want to imagine what it's like to have a falling-out with a friend . . . in tenth grade, Johnny D'Angelo kissed me behind the bleachers after football practice."

I hung up to a screech of "He did what!"

Chapter 5

"One extra for breakfast," Edna said. "A guest has only just arrived. Something about not being able to make it last night. He'll have the full English with fried eggs over easy."

I tossed another sausage into the sizzling frying pan. At the B & B a full English breakfast is our advertised specialty: eggs, bacon or sausage, crispy fried potatoes, grilled tomatoes and mushrooms, tinned baked beans, unlimited amounts of toast. A slightly lower-fat, slightly modernized version of the fried breakfast my grandmother made for my grandfather every Sunday of their married life.

We were in full breakfast swing. As well as the full English, we offer a lighter option and always have freshly baked pastries available along with fruit, cereal, and yoghurt. I'd made muffins with local Cape Cod blueberries when I started work at six and then began prep for the hot breakfasts. Edna came in at six thirty, put together the fruit salad, and carried it out to the dining room along with boxes of cereal and containers of yoghurt. When guests began to arrive at seven, I finished the cooked breakfasts to order, and Edna served and cleaned up.

It was five to nine now. Breakfast service finishes at nine, and I was never pleased when someone came in at the last minute expecting to be fed. I prepared the plate for the late arrival, and Edna carried it through along with a side of toast. I took my apron off, hung it on the hook by the door, poured myself a cup of coffee, and folded a warm muffin into a napkin for myself. Seeing the signs of leaving, Éclair stretched and came out from under the kitchen table, stubby tail wagging, ears up. She spends the mornings under the table, hoping I'll drop something tasty. I never do, but her optimism could serve as an inspiration to us all.

Edna came into the kitchen in a rush and dropped her tray on the table. "Lily, you'd better come."

"Why? What's happening?"

"A woman's arrived and she looks like she's spoiling for a fight with some of our guests."

I had a sinking feeling as to who this woman and the guests might be. I told a disappointed Éclair to wait and hurried into the dining room. Only two tables were still occupied. A group of four in the center of the room, lingering over their coffee while they studied maps and guidebooks, and a table for two tucked into a corner by the French doors overlooking the back lawn, the bluffs, and the bay.

As I feared, the intruder was none other than Rachel Morrison. She stood next to the table for two, gesturing wildly and yelling at her half sister. Rachel wasn't her normal well-groomed self today, dressed in yesterday's clothes with no makeup and her hair gathered behind her head in a messy ponytail.

"Is something the matter here?" I asked in a calm voice.

"This is none of your business, Lily," Rachel said.

"I'm afraid it is."

She ignored me and pointed an index finger, the polish

bright red, at her sister. "I know you have it. Lily told me you found it yesterday in the tea chest. Give it to me."

Kimberly picked up her coffee cup and calmly took a sip. By contrast, she was nicely put together and ready for a day's vacation in a pretty yellow sundress. "Sorry. Don't know what you could possibly be talking about, Rachel."

"You can't pull that one on me. Lily, you're a witness, right? You saw Kimberly take the envelope out of the tea chest."

"I, uh . . ."

"I must insist you take your disagreement elsewhere." Rose tapped her way across the room, leaning more heavily on her cane than usual. Playing up the feeble old lady bit to perfection, as she could do when it suited her. Her cat, Robert the Bruce, followed her. He leapt onto an unoccupied table to get a better view of the commotion. The guests at the other table had stopped planning their day to stare, and a couple stood in the doorway, also watching.

"I'm happy to be on my way," Rachel said. "Once I have what's mine."

"Yours?" Kimberly sneered. "Don't be ridiculous."

"I thought you didn't know what I'm talking about."

"Don't play gotcha games with me, big sister. You're no good at it."

Rachel's arm flew out and she knocked the coffee cup out of Kimberly's hand. It hit the wall and shattered in a spray of hot liquid. Kimberly yelped and half rose from her seat in fright.

The man sitting opposite Kimberly, the one with an untouched plate of my full breakfast, leapt to his feet. I'd paid him no notice: my attention had been focused on the sisters, and Rachel had been blocking my view of him.

I noticed him now. None other than Wesley Schumann. My ex-boyfriend. He grabbed Rachel's arm. She yelled at him to let her go and tried to pull away, but he held on. His face was tight and his eyes narrow with an anger I was well acquainted with.

"What are you doing here?" I said, as if that was important at the moment. Rachel told me yesterday Wesley had married a woman she didn't care for. She hadn't mentioned the woman was her own half sister. Proof, if I needed more, that the sisters didn't exactly get on.

He gave me a lazy grin without letting go of Rachel. "Hi, Lily. I heard you'd moved to this town. I hoped I'd run into you."

Rachel snarled at him. "Let go of me or I'll have you charged with assault."

"Do call the police." Kimberly perched on the edge of her chair. "You'll lay charges, won't you, Lily? This"—she sniffed—"*person* has been asked to leave, and she's refusing to do so."

"You can all leave," I said. "Take your squabbles elsewhere."

"I haven't had my breakfast yet." Wesley gave me a wink, so totally inappropriate in the circumstances, I gaped. He was not much taller than me at five feet nine, but his slim hips, broad chest, muscular arms made him look bigger. Wesley was a good-looking man, with sculpted cheekbones, large dark eyes surrounded by thick black lashes, olive complexion, strong jaw, full lips. When it was almost too late, I'd finally noticed the way those lips could curl in a smirk and how the dark eyes turned even darker in an instant before he flew into a rage. "I'm looking forward to it," he said. "I know it'll be good, if Lily cooked it."

Rachel realized his attention had wandered and she pulled her arm free of Wesley's grip. She made another lunge for her sister, her long red fingernails outstretched. "I want that envelope, and I want it now!"

Kimberly jerked backward, trying to take herself out of

Rachel's way, and her chair toppled over. She grabbed at the table in an attempt to keep herself upright, but all she got was a fistful of the starched white tablecloth. She pulled it after her as she fell. The entire table setting hit the floor along with Kimberly and her chair. Glassware shattered, pink and red china cracked, water and coffee spilled. Salt and pepper shakers rolled across the wide-planked wooden floor, and Wesley's full English breakfast spread across the gray and pink rug. Egg yolk and baked beans spattered on the flower-patterned pink wallpaper. The sound of Éclair's frantic barking came from the kitchen, and Robbie arched his back and hissed. The other guests leapt to their feet and scurried for the safety of the doorway.

"We might need assistance here," Edna calmly said into her phone. Rose pounded her cane on the floor and yelled, "Get out of my house."

Rachel dove toward Kimberly, who lay flat on her back, eyes wide with shock, wrapped in a tangle of tablecloth, dishes, food, and chair.

"Get her away from me." Kimberly's legs kicked in the air as she attempted to scramble backward on her rear end. "She's finally lost what's left of her tiny mind."

Wesley grabbed Rachel around the waist and almost jerked her off her feet. "That's enough of that."

Rachel struggled against him, but Wesley was a strong man. He half lifted, half dragged her across the room. Rachel screamed obscenities, but I couldn't tell if they were aimed at Kimberly or at Wesley. Probably both.

"Edna," I said, "see to Kimberly. Rose, stay here." I ran after Wesley and Rachel as Simon burst out of the kitchen, Éclair hot on his heels.

"What's going on?" Simon yelled.

"Come with me," I said.

Wesley manhandled Rachel out of the dining room. Simon followed them, and I came last, shutting the double doors behind us as Éclair scrambled after me. Additional guests stood on the stairs, and others were gathered in the hallway, attracted by the noise.

"Do you need us to call nine-one-one?" someone asked me.

Éclair kept barking. A woman dropped to a crouch next to her, murmuring, "There there, you sweet thing. No need to fuss." The barking turned into small yips as the dog allowed herself to be stroked.

Rachel's face was pure white except for two spots of bright red on her cheeks. Her perfectly sculpted eyebrows were fused together, her eyes bulged, the veins in her neck pulsed, and her lips were twisted into a snarl.

"The police won't be necessary, will they, Rachel?" As I stared at her, some of the rage began to melt from her face. She gave her head an almost imperceptible shake. "No, no cops."

"Wesley," I said, "you can let her go now. Please."

Wesley ignored me and gave Rachel a shake. "Are you crazy?"

"You were asked to let her go, mate," Simon said.

"Rachel?" I said.

She grumbled something noncommittal. Wesley relaxed his grip, and Rachel pulled herself free with a huff.

I let out a long breath. "I suggest you leave. If you have a dispute with your sister—"

"My half sister."

"I truly do not care about your family relationships. You aren't going about resolving your differences in the right way."

"There is no right way, not when dealing with her." All the fight went out of Rachel in a flash. Her eyes filled with tears, and she dropped into the chair behind the reproduction antique desk with a sob. "I would have thought you had better taste in women, Wesley."

"I wouldn't have told you where we're staying if I knew you were going to go crazy," he said.

"You're wasting your time with her. She'll never get it. I'll see to that."

"Like I said"—Wesley twirled his index finger in the air next to his right ear—"craaaa-zy."

"Why don't you go and see if Kimberly's okay?" I suggested.

Wesley looked at me for a long time. Then he smiled and said, "You're looking good, Lily. Really good. I've missed you."

Simon threw me a questioning look.

"That's neither here nor there," I said. "Please go back to the dining room."

He didn't move. Finally, Simon stepped forward. He stood beside me, close but not touching me. "You heard what Lily said, mate. I suggest you do it."

"Who are you, her bodyguard?"

"Her gardener."

Wesley sneered. "In that case . . . wouldn't want to keep you from your roses."

"They'll wait," Simon said.

"Besides," Wesley said, "I haven't had my breakfast yet."

"Kitchen's closed," I said.

He turned his attention back to Rachel. "Stay out of our way. If you know what's good for you." He crossed the hall in quick angry strides, threw open the door, and went into the dining room. Show over, the other guests wandered away. Éclair sniffed at Simon's pant legs, wondering what he'd been up to in the garden.

Rachel's shoulders collapsed, and she put her head in her hands. "Sorry. I guess I overreacted."

"You think?" I said.

She wiped her eyes with her hand. "What room's she in?"

"What?"

"Quick. What's Kimberly's room number? I'll get what I'm after and be out of your hair."

"I'm not telling you that."

"Come on, Lily. Help a girl out."

"That would be unethical, not to mention possibly illegal."

"I won't tell anyone you told me."

"Lily said no," Simon said.

"I have no time to waste. She'll burn it."

"Burn what?" Simon and I chorused.

Before Rachel could answer, the dining room doors opened once again, and Rose and Edna came out, followed by Robbie. "They left via the French doors." Rose turned the full force of her piercing blue eyes on Rachel as she spoke to me. "Do you know these people, Lily?"

"Sadly, yes."

Chapter 6

"Thanks for coming so quickly," I said to Simon.

"Happy to help."

"You weren't hired to work as a security guard, but it seems to be turning out that way."

"Other duties as assigned," he said with a chuckle and a touch to the brim of an imaginary cap.

The guests went back to minding their own business, and Simon and Edna returned to work. I took Rose into the drawing room, followed by Éclair and Robbie, and shut the door. I told Rose about the circumstances of first Kimberly's and then Rachel's visits to Tea by the Sea. I then, briefly and reluctantly, mentioned that Wesley and I had worked together for a while, glossing over the circumstances of our relationship and breakup. When I finished, I said, "They're booked in here for three more nights. You can ask them to leave. If you don't want to do that, I will."

Rose folded her hands together and rested them on her cane. She was dressed for the day in a purple T-shirt and voluminous black pants with a pattern of yellow sunflowers. Her short gray hair was combed into spikes, but she'd been interrupted before applying her makeup. "They didn't do anything to warrant being kicked out, love. It was the other woman, the sister, who caused the trouble."

"Maybe, but I don't trust Rachel to stay away."

"I'll admit, that's a concern. This envelope they're talking about. You don't know what's in it?"

"Not a clue. And I'm not interested enough to speculate."

Rachel didn't return, and the rest of the day passed uneventfully. The beautiful summer weather continued, and Tea by the Sea was satisfyingly busy all day. When I first arrived at work, I worried Wesley would come in under the pretext of wanting to see what I'd done with my own restaurant, but that didn't happen. I put Kimberly and Rachel and their issues out of my mind and got on with my day.

But, once again, fate intervened and the feuding sisters became my problem.

I was curled up on the couch watching a not-very-good cooking show, sipping a cup of tea, Éclair cuddled into my side, when I became aware of an argument raging outside my cottage. Éclair's ears pricked up, but she's used to people wandering around the property at all times, so she didn't bother to rouse herself from the couch to investigate. My cottage sits at the north end of the B & B property, close to the house and overlooking the bluffs. Guests regularly go for a stroll through the gardens or along the cliff edge after dinner or before turning in. All too often people bring their arguments and petty feuds with them, even on vacation. I turned the sound on the TV up and tried to ignore them, but the voices got louder as they came closer. I recognized the high-pitched whine of Kimberly Smithfield. I groaned and said to Éclair, "I wonder who she's arguing with this time. Wesley probably. None of our business."

I couldn't make out what they were saying, which was

just as well, as I didn't want to know. Nor could I tell if the second person was a man or a woman. I should say, Kimberly's voice got louder. The other remained low and indistinct, but I could detect the bite of anger in it. I turned the sound on the TV up another notch.

Kimberly yelled. She sounded so close, I started. "You're out of your mind if you think I'm ever going to agree to that. Don't you dare. Let go of me. I—"

Éclair barked and leapt off the couch. She ran to the window, shoved the drapes aside with her nose, put her paws on the window ledge, and continued barking. On the TV, a woman wept over a sunken soufflé. I cared about neither the soufflé nor Kimberly's problems, but I picked up the remote and turned off the TV. We couldn't have people fighting near bedroom windows and possibly disturbing other guests.

But the voices had stopped, and all was quiet once again, except for Éclair, her barks getting increasingly frantic. She wasn't normally a barker—another thing we can't have on B & B property is a noisy dog. I pushed myself to my feet. Bedtime, anyway. "Shush, you. It's nothing but a couple of guests forgetting they're not at home. They've gone now."

She ran to the door. I washed my teacup and went to brush my teeth and put on my pajamas. When I came out, Éclair was still at the door. Her barking had turned into a low whine, and she'd lowered the front of her body to scratch at the door with her forepaws. She cocked her head at me when I came in. No doubt thinking, and not for the first time, that I'm mighty stupid.

I finally got the message. I scooped my phone off the coffee table. I threw open the door, and Éclair shot out. She flew down the porch steps and ran to the gate, where she continued whining. I stepped onto the porch. I could see no one. The bay was a dark, shifting mass; clouds covered the moon and stars; a handful of lights glowed from behind curtains in some of the bedrooms in the big house and above the door to the kitchen.

A few feet from my gate, an unmoving shape lay on the grass. It looked to be a small bush or a large boulder, but I walked next to or across that spot several times a day, and I knew nothing should be there. I ran through the gate, fumbling for the flashlight app on my phone. I flicked it on and focused the light on the ground.

Kimberly Smithfield lay at my feet, her eyes staring up into the night sky. The neatly cut grass beneath her head glimmered with moisture, and she did not move.

Chapter 7

I leaned on the railing of my porch watching the activity on the lawn. Éclair had been confined to the cottage, and she was letting me know she wasn't happy about that. My grandmother had taken a chair close to me. The night was warm, but she'd wrapped a blanket over her lacy white nightgown. Bright lights illuminated the scene, and guests, most of them in their own nightwear, clustered at the edge of the police circle, also watching.

I had called 911 immediately on finding Kimberly. While waiting for help to arrive, I did what I could to try to revive her, although I feared my attempts were useless. Her eyes were open and unseeing, and I could detect no pulse. Then I was surrounded by men and women in uniform, as well as my grandmother, and politely asked to get out of the way.

"Do you know this woman, Ms. Roberts?" Officer LeBlanc asked me.

"Yes, but not personally. She's a guest here. At the B & B. I heard her arguing with someone not long before I found her. I . . . you might want to call the detectives."

He fingered the radio on his shoulder and turned away.

With a pang, I thought of Wesley. Someone had to tell Wesley. How long had he and Kimberly been married? Not long: she'd earlier said something about a honeymoon. The poor man would be devastated.

Detectives Amy Redmond and Chuck Williams soon arrived. They spoke briefly to the officer protecting the scene from curious onlookers, pulled back the blanket the medics had placed over Kimberly's face, studied her silently, replaced the blanket, and then climbed the steps to my porch.

While waiting for them, I'd been glad of the chance to slip inside and hastily change into yoga pants and a big loose T-shirt. Far more suitable for giving evidence to the authorities and trying to calm guests than in my summer pajamas.

"Good evening," Rose said in her haughtiest English accent. My grandmother had been a Yorkshire kitchen maid in her youth—that upper-class accent didn't come naturally to her, but she employed it on occasion to put people in their place. I really, really wished she wouldn't. She and Detective Williams had butted heads the first time they met, and she now went out of her way to antagonize him.

"You again," Williams replied.

"I fear it is us, once again, Inspector." Rose knew full well Williams did not have the rank of Detective Inspector, as though he were a character in a British mystery novel or TV show. She used it simply because it annoyed him.

"Lily," Redmond said. "We've been told you called this in. Is that right?"

"I did."

"Do you know this woman? Do you know what happened here tonight?"

"She's a B & B guest by the name of Kimberly Smithfield. She's here with her husband, Wesley Schumann. I was inside, watching TV, when I heard her arguing with someone, but I didn't see who that person was. The argument ended . . . abruptly. Éclair, my dog, set up a heck of a fuss, so I came outside to see what was going on. Whoever had been here with Kimberly had gone. I found her"—I pointed—"lying on the ground. Before you ask, I can't identify the person she was with. I can't even say if it was a man or a woman. Kimberly was angry, yelling, but the other person kept their voice low and I had the TV on."

"You say she's here with her husband? Our first order of business is to speak with him. Mrs. Campbell, do you know if he's in their room at the moment?"

"No." Rose began to stand, and I gave her my arm. She smiled her thanks. "Lily called me after she'd called nine-one-one to let me know you people would soon be arriving." She indicated her nightwear. "I was enjoying a last cuppa before bed. I didn't see anyone in the hallway when I left my rooms, or outside. I'll check their registration information for you."

"I can do that," I said. "I should come with you when you speak to her husband, Detective. I have to tell you that although I'd not met Kimberly until this week, I know Wesley. We were . . . coworkers and . . . friends when I lived in Manhattan."

"That won't be necessary," Williams said. "I . . . We'll handle this case ourselves. This time."

"What sort of *friends*?" Redmond asked, ignoring her partner. As she did regularly.

I grimaced. "We were in a relationship."

"When did that end?"

"Over the winter. Before I moved here."

"Then you can come with us."

While we talked, Chuck Williams scowled at Rose, who smiled sweetly in return, but Redmond kept her eyes on the activity on the lawn. An older man carrying a large black bag was allowed to pass the yellow tape. "Detective

Williams," Redmond said. "The pathologist's here. Why don't you check with him while I notify the husband?"

"Yeah, okay." He lumbered away.

Williams was in his late fifties, overweight, a few strands of greasy hair pasted to his scalp, flabby face, loose jowls, tired eyes. Tired of work, tired of life. He'd spent his entire career in North Augusta, and these days he wanted nothing more than to ease his way into retirement. Redmond, in contrast, was in her early thirties, recently arrived on the Cape from Boston. She was tall and lean and muscular with cropped hair dyed bright yellow and possessed of all the energy her partner lacked.

"Can I walk you back to the house?" I asked Rose.

"You may, but I won't be seeking my bed. The guests need to be assured we don't have a serial killer running amok. Perhaps coffee and pastries laid out in the dining room? Detective, will you want refreshments for your people?"

"Eventually, that would be good. Thanks, Mrs. Campbell. But first, I need Lily to come with me." Redmond knew that when Rose offered her guests sustenance, she had no intention of providing it herself. That task would be up to me.

I averted my gaze as we passed the body of Kimberly Smithfield. I hadn't liked the woman much—okay, I'd intensely disliked her—but she didn't deserve to die so young, and at the very beginning of a marriage.

"What's happening?" guests called when they saw us. "Mrs. Campbell, is it safe to stay here?"

"Perfectly safe." Rose had resumed her reassuring salt-of-the-earth, working-class Yorkshire accent. "A private matter. Highly distressing, but no need for you to concern yourself."

"Is that right, Officer?" a woman asked. "Have you caught the person who did it?" Amy Redmond was dressed in slim-fitting dark jeans, a bright red T-shirt under a blue leather jacket, and Converse sneakers. She was young and pretty with several piercings in her right ear and hair cropped so short it stood up. Despite all that, her bearing virtually screamed COP.

"Why do you think someone did it?" she asked. "Do you know what went on here tonight?"

"Well . . . no, but I thought . . . I mean, look at all these police. That means you believe it's murder, right?"

Whispers of murder spread through the crowd of onlookers.

"The authorities respond to any report of a sudden unexpected death," she said. "Don't read too much into it."

"My granddaughter will have the coffee on in a tick," Rose said. "And some of her delicious baking, too. We'll serve it in the dining room."

"Can't say no to that," a man said.

As we rounded the house, I quickly tallied up what baked goods I had on hand. I'd made a second coffee cake on Saturday, which I planned to serve tomorrow. That, plus the few blueberry muffins left over from this morning, would have to do. "Coffee cake's in the freezer," I said to Rose as we rounded the house. "Set the oven to 350 degrees and put it on a baking sheet."

"I'm sure you won't be long, love. My guests need my comforting presence."

"They need the food you've promised them more."

Headlights washed the driveway as a car approached. "That might be him now," I said. "Wesley Schumann." The car was a bright red Mercedes-AMG. It was new since I'd dated Wesley, but perfect for him—expensive, ostentatious, impractical.

His head turned as he passed the police cars and vans clustered at the side of the house, blue and red lights breaking the night. He parked the car and jumped out. Redmond and I headed toward him, while Rose went into the house, followed by most of the guests. A few hung back, perhaps hoping Redmond was about to bring down the "suspect" and they could capture the drama on their phones.

"Lily? What's going on?" Wesley's handsome face was a picture of confusion, accented by a touch of concern. His eyes flicked to Redmond. "Who are you?"

"Detective Amy Redmond. North Augusta PD." She flashed her badge. "I wonder if I might have a few words. Are you Mr. Wesley Schumann?"

"I am. What's happening? Lily?" He glanced behind me. "Has Rachel been here again?"

"Who's Rachel?" Redmond asked.

"My sister-in-law. Rachel Morrison. She and my wife had a minor disagreement earlier today."

"Is that so? Why don't we go inside and talk in some privacy? Lily, can we use the drawing room again?"

"Of course." I touched Wesley's arm lightly. I looked into his face. He blinked, and then the edges of his mouth turned up. He put his hand over mine. "Lily." His voice was low and soft, full of something I didn't want to understand. I pulled my hand away, turned around quickly, and led the way into the house.

More guests had gathered in the front hall. "I don't see Kimberly," Wesley said. "Is she okay, Lily?"

I said nothing as I shut the door to the drawing room behind us.

"Please," Redmond said, "have a seat, Mr. Schumann."

"I don't want to sit. I want to know what's going on." He spread his legs and folded his arms over his chest.

Redmond's eyes flicked to me, telling me to go ahead. I said, "I'm so very very sorry to have to tell you this, Wesley, but Kimberly died earlier tonight."

He threw up his hands. "Died? What do you mean she died? Don't be ridiculous, Lily. Did Lily tell you she and I were together until earlier this year, Detective? If you must know, she dumped me, out of the blue, and ran off to this provincial backwater. But I got over it. It wasn't hard. I'm sorry, Lily, but I'm married to Kimberly now, and I'm not amused by your joke."

"She's not joking, sir," Redmond said. "Your wife suffered a fall and appears to have struck her head."

Comprehension slowly dawned, and Wesley dropped into Rose's favorite wingback chair. "That's . . . that's . . ."

"I am sorry," Redmond said.

"Are you sure? I mean, where is she now? Can I see her? Did anyone see what happened?"

"At the moment the scene is secure pending our investigation. Your wife will be taken to the North Augusta Hospital in due course. If you want to go to your room and rest, I'll call you when you can see her."

"I don't want to go to my room and rest. I want to do something."

"You and your wife didn't go out together tonight?" Redmond said. "Why is that?"

"I had a business dinner. Kimmy's bored by business. We're on sort of a honeymoon, but we're calling it a working honeymoon."

"What type of business are you in?"

"Restaurants. I'm a chef. I own a Michelin-starred restaurant in Manhattan, and I'm interested in expanding onto the Cape. My wife is . . . I mean Kimmy was from this area and we intend . . . intended to spend much of our time here."

"From this area? You mean North Augusta?"

"Her family home's in Chatham, although she's been living in New York City for the past couple of years."

"My partner and I will need to talk to you in more detail later, but first I need to check what's happening outside. I trust you'll remain here tonight?"

Wesley nodded. "Nowhere to go."

"Do you have anyone you can call?" I asked. "To come and be with you?"

"How about you, Lily?"

"Me? I don't think so. I'm needed in the kitchen."

"If you're cooking, I'll help."

"I'm reheating. Rachel needs to know about this. Can you call her?"

"Rachel?" he said. "You haven't told me exactly what happened, Detective. If you have reason to believe my wife was murdered, you won't have far to look."

"Meaning?" Redmond asked.

"Kimmy and Rachel had a falling-out recently. A falling-out that climaxed in Rachel physically attacking Kimberly only this morning. Lily herself was a witness to that."

Redmond glanced at me, and I said, "It wasn't much of a deal."

"Only because I intervened and physically dragged Rachel away," Wesley said. "I'd say she was mad enough to kill. I've known Rachel longer than I have Kimberly, Detective. It was through Rachel that Kimmy and I met in the first place. Rachel's notorious for her temper."

That was news to me, but I said nothing. I didn't know her all that well, not at all on a personal level, but I did know she had a solid professional reputation.

"What was this argument about?" Redmond asked.

"Money. Parental favoritism. All the usual stuff. A lifetime of grievances. They have different surnames because they have different fathers. Rachel's the elder sister and she's always resented Kimberly. That resentment only increased as they got older. Their mother died quite recently, and this morning all the animosity between the two of them came to the boil. Rachel's not the sort to back down graciously. Being thrown out of a public place would have only made her angrier. If someone killed my wife, Detective, you don't have to look far to find out who did it."

"Do you know where your wife's sister is staying?"

"No, I don't. Their family home's in Chatham, but, as I said, things aren't good between them, so I don't think Rachel would have gone there. Then again, she might have, knowing Kimmy was going to be away for a couple of days."

"Kimberly has occupancy of the family home, but the elder sister does not?"

"Their mother's will is . . . complicated."

"Do you have her phone number?"

"Yeah, I do. We've done business together in the past." His eyes widened and his face crumbled. "Oh, my gosh. I've just realized. It was me who told Rachel that we're staying here. I didn't realize how much she had it in for Kimberly, so when she called yesterday and asked where Kimmy was, I thought nothing of telling her. I should have realized that if Kimmy hadn't told her, it was because she didn't want Rachel to know."

"You can't blame yourself," I said. "We don't know if Rachel had anything to do with . . . whatever."

"Thanks, Lily, but I do blame myself. I knew they didn't get on, but I never realized how far Rachel would go."

"Number, please," Redmond said.

He gave it to her and she walked toward the windows and placed the call with her back to us. Wesley looked at me. I couldn't read the expression on his face, but I didn't see a lot of sorrow there. That, perhaps, was still to come.

Rachel's phone rang for a long time before going to voice

mail. Redmond introduced herself and said she needed Rachel to contact her as soon as possible. When she'd hung up, she said, "Lily, you can make that coffee now. Mr. Schumann, what room are you in?"

"Two-oh-two. But if Lily's baking, I'll stay here." He gave me a quick wink that I considered totally inappropriate. But, I reminded myself, we all grieve in our own way. Flirting came as naturally to Wesley as breathing, and the death of his wife might not have fully sunk in yet.

Chapter 8

I didn't get to bed that night. I served refreshments to guests who were more interested in police activity than enjoying a good night's sleep. Wesley attempted to follow me into the kitchen, but I chased him off, and he gave in without too much of a fuss, saying he had calls to make.

As well as serving our guests, I laid out a giant pot of coffee on the veranda, along with some of the muffins, and invited the police to help themselves. Which they did, eagerly. With all the activity outside my bedroom windows I didn't even try to get some sleep. I felt it would be somehow disrespectful to crawl into my comfy bed while Kimberly lay in the dark. Éclair had calmed down, and she was taking the presence of all these people in stride, so we sat together on the porch, watching and thinking. That is, I was thinking. The dog soon fell asleep. Her legs moved as she dreamed she was chasing squirrels or romping along the stony beach. Redmond and Williams came and went. I assumed they were interviewing Wesley and other B & B guests, but I was not invited to listen in. I didn't even try to sneak into the secret room next to the drawing room and eavesdrop. I could see no reason Kimberly's death would threaten Rose and my businesses, and thus no reason to get involved. Word that a death (another death) had happened on our property wasn't good, but Victoria-on-Sea and Tea by the Sea had weathered such storms before and business continued to boom.

It was almost time for me to head into to the kitchen to start the breakfasts, when Kimberly was finally taken away. I rose to my feet to watch her go, and I hushed Éclair into a respectful silence.

Neither Redmond nor Williams had spoken to me again, and I didn't see Wesley. Redmond hadn't asked me if I knew Rachel. I should have voluntarily told her what had occurred when Rachel came to the tearoom in search of her sister, but something held me back. Maybe, I told myself, it would be better for Redmond to hear Rachel's side of the story first.

"Twitter is abuzz," Edna said as she tied her apron strings behind her.

"You heard what happened here last night?" I used an ice cream scoop to drop thick muffin batter dotted with fresh blueberries into tins. As I hadn't slept last night, I hadn't needed to get up early to replace the baking used last night. A tray of apple and cinnamon muffins were already in the oven, and the sweet scent, mixed with coffee freshly brewing in the pot, filled the small kitchen.

"Of course I heard, but no specific details." Edna's husband, Frank, is the editor in chief of the *North Augusta Times*. "What did happen?" She laid a bunch of bananas on the cutting board and rummaged in the fridge for melons and pears.

The door flew open and Bernie rushed in. She was dressed in baggy sweatpants and a T-shirt in need of a wash and hadn't taken the time to comb her hair. "Is it true? You've had another suspicious death here?"

"You're up early," I said.

"I had a good writing day yesterday and wanted to get an early start. I'm thinking of turning Rose's interfering, stuck-up blue blood brother into the killer. What do you think?"

"That's not in your outline."

Bernie helped herself to a cup of coffee. "Never mind the outline. A writer has to go where inspiration leads her."

I said nothing. Bernie's problem was that inspiration led her *everywhere*. And often at the same time.

"As long as you're here." Edna pushed the cutting board, knife, and big glass bowl across the table. "You can work. Make the fruit salad. But first, enough of your Rose character and her troubles. The Smithfields are a well-known family on the Cape. They've been here for generations and have tons of money, although rumor says they haven't been doing so well lately. They own a big house and property near Chatham, as I recall. Natural enough that Kimberly's death would be major news, among the locals, anyway. Can you tell us what happened?"

"I don't know what happened," I said. "I heard people arguing outside my cottage last night, and when I went outside to see what was going on, I found Kimberly. Dead. Before you ask, I didn't see or hear who she'd been arguing with."

"Whom," Bernie corrected. "Do you think it was her sister? She has a screw loose. They both do. Did."

"I don't know, and I'm not speculating. Wesley told the police about the fight between them yesterday, and the detectives will take it from there."

"What fight? Wesley? You can't possibly mean Wesley Schumann?"

"Sadly, I do. He's staying here, and not only that, he recently became Mr. Kimberly Smithfield. Very recently. They were on what he called a working honeymoon."

"I didn't see that one coming," Bernie said.

"Who's Wesley Schumann?" Edna asked.

"Lily's ex. A truly nasty man, in my humble opinion. Fabulously handsome, and thus proof that you can't tell a book—or a man—by its cover. He's a big-name chef, and thus also proof that not all men who cook are a good catch. I never liked him, but I never let on how I felt to Lily while they were together."

"You never stopped telling me you didn't like him," I said.

"Perhaps I wasn't as subtle as I thought I was. I celebrated the day you left him. Jerk."

I smiled at her. Maybe I'd stayed with Wesley longer than I should have precisely because Bernie was so dead set against him. But I finally saw the light. Sometimes our closest friends know us better than we do ourselves.

"Mornin', all." Simon headed directly for the coffeepot. "You're not usually here this early, Bernie."

"Exciting things have been happening. Tragic, yet exciting. Did you hear?"

"Hear what?"

"That fruit isn't going to slice itself, Bernadette," Edna said.

Bernie picked up the knife and waved it in Simon's direction. "Lily was about to tell us all about it."

"You remember the fight in the dining room yesterday at breakfast?" I asked.

"How could I forget?" He plucked the knife out of Bernie's hand before she could do damage to more than the fruit, sat down, and began slicing bananas.

"One of the participants in that kerfuffle died last night," I said. "The police suspect murder, and I'm inclined to agree. I was an auditory witness."

"What does that mean?"

"I overheard part of the disagreement, but I didn't see it,

nor can I say who else was involved." I went on to explain what had happened, ending with Wesley accusing Rachel of killing her sister.

"You attract trouble everywhere you go, Lily Roberts," Edna said.

"That's only since I arrived in North Augusta. I used to live a calm, uneventful life."

"As a pastry chef at Wesley Schumann's restaurant. Not," Bernie said.

"What's the name of that restaurant?" Simon said.

"Are you thinking of going there?" Bernie asked. "The food's nowhere near as good as its reputation suggests. I figured he bribed the reviewers." She winked at me. "Although the desserts were mighty good."

"I'm wanting to know, so I can avoid it. If I'm ever in Manhattan wanting to dine at a Michelin-starred place. Which, I'll admit, is unlikely."

"West Steak House. West, from Wesley, and steak because that's his specialty, although he was starting to feature more seafood, as I recall," Bernie said.

"Which might be why he's wanting to open his new place, or places, on the Cape," I said. "Concentrate on the seafood part of the menu."

Éclair had taken her usual spot beneath the kitchen table, and she leapt to her feet. A fraction of a second later, I heard the *tap-tap* of Rose's cane in the hallway. The door opened and Robert the Bruce flew across the room to land on the table next to Simon. I picked the beast up and put him on the floor. That a cat was in residence, and had the run of the place, was prominently mentioned on all our advertising and booking information. Nevertheless, I didn't want cat hair in the fruit salad. I didn't want cat hair anywhere, but I'd lost the argument about allowing Robbie into the kitchen the day I arrived.

Robbie snarled at Éclair; Éclair yipped in response.

The cat, as could be expected, was followed by Rose, still in her nightwear. She dropped into a chair, and Robbie leapt into her lap. He might have given me a supercilious smirk as he did so.

"You're up early," Edna, Simon, and Bernie said at the same time. Then they laughed.

"I didn't sleep well," Rose said. "I often don't these days. Last night in particular with all the comings and goings. Any developments, love?"

"Not that I've heard," I said.

"Is the tea ready, Edna?" Rose asked.

"I have no idea, Rose, as I never make tea unless one of our guests requests it and so far today, no one has."

Rose and Edna engaged in a never-ending, ongoing battle. Rose had never had servants in all her life—in her youth she'd been one—and she wanted to enjoy being the boss of Edna now. Edna had taken the job of B & B kitchen assistant to help out her bridge club companion, Rose, mainly because she was a high-energy woman and she wanted something to do in her retirement along with her many charity gigs. She was *my* assistant, she maintained, not Rose's lady's maid.

Neither of them would ever give an inch, so I took it upon myself to fill the kettle. Then, muffins in the oven, I began tossing ingredients into the blender to make gluten-free pancakes. Every evening before retiring, Rose leaves me a note telling me the number of guests we have and if any have special dietary requirements. Last night's note said we had two gluten-intolerant guests this morning.

"Do you think Kimberly's death has something to do with that envelope they were both so desperate to get their hands on?" Simon asked.

"What envelope?" Rose and Edna asked.

I quickly gave them the bare bones of the story. "I don't

know, and I don't want to speculate. This has nothing to do with us. I intend to keep well out of it."

Bernie and Rose exchanged a look.

"*We* will keep well out of it," I said. "That includes you two."

"Whatever you say, love," Rose said. "Edna, I trust you'll keep us informed as to what the members of the fourth estate learn. In the meantime, I'll have my tea now."

"Kettle's starting to boil." Edna carried the boxes of cereal and individual containers of yoghurt into the dining room. I poured the hot water over tea bags in a sturdy brown betty pot and left it to steep. In true Yorkshire working-class fashion, Rose likes her tea strong enough to support a spoon. Along with an excessively large amount of sugar. "I mean it, Rose. We are not getting involved."

She sighed and continued stroking Robbie. "Probably for the best."

"I agree with Lily," Bernie said. "This time. The less you have to do with Wesley Schumann, the better."

"I'm not about to be tempted to go to back to him," I said.

"Glad to hear it."

"Go back to him? You mean to work at that restaurant?" Simon asked.

"Surely not," Rose added.

"Fear not," I said. "I'm not looking for another job." I was saved by a ringing in my apron pocket from having to tell them I meant go back to him relationship-wise. I pulled my phone out and saw Amy Redmond's number. I lifted my eyebrows and formed my mouth into a round O for the benefit of the people watching me as I answered. "Good morning, Detective."

"Lily. I haven't been able to get in touch with Rachel Morrison. She's not answering her phone at the number

Mr. Schumann gave me. We have people calling the hotels and motels this morning, and officers watching for her plates. If she contacts you, I need to know about it."

"No reason she should."

"Perhaps not, but Mr. Schumann told me you and she were friends when you lived in Manhattan."

"Not friends. Business acquaintances."

"Irrelevant. I'm asking you to let me know if you hear from her, or if she returns to your place under the pretext of wanting another talk with her sister. Will you tell your grandmother that also?"

"I will."

"Thanks. I'll be around later to talk more about what you might have seen or heard last night, but I have some leads to follow up this morning first."

"Has it been confirmed that Kimberly was murdered?"

She didn't bother to say good-bye before hanging up.

Chapter 9

Breakfast finished in good time, and I was able to get away promptly at nine. Edna told me Wesley had not come in. Rose went to her suite to get ready for the day, and Bernie headed back to the world of "her" Rose and Tessa. I didn't feel much like sitting on my porch watching the bay come alive this morning, so I took Éclair home, told her to have a nice day, and headed up to the tearoom to get an early start. I felt a touch of guilt at the look on the dog's face when she realized she wasn't going to get her morning romp in the yard, but I gave her an enthusiastic scratch behind the ears in an attempt to compensate and promised an extra-long walk this evening. She didn't look entirely placated.

I let myself into Tea by the Sea via the front door and walked through the dining room, flicking on lights and checking that everything was as it should be. It was dim and quiet and so very peaceful. The tables were laid, everything ready for a busy day. The calm before the storm.

Afternoon tea, as invented, so the story goes, by Anna, Duchess of Bedford in 1840, and eagerly enjoyed in the twenty-first century, is not an everyday occurrence for most people. It's a treat, an indulgence. Something to be enjoyed as a special outing when on vacation or to mark a birthday or anniversary. It's not cheap, but it doesn't attempt to be. Here at Tea by the Sea, the tables are set with fine china, polished silverware, ironed linens, and fresh flowers. The food is prepared by hand, from scratch every time, using the freshest available local ingredients. The tea selection is individualized and sourced from tea specialists, not bought in bags of a couple of hundred at the supermarket. When I first had the idea of opening my own restaurant specializing in afternoon tea, this was exactly what I'd dreamed of. I was so proud of it.

We cater mostly to tourists, and I knew the off-season months would prove challenging. I might have to expand the menu or even start catering (shudder), but I'd cross that bridge when I got to it.

I went into the kitchen, put on my apron and hairnet, and began getting out mixing bowls and ingredients. As always, I made scones first. We can run out of most other things, except for tea, but at a tearoom we must never run out of scones.

I had a batch of currant scones in the oven and was folding the dough to make plain ones when someone began rapping on the kitchen door. Thinking Cheryl had forgotten her keys, I fumbled to unlock the door and open it with sticky hands.

Rachel Morrison stumbled in.

"What on earth are you doing here?" I asked.

"Lily. Lily. You have to help me." Her long hair was tucked into an enormous straw sun hat, and huge sunglasses hid her expressive eyes. She held out both her hands to me, palms up. I glanced at my own, covered in scone dough, and ran for the sink. I washed my hands and dried them on a dishcloth while I kept one eye on Rachel. She pulled off her hat, propped the glasses onto the top of her head, and leaned against the butcher block in the center of the room, breathing deeply. "Thank heavens you're here."

"Never mind me, I belong here. What are you doing here?"

"Do you have any coffee? I'm desperate, but I've been afraid to go into a coffee shop."

Even in a tearoom we have to have coffee on the menu. Hard to believe, I know, but some people don't care for tea. I began to prepare a pot.

"It smells nice in here," Rachel said. "Sugar and spice and everything nice."

"Do you know the police are looking for you?" I asked.

She nodded.

"Do you know why?"

"I'm guessing it's because they think I killed Kimberly."

"Did you?"

"No. I didn't even know, not for sure, it was about Kimberly until now. You just told me, Lily."

"Please don't play games with me." I'd been trapped in this kitchen before by a killer, so I like to think I've developed an instinct for that sort of thing. Maybe I'm naive, but I felt no danger from Rachel. "Would you like something to eat? I can offer you a sandwich."

"Coffee'll be fine."

"How did you hear?"

"Twitter, of course. Not that Kimberly's name was mentioned, but it says a woman on her honeymoon, guest at a North Augusta B & B. Some indeterminant, grainy pictures taken with a phone of police moving around in the dark. I might not have thought anything of that, plenty of B & Bs in North Augusta, and plenty of honeymooners, but I got a call, a bunch of calls, from some detective demanding I call her back. *Immediately*. I put two and two together and . . . here I am. I noticed some sort of yellow tape fluttering in the wind at the side of your property, but I don't see any cops."

"They'll be back."

I served the coffee, took one for myself, and put cream and sugar on the butcher block. Rachel picked up her mug with a muttered, "Thanks," and took a long drink. She wrapped her hands around the mug and studied my face. I said nothing. "I need your help," she said at last.

"The only help I'm going to give you is to tell you to call Detective Redmond. She's a good cop. Tough but fair."

"Not yet. I need to know what's going on."

"The police aren't saying Kimberly was murdered."

"What else could it be? She was young, healthy. She had a pure black heart, but only figuratively speaking, and figuratively never killed anyone. More's the pity."

The rooster timer crowed and I took the scones out of the oven. I then returned my attention to finishing the next batch. "My assistants will be here soon, followed by hordes, I hope, of hungry people knocking down my doors. You can't stay here, and I wouldn't hide you, anyway."

Rachel sighed. She studied the coffee in her mug. "Okay. Not your problem, right?"

I said nothing. I was about to get out my phone and call Redmond, when Rachel said, "You probably want to know what all that stuff about the Peter Rabbit tea set was about."

I have to admit, I was curious. I decided to delay the phone call. "If you want to tell me."

"No reason not to. As I told you, my father died when I was very young, and my mother married Julian Smithfield. Shortly thereafter they had Kimberly, the bane of my existence. A couple of years after that they had a son, Stephen. My mother loved all her children equally, but Julian and I—I never called him *Dad*—never got on. I suspect I reminded him of my father, and that my father was my mother's one true love. My father was tall and handsome, Julian short and dumpy and a lot older than Mom, so maybe he was jealous of a dead man and took it out on his daughter—meaning me. Hard to say. Mom and Julian didn't have a good marriage, far as a kid can tell, anyway. We were provided with everything we could want, and there was never any abuse, to us or to my mother, but it wasn't a loving house to grow up in. It might not be a real memory, but I believe I remember more laughter, more affection, between Mom and my dad than between her and Julian. That's my sob story, anyway."

I rolled and folded scone dough, patted it into a thick rectangle, and then reached for my cutter. One thing about being a baker—I can work and listen at the same time.

"When my real dad was alive we lived in Boston, but when Mom and Julian married, we moved to Cape Cod. Julian had a lot of money. Family money, most of which was made by his grandfather way back when. I never wanted for material things; I was sent to private schools, had horseback riding and sailing lessons, my college tuition was fully paid for. My mother loved me, and I always knew that, but things were tense between me and Julian, even when I was a little kid. Fast forward to now. Julian died five years ago. Heart attack. He dropped dead on the golf course. All his money went to my mom, as it should have. Life continued. My half brother, Stephen, was always in trouble of one sort or another. Rich-boy problems: drugs, running with a bad crowd, no job to speak of, no ambition. Too much money. Before his father died, Stephen went to California to try to make it as a musician. Nothing came of that, and I didn't have any contact with him until our mother died and he came home for the funeral. That was two months ago."

"I'm sorry."

"Thanks. Mom was ill for a long time. Pretty much confined to the house in her last year. Shortly after Julian died, Mom rewrote her will. She shared it with us, so I know what it said. The bulk of the estate was left to Kimberly and me equally, after making a small but adequate provision for Stephen and the usual bequests for longtime staff such as the gardener and the housekeeper. Stephen got enough to provide him with a modest income, and no more. Mom told us at the time that Stephen would be likely to contest the will, and she was sorry if it caused problems for us, but she believed he simply couldn't handle money."

"And that's what happened?"

Rachel laughed without mirth. "No. Stephen came to Mom's funeral. He looked good and he seemed good. He says he's off the drugs, he's given up trying to make it as a musician, and he's got a job he likes working as a salesclerk in a super high-end women's clothing shop in LA. He always loved fashion. He told me he'd done some bad things when he was on the drugs, and Mom was right to cut him off. But . . . it turns out I've been cut off, too."

"I don't understand. You just said—"

"Mom rewrote her will again about three months before she died. I didn't know about it, and I didn't see it until after her death. She left everything to Kimberly, except for the same small bequest to Stephen. Nothing to me. Zippo."

"Why?"

"Because her mind was failing and Kimberly told her to. Why else? I was in France for several months around that time. I didn't want to go, not with Mom being sick, but it was a huge commission for a restaurant that was going to be the talk of the Paris dining scene, and how could I pass that up? Kimberly must have convinced Mom that it was Julian's family money, and I am not part of Julian's family.

Therefore, I deserve nothing. I wouldn't put it past her to have told Mom I'd run off to France on a whim, not caring about her."

"Is this will legal?"

"Perfectly legal. The family lawyer was called to the house. The will was witnessed by our housekeeper and the lawyer's assistant."

"You must have been furious."

"Less than you'd think. Do I want money? Who doesn't? Do I want anything that had been Julian's? Not really. I make a good living, Lily. A very good living, and I love everything about what I do. Although it rankled, badly, to think Mom thought poorly of me at the end."

"Did you see her before she died?"

"Yes, I got back in time. You'd have liked my mom, Lily. She loved her afternoon tea, sitting in her chair by the window in the sunshine." Tears formed in Rachel's eyes. "At the end she went downhill quickly. She might not have even remembered rewriting the will." She wiped angrily at the tears. "More than that, it's knowing Kimberly pulled a fast one on me, manipulated our mother against me, that really hurts. I decided to put her and the memory of her odious father behind me for good and get on with my life."

"Obviously that didn't happen."

"No. Turns out Mom realized what she'd done and had a change of heart. She called in Helen, that's Helen Chambers, the housekeeper, and said she wanted to write another will. This time with me back in it. Helen called the lawyer, but he was away on vacation. Mom pointed out that she had no time to waste, so she handwrote a new will with Helen's help. It was witnessed by the gardener's assistant and the private nurse."

"And?"

"The new will disappeared. Couldn't be found after Mom died. Kimberly can't deny there was a new will, because it was witnessed, but she claims Mom must have changed her mind and tossed it in the trash. A will that can't be produced in court has no legal validity, Lily. Mom wrote it out herself, and after being witnessed, she put it in an envelope and sealed it. The witnesses only signed the last page, so they can't testify what it said, and Helen says Mom didn't tell her specifically what she was writing."

"It was in the Peter Rabbit tea chest."

"Yup. I decided it wasn't worth my time and stress to contest the earlier will, if that was Mom's wish. The second will, I guess we should call it. But I can't let myself be out-and-out cheated by Kimberly. We weren't speaking by then, but she agreed to let me come around to the house—now her house, as she informed me—to pack up the few of Mom's possessions I'd like to keep. The only thing I really wanted was the Peter Rabbit tea chest. It had been Mom's when she was a little girl, and some of my earliest memories are of us having tea parties when we lived in Boston and my dad was still alive." Rachel wiped at her eyes again, dug into her pocket, pulled out a tissue, and lustily blew her nose. I finished arranging the scones on the hot baking sheet, popped them in the oven, and set the rooster timer, giving Rachel a brief moment of privacy. Eventually she put the tissue away, gave me a weak smile, and continued.

"We never used the tea set again once she married Julian, and it was abandoned upstairs in the attic, gathering dust. I don't know why, but in her last months, she got it out again and had it cleaned. We used that tea set a couple of times when I came home after my trip to France. Kimberly joined us once, and she was insultingly patronizing to Mom about using it. She thought Mom was regressing to her childhood, but she wasn't. She wanted to be near things she'd loved over the years. When I was little, she showed me where the lining had been ripped and resewn. It had been her teenage hiding place, she said, where she kept her diary away from the prying eyes of her nosy older sister. It didn't occur to me that Mom would have put the third will in there. Not until I came to get it and it was gone. Kimberly had sold the things she didn't want—the tea sets and silver and Royal Doulton figurines—to antique dealers before I even had a chance to get my hands on what I wanted."

"Not nice."

"I told you, Kimberly was never nice." Rachel held out her cup. "More coffee?"

"Sure." I poured another round. I had to keep working, so I told Rachel to continue as I assembled the ingredients to make coconut cupcakes.

"Then I made a mistake. A bad one. I got angry, really angry, about the tea chest being sold out from underneath me. Kimberly sneered and said it was nothing but an old toy, and I told her about the sentimental value it had for Mom, including her hiding her diary in it when she'd been a girl. And then I stormed out of the house, vowing never to return. I know my dear half sister well, and it was obvious she was worried about what had happened to the new will, even though she pretended it was of no consequence. Imagine her shock on hearing Mom had rewritten her will, and then her relief when it couldn't be found. She hadn't destroyed it, and she didn't believe Mom had changed her mind, so she must have spent a lot of restless nights wondering what had happened to it. And then I pretty much out-and-out told her where it might be found."

"The trail led to the antique dealer, and then to me."

"Right. And I arrived too late. You'd given it to her."

I whirled butter and sugar in the mixer and thought. Had Rachel confronted Kimberly at Victoria-on-Sea last night and demanded she return the envelope presumably containing the third will? Possible. Had Kimberly told her she'd destroyed it? Also possible. If so, and if Rachel had lashed out at Kimberly and killed her, then why was Rachel still in North Augusta? Wouldn't she have run for the nearest lawyer?

What would Rachel's legal situation be in light of Kimberly's death, as regards their mother's estate? If Kimberly hadn't yet written a will of her own, it's entirely possible their mother's will (whichever one had legal standing) directed what would happen to the funds should one of her children predecease her or die intestate. On the other hand, Kimberly was married, and if she didn't have a will, shouldn't most of her estate automatically go to her widower? I know nothing about the laws of inheritance, but it seemed to me that Rachel had more than one reason to kill her half sister.

"You need to call the police," I said.

A car turned into the driveway and parked next to the kitchen door. I glanced at my watch. Ten o'clock. Marybeth and Cheryl had arrived for work.

"No." Rachel put down her coffee cup.

I switched off the mixer. "Then I will."

"You do what you have to do, Lily, but I have no intention of going to jail. I didn't kill Kimberly. I didn't find my mother's last will and testament, but I intend to keep looking. People other than Kimberly don't want that will to come to light. Kimberly's new husband comes to mind."

"Wesley? What does he have to do with it?"

"Why do you think he married Kimberly? He needs funding for the restaurant empire he intends to create. A quick marriage to a woman who's recently come into a substantial inheritance, and then the wife conveniently dies. And the vengeful sister goes to prison for it. Neat and tidy. For him."

The door opened and Cheryl and Marybeth came in. They started when they saw Rachel, who'd put her sun hat and dark glasses back in place. Rachel slipped past them without another word.

I reached for my phone and called Detective Redmond.

Chapter 10

"Someone's asking for you, Lily," Marybeth said.

"This is starting to become a habit. One I don't care for. Tell her no. I am not available. I will never be available." I chopped at a chicken I'd poached in Darjeeling yesterday to use for sandwiches.

"It's not a her; it's a him." Marybeth grinned at me. "I wouldn't mind seeing a lot more of him. If you get my meaning."

"I'm afraid I do. Okay. Show him in."

She was back a moment later with, as expected, Wesley Schumann.

It was a few minutes after eleven, and the tearoom had just opened. Earlier, I'd called Amy Redmond as I watched Rachel drive away. I told her Rachel had been here, but she'd left without telling me where she was going.

"Why did she come to see you?" Redmond asked.

"I don't quite know. She told me some things about her and her sister's relationship, and it was not a good one."

"I'm at the police station now, and I have a few things to deal with first. I want to find out more about this not-good relationship. I trust you'll be at Tea by the Sea all day?"

"Where else would I be?" I'd said.

"Nice place, Lily," Wesley said now. "I always knew you could make it on your own if you put your mind to it."

I kept my head down and continued chopping. As I remember, Wesley had disparaged every mention I made of eventually having my own restaurant, to the point that I gave up talking about it. Although I didn't give up dreaming about it. "You're a talented pastry chef, Lily," he'd say. "But you don't have the drive or the ambition, never mind the sheer guts to compete in this business."

"Thanks," was all I said now. "I'm happy with it."

"Are you? Happy, I mean? Living with your grandmother? Making breakfasts in a B & B, of all places? Living in this provincial backwater? Not a lot of space in here."

"Enough for me."

"May I?" He indicated the scones cooling on a rack.

"Help yourself."

He took one and broke it apart. Like the chef he was, he closely examined the interior before tasting it. He popped a piece in his mouth and chewed carefully and thoughtfully. "Top-notch," he said at last.

"Thanks," I said, meaning it. Praise about food from Wesley was rare, and heartfelt when given. "I haven't had a chance to say I'm sorry about your loss. You must be devastated."

"I'll get over it."

I stopped chopping and started at him. His hair was perfectly arranged to look casual, and a touch of stubble blackened his strong jaw. His eyes were clear. He wore slim dark gray pants and an open-necked light gray sweater with the sleeves rolled up. Bare feet were stuffed into Italian loafers. *Grief* was not the word that came to mind.

The edges of his mouth turned up in that slow smile I knew so well, and he winked at me.

He winked. In that way that had, once upon a time, turned my bones to jelly and set my blood on fire.

I blinked. "Wesley? Are you okay? Need I remind you that your wife has died."

"We hadn't been married for long."

"I don't think that makes it any easier."

"Put that knife down."

"What?"

"That knife. Put it down."

I did so. He crossed the room in two quick strides and took my face in his strong hands, scarred by numerous kitchen encounters with hot metal and butcher knives. He stared into my eyes, saying nothing.

I averted my gaze and pulled myself away. "I have work to do. We're expecting a full house all day."

He ran a finger lightly over my cheek. "Lily. My Lily. I've missed you. So much."

"Wesley, stop it."

His eyes sparkled. "You're afraid your staff will come in. Like that time—"

I picked up the knife once more and focused my attention on the chicken. "Cape Cod isn't a provincial backwater. Didn't I hear you're intending to open a restaurant near here?"

"Two. One in Provincetown and one in Orleans. If things turn out, I'm looking at Hyannis also. Plans are well under way, and I'm excited about it. I want you to come and work for me, Lily. I'll give you free reign with the dessert menu. We can talk about offering afternoon tea service on summer weekends, and you can be in charge of that."

"Four orders of the full tea, and two for light tea." Cheryl came into the kitchen.

"I'm behind on the chicken sandwiches," I said. "Get the tea on while I finish them."

Without asking, Wesley began arranging scones and pastries on the three-tiered stands. Cheryl squeezed around him to get to the airpots and tea canisters.

"Two cream tea and two children's tea," Marybeth said. I turned in time to see Wesley smile at her, and her blush as red as the strawberries we added to the children's service. Marybeth went into the pantry and came out with pieces of the Peter Rabbit set.

I glanced at Wesley to see his reaction, but he showed none. He must not have known how much trouble Kimberly and Rachel had gone to in trying to find that tea set.

"Wesley," I said. "You have to leave. My staff and I have work to do and you're in the way."

"Will you think about what I asked you?"

"No, I won't. I'm happy here, very happy, and even if I wasn't I wouldn't leave my grandmother."

"I can help with your grandmother."

I tried to make a joke. "No one can help with my grandmother."

"She's got that right," Cheryl said, and Marybeth laughed.

"Give me a minute, Lily," Wesley said. "Let's go outside. I won't take much of your time."

Cheryl and Marybeth watched us out of the corners of their eyes as they made tea and assembled the food.

I knew Wesley wouldn't leave until he said what he wanted to say, so I sighed and said, "One minute. No more." I led the way out the kitchen door.

The sun was strong, and Wesley and I stood in the shade of an ancient oak. Traffic was light on the main road. A car slowed and turned into our driveway.

"I'm asking you to do more than work for me, Lily," Wesley said. "Things can be the way they used to be between us."

I gaped at him. Wesley's wife had died little more than twelve hours ago, and he was asking me to get back with him? "You're in shock," I said at last. "Kimberly's death was so sudden. So unexpected. I—"

He reached for me, but I dodged out of the way of his hands. "Forget Kimberly. As soon as I saw you again, yesterday morning in that overdecorated breakfast room, I knew you were the only woman for me. I've always known that. When you left me so suddenly, with no reason, I was in shock, yes. Maybe I turned to Kimmy because of it, but—"

"You're nuts."

"Lily. I need you, but most of all—you need me."

Suddenly, I was angry. All the hurt this man had caused me came flooding back. I was here, standing under the big old oak at Tea by the Sea, my sanctuary, and here he was—at me again. The ego, the arrogance, the unwillingness to see anyone else's point of view. "If you want a reason, Wesley, I'll give you a reason. I left you because you're not a nice person, and I finally realized that. You're not nice to anyone who's not in a position to do you any favors. You're not nice to your staff, to your friends. You were not nice to me when I was your girlfriend. To prove my point, you can't even be nice to your wife after she died."

A dark shadow replaced the amusement in his eyes, and his face tightened.

"I don't want to work with you again. Or have anything else to do with you."

He was standing between me and the kitchen door. As I moved to go around him his hand shot out and grabbed my arm. He pulled me close to him and stared into my face. His eyes were very dark. "You don't know what you want."

I pulled at my arm, but he didn't let go. His grip was strong, his face tight with anger.

"Well, well. Look who's here." Bernie came around the building, smiling broadly. "Wesley Schumann. How's it going, Wessie, old pal?"

Wesley, well I knew, loathed being called Wessie.

He released me, and I edged toward the door, trying not to rub at my arm.

"Bernadette Murphy," he said. "I should have known you'd pop up soon. As interfering as ever."

"I try. I heard about your loss. My condolences."

He said nothing.

"If you two are done talking, I'm here and ready to pitch in like we arranged, Lily."

"Yeah. Right. Good. Let's get to it, then."

I bolted into the kitchen. Wesley called after me, "You will be very sorry, Lily Roberts."

Bernie slammed the door shut behind us.

"Seems as though I arrived in the nick of time. As usual. What was going on out there?" Bernie asked.

My heart was pounding, and I fought to control my breathing. "I scarcely know. He started by asking me to work for him in his new restaurants, and then he was telling me he missed me and wanted us to pick up where we'd left off. Personally."

"Weird."

"Very weird. I mean . . . Kimberly? And then, when I said a firm no to both those things, he got . . . angry."

Marybeth had taken over finishing the poached chicken sandwiches and had sliced them into neat triangles. She was now assembling roast beef on crostini, adding a touch of Dijon and a handful of bright green chopped herbs. Her ears were almost flapping as Bernie and I came into the kitchen.

"Royal tea for four," Cheryl called.

I got four champagne flutes down from the shelf. My hands were shaking.

"Are you okay, Lily?" Cheryl asked me. "You've gone very pale."

"I'm fine. Now. Thanks to Bernie."

"I'll accept this as my reward." Bernie helped herself to a scone. "Any jam?"

"Jar on the second shelf," Cheryl said. "Lily, you've gone pale. Do you want to sit down? We can manage for a while."

"No need. I need to get started on the chocolate chip cookies for the children's tea. Are you okay working on sandwiches, Marybeth?"

"Yup."

"Thanks. We'll need peanut butter and jam pinwheels next."

"I'll get out of your hair, then." Bernie slathered jam on her scone.

I smiled at her. "Thanks for your intervention. And I mean it. I'd have been okay, I think, but it was getting mighty tense out there. I don't know what came over him."

"Ego came over him, Lily. Ego, arrogance. He left here humiliated, and his injured pride won't let him forget it. I'd like to see him gone completely. Can I tell Rose to kick him to the curb?"

"Not necessary. He's supposed to be checking out tomorrow. He'll go on to bother someone else. What brought you here, anyway?"

"I'm taking a break, and I thought I'd drop by to see if there's been any developments. When I drove up, I saw you and him talking, and I thought I'd . . . uh . . ."

"Eavesdrop?"

"Offer him my condolences. Obviously that turned out

not to be necessary. Jerk. Now that I'm here, I see Matt's car in his driveway. I'll pop over and say hi."

Matt Goodwill was our neighbor. He and Bernie seemed to be becoming quite fond of each other. I grinned. "Shouldn't you be getting back to the book?"

"All work and no play makes Bernie a dull girl," she said with a twinkle in her eye. The twinkle disappeared. "Marybeth, I'm leaving you in charge of Lily. Any more signs of trouble, you have my number."

Marybeth leapt to attention and saluted. The effect was somewhat spoiled by the peanut butter–covered knife clasped in her hand.

Bernie waved her scone in the air and left.

My next callers were Detectives Redmond and Williams. Bernie popped her head back into the kitchen to tell me the police had arrived at Victoria-on-Sea, but more than an hour passed before they appeared in the tearoom asking for me. I assumed they'd been talking to Wesley and interviewing B & B guests who might have heard last night's disturbance or who'd seen someone Kimberly had been talking to shortly before she died.

"What's it like in the dining rooms?" I asked Cheryl as I took off my apron and shook out my hair. "The detectives will want to talk to me in some degree of privacy, and I don't want them getting the idea of hauling me down to the police station."

"The patio's full, but we have some space inside. The small alcove's free. Do you want me to bring you a cup of tea?"

"That would be great. Tea for me and Redmond. Coffee for Williams. Anything you can spare to eat would be great. But not too much."

I met the detectives in the vestibule and showed them to

a table for four in one of the alcoves. Redmond greeted me politely, but Williams gave me such a sideways look, I wondered what was up. Surely they were here only so I could tell them what I'd heard from Rachel?

We sat down. Marybeth brought tea and coffee and a plate of shortbread cookies.

"Did you find Rachel?" I asked when my assistant was out of earshot.

"She's not answering her phone," Redmond said. "We've put a BOLO on her car, but she's either parked it in a garage somewhere or is keeping to the back roads."

"She won't get far." Williams added three heaping spoons of sugar to his coffee. My teeth ached just watching him.

"What did she have to tell you?" Redmond asked me.

I repeated Rachel's story as best I could, painting a picture of motives for murder: money, hatred, sibling jealousy, revenge. I didn't think she'd killed her sister, but I didn't say so. My impression would count for nothing with the police. Heck, it didn't account for much with me. I'm not known as a shrewd judge of character.

As proof of that, I'd dated Wesley Schumann for a long time, hadn't I?

While I talked, Redmond sipped her tea and Williams drank coffee and ate most of the shortbread. Conversation flowed into the alcove from tables in the main room. Cheryl greeted new arrivals, showed them to their places, and thanked people for coming. Chairs were pulled up or pushed back, tea was poured, silverware clinked, people laughed.

"Rachel Morrison didn't say anything about where she might be going next?" Redmond asked.

"No. She asked me not to call you, but . . ." I shrugged. "Obviously I did. Her family home is in Chatham. You could try there."

"We sent someone around. The housekeeper told them

she hasn't seen Rachel for several weeks. The sisters didn't have a good relationship. Kimberly moved into the house more or less permanently after the death of their mother, and Rachel stayed away."

"What's your connection with the dead woman's husband?" Williams asked me.

"Wesley? I worked at West Steak House, his restaurant in Manhattan. I told Detective Redmond about that last night. We dated for a while. We broke up when I moved here."

"Why did you break up?"

"Because I didn't want to be with him anymore."

"Who ended it?"

"Why are you asking me that?"

"Just answer the question."

"I did. If you want further details, I ended it after he attacked me with a butcher's knife."

"Were you hurt?" Redmond asked.

"No. And in fairness to him, it was more a matter of screaming at me and waving the knife in the air than intending to use it to harm me. We were in the restaurant kitchen, surrounded by kitchen workers. One of the sous chefs intervened, no harm done, but the entire incident was a matter of the straw that broke the camel's back, and I realized I'd be better off without him. I quit my job on the spot and left him at the same time."

"That's not what he says," Williams said.

"What does he say?"

"Mr. Schumann told us he ended things with you because you were clingy and increasingly demanding."

My mouth flapped open. Redmond studied me over the rim of her teacup.

"He says you wanted to get married and he didn't," Williams continued. "You were getting pushy about it. When he ended things with you, you lost your temper and told him you'd never give him up. He said he reluctantly had to fire you because the quality of your work was slipping as the personal relationship deteriorated."

"That's . . . that's not right."

"Mr. Schumann also told us you were angry when you found out he'd married Ms. Smithfield. Did you kill Kimberly Smithfield, Lily?"

I stared at him. I looked at Redmond. Her cool gray eyes studied me.

"That's beyond preposterous," I said when I could speak again. "Wesley was in my kitchen only this morning asking me to work for him at his new restaurant. Asking me also, if you must know, to get back with him personally. I turned him down flat. On both matters."

"He told us he came to see you this morning wanting to reconnect with an old friend, thinking you'd have gotten over your anger at him and would offer him condolences on his grief."

I sputtered.

"Did anyone overhear this morning's conversation?" Redmond asked.

I thought. Marybeth and Cheryl had been in and out of the kitchen constantly, but did they actually hear what Wesley said? Maybe not. Bernie would tell the police what I told her, but she hadn't heard Wesley's exact words. She had seen him grabbing me, though. "When did he tell you all this?"

"Just now," Redmond said. "We had further questions about his wife's activities and whereabouts yesterday, as well as her business and personal relationships."

Wesley had told the police these lies about me *after* he'd asked me to get back with him. What had Bernie said? He left humiliated, and I'd better watch out.

He'd been in a rage when I turned him down. Had he

truly been angry enough to want to hurt me? Did he think he could frame me for Kimberly's murder that easily? Did he think I'd be so grateful if he changed his story that I'd agree to get back with him in thanks?

Or had Wesley himself killed Kimberly and leapt at the chance to get revenge on an old girlfriend while at the same time turning suspicion onto someone else?

"He's lying," I said. "There were witnesses to the previous incident in his restaurant I told you about, and witnesses to his and my conversation this morning. Even if Marybeth, Cheryl, and Bernie didn't hear the exact words, it would have been obvious he isn't exactly mourning his wife. I'd say his attitude borders on the blasé."

"We all grieve in our own way," Williams said.

"Don't give me that, Detective," I snapped. "Some of us grieve in public, some quietly. Some show emotion, some don't. No one truly grieving tells an old girlfriend he should never have married the dead woman."

"Did he say that?" Redmond asked.

"Words to that effect."

She stood up. "If you hear from Rachel again, or if you remember anything that might be of help to us, give us a call."

Williams made no move to also get up. He kept looking at me.

"Detective?" Redmond said. "Are you ready to go?"

"Yeah." He lumbered to his feet. "I'd advise you to think things over and come clean, Lily. You're the only person who heard this so-called argument between the dead woman and another."

He walked out of the alcove. I stared after him. When I looked back at Redmond she gave me an encouraging nod. "Forget it. Schumann's an open book. It was obvious to me last night that he cares for you. And then this afternoon he does a one-eighty and tries to paint you as a vicious harridan who won't leave poor innocent him alone. Not hard to guess you turned him down flat."

"Your partner doesn't seem so sure."

"I'll handle him," she said.

Once they were gone, I leaned back in my chair and stretched and tried to work some of the kinks out. My neck was a ball of tension. Amy Redmond had tried to sound as though I had nothing to worry about, but I wasn't so sure. If Wesley managed to convince Chuck Williams that I had reason to kill Kimberly, would Williams bother searching for the real killer, or spend all his time trying to find proof against me? The police had more than one case on their plate at a time, and Williams was the senior detective. If Redmond was assigned to something else, would I be left hanging in the wind?

"You okay, Lily?" Cheryl asked as she cleared the used dishes off the table.

"No, I am not. About the last thing in the world I wanted was to get wrapped up in another murder case. Seems like what I want doesn't much matter."

Chapter 11

We were busy enough for the rest of the day I managed to put Wesley Schumann out of my mind as I made scones and pastries and small cakes and put together sandwiches. Marybeth and Cheryl passed on a good deal of praise from happy customers and told me tips had been exceptionally good today, which pleased me a great deal. They were both marvelous employees, loyal and hardworking, and I wanted them to do well out of my venture.

A bus tour of twenty people arrived at four o'clock, giving us a frantic ending to the day, but by six the last of the well-fed guests were out the door. Marybeth was clearing off the patio tables, and Cheryl hummed softly to herself as she unloaded the dishwasher.

I slipped the day's final tray of scones into the oven and set the rooster timer. Bernie had called me from Matt's place, suggesting we go out for dinner and invite Simon to join us. I was looking forward to the evening. I'd have just enough time to get the scones out of the oven and into the freezer, run home to let Éclair enjoy a short romp, and change.

I hadn't forgotten that I'd earlier decided I might have

to get involved in the situation regarding Kimberly's death; I was planning to talk it over with my friends, see if anyone had any ideas as to what might have happened. Because I certainly didn't.

Marybeth came in with her laden tray and dropped it next to the sink. "Some fancy convertible just drove up to the house," she said. "That guy got out, the handsome one who was in here earlier."

"Wesley," I said. "I was hoping he'd gone."

"No such luck." She left the dishes to her mother and dragged the vacuum cleaner out of the closet.

I opened my iPad and checked the reservations list for tomorrow. Another busy day. Busy was good. Next, I called up the weather report. Hot and sunny. Hot and sunny was also good. It brought the tourists out in force and allowed us more seating space when we could use the patio.

My phone rang. Rose.

"Lily, love, can you come up to the house?" Her voice was strained.

"What's happened? Is something wrong? Are you okay?"

"I'm perfectly fine, but we have an . . . issue, and I need your support."

"On my way." I shoved my phone into my pocket.

"What's wrong?" Cheryl asked.

"I don't know. I'm going up to the house. Can you take those scones out of the oven when the timer sounds, please? Give them fifteen minutes to cool and then put them in the freezer. If I'm not back when you leave, lock up."

"You'll call and tell us if you need anything?"

"I will. Thanks." I tossed my apron and hairnet onto the butcher block and ran through the restaurant. Marybeth glanced up from her vacuuming, but I kept going and broke into a run. Rose hadn't sounded more than irritated, but she could sometimes take English stiff upper lip to extremes. Particularly if guests were with her.

I ran down the driveway, heading for the big house.

Victoria-on-Sea is a true beauty and I could see why Rose loved it so much. Perched close to the cliffs, framed by the blue sky and the sparkling waters of Cape Cod Bay, it was painted a clean fresh white with a gray roof. Numerous turrets and dormer windows added interest to the exterior, as did copious amounts of gingerbread trim. A wide veranda, roof supported by white pillars, ran the length of the house. The steps and railing were accented with terra-cotta pots and iron urns containing variegated hosta, multihued coleus, trailing sweet potato vines, and red and white geraniums.

A couple of cars, including Wesley's Mercedes, were in the guest parking area, but most people would still be lingering at the beach, returning from their fishing or whale-watching trips, or have gone out for an early dinner.

The door to the garden shed tucked against the southern edge of the property was closed, and Simon's motorcycle wasn't in its regular place next to it. The shed had been in use for a long time. A remnant of the days before prefabricated buildings, it was still in good shape, handcrafted out of whole logs with a shingle roof. The small windows on either side of the double-hinged wooden door contained boxes overflowing with tumbling ivy and purple fuchsia.

Even in my haste and my worry, I was able to enjoy the beauty of the gardens in the long soft light of early evening. They'd been laid out many years ago in a traditional English cottage garden format, with neat hedge rows, curving flagstone paths, benches for relaxing, statues to provide points of interest, a formal rose garden, herb and kitchen gardens. The scent, mixed with traces of salt off the sea, was intoxicating.

I ran up the steps to the veranda and through the front door.

Rose was seated behind the reception desk. Robert the Bruce stood on the desk, his ears up and his back arched. A woman and two teenagers lingered on the stairs eavesdropping, and an angry Wesley loomed over Rose. Her face was calm, her posture relaxed. She realized he meant her no harm. Not physically, anyway.

". . . entitled to my privacy." He whirled around when he heard me come in. He was dressed in the clothes he'd had on when he came to the tearoom earlier; a laptop bag thrown over one shoulder. "What do you know about this, Lily?"

"Considering I have no idea what's going on," I said, "I know nothing about it. Rose, are you okay?"

"Perfectly fine, love. It seems we've had an . . . incident."

"More than an incident," Wesley snapped. "I'm calling the police."

"Cool," the teenage girl said. "I want to be a cop, but it was my bad luck that I missed what happened last night."

I gave the onlookers my best professional smile. "Everything is in hand. Please don't let us keep you from your evening plans."

"This doesn't have anything to do with what happened to that poor woman yesterday, does it?" the girl's mother asked.

Neither Rose nor Wesley replied, so I said, "If your assistance is needed, we'll let you know. Thank you."

She finally got the hint and headed up the stairs. Her son went with her, but the girl stayed where she was, eyes wide with interest. Her mother snapped at her to get a move on, and she reluctantly followed them.

"Let's go into the drawing room and talk there," I said to Wesley.

"I don't want to go into the drawing room," he snapped at me. "I might sue."

Robbie hissed. Rose put her hand on his back and stroked him. He didn't relax.

"That would be your prerogative," I said. "But first can you please tell me what's happening?"

"Better still," he said, "I'll show you. Let's go to my room."

Maybe not such a good idea. I wasn't going to venture into Wesley's room, particularly not when he was so angry. Angry about what, I still didn't know. "No."

"I'll come with you," Rose said. "I want to see for myself."

I reasoned that I should be okay with my grandmother acting as bodyguard, and we followed Wesley up the stairs. Robbie leapt off the desk and ran on ahead.

Wesley and Kimberly had been given room 202, a suite with a sea view and a spacious balcony. The door was half open, the wood around the handle smashed. I exchanged a worried glance with Rose, cautiously pushed the door aside, and stepped through it.

I stopped dead. Rose crashed into the back of me. "Goodness," she said. Robbie hissed once again.

Goodness was right. The room had been tossed. Drawers were pulled open, the contents spilling out. Clothes, Kimberly's as well as Wesley's, had been pulled off their hangers and thrown aside, pockets turned out. The bedspread had been torn off the bed and the sheets, too. The side tables and the sofa were partially pulled away from the wall, the cushions tossed on the floor. The paintings were either hanging askew or off the wall altogether.

"I . . . I don't know what to say," I said.

"Obviously, someone's been searching for something," Wesley said.

"You don't know what they were after?"

"Not a clue."

It had to be the lost third will. I didn't say so. "Did you lock your room when you left?"

"Of course I locked it. What do you take me for?"

I didn't answer that, either.

"I got here a few minutes ago and immediately realized something was wrong with the door."

"It's been forced," Rose said.

"What time did you leave?" I asked.

"I went up to your childish little tearoom to talk to you around eleven," he said. "After that I got the car and went into town without coming back in here. I had a lunch meeting in Truro and then people to see in Provincetown. Potential investors in the new restaurants. I returned ten, fifteen minutes ago and found . . . this."

"I am so sorry," Rose said. "Nothing like this has ever happened before. I—"

"That's the point," I said. "Nothing like this has ever happened here before. If you brought something worth stealing, Wesley, you brought the person who's looking for it with you."

"You're not turning this on me, Lily. My wife died yesterday. She was a woman of considerable means, and I'm guessing one of your staff decided to have a poke around and see if she left anything of value behind."

Rose straightened to her full formidable five feet nothing. She thrust her chin forward and her eyes blazed. "Now see here, young man. My staff are all as honest as the day is long."

Under the force of her fury, Wesley took a step backward. Unfortunately, he wasn't intimidated into silence. He smirked at me. "By staff, I'm including Lily."

"Whatever," I said. "My alibi, not that I need one, is iron clad. I was in my restaurant all day."

"In the kitchen, where the only people who saw you are dependent on you for their living."

"Are you suggesting . . . ?" Rose sputtered.

"Yes," I said, "he is. Pay him no attention. I suggest you call the police, Rose, and report this. Due to the death of one of the people who occupied this room as recently as yesterday, they'll be interested. Very interested. You should also call Jean and ask her when she cleaned in here. She would have said something if she'd found the room in this state. That'll give the police a timeline."

Wesley picked up a shoe. One of Kimberly's, a sandal with far too much bling for my taste.

"Don't touch anything," I said. "The police will want to see everything in situ. If you take a seat in the drawing room, I'll bring you a coffee or tea while we wait."

He threw the shoe aside. "Never mind. I have dinner plans with an important investor, and I have no intention of canceling or being late. The police can track me down, if they want to bother. Small-town cops, useless the lot of them." He headed for the stairs at a rapid clip.

"I sense," Rose said once his footsteps had faded away, "that man has some conflicting emotions toward you, love."

"Nothing conflicting about it. He wants me to grovel and when I won't, he lashes out. Never mind that. This is a big problem. I'll make the call."

I phoned Amy Redmond and told her what had happened. She said she'd be right over.

"If Wesley decides, out of pure meanness, to make something out of this," I said to Rose, "it can cause us problems. First a death, and now a guest room being ransacked."

"If he wants to cause problems," Rose said, "he should have stayed to wait for the police. Leaving, business dinner or no, indicates to me he doesn't consider the issue to be all that important. Nor is the sanctity of his property. He left without asking that the door be sealed pending the police arrival. I will mention such to anyone who asks."

I gave her a fond smile. Excitement over, Robbie headed for the stairs and Rose and I followed.

"Do you have any idea what someone might have been after?" my grandmother asked.

"I suspect I do. Kimberly's mother died recently, and her will's being contested. It's rumored she wrote a final will which changed the primary benefactors. That will has conveniently disappeared. I can't see it could be about anything other than that."

We took seats in the drawing room to wait. Rose settled in her favorite chair, and I perched on the window bench, keeping an eye out for the police. Had Kimberly told Wesley about the existence of a third will? Perhaps not, not if she suspected he'd married her to get his hands on her inheritance. If she hadn't, might Rachel have told him? Possible. He'd spoken to her recently, when he told her he and Kimberly were staying at Victoria-on-Sea. Rachel might have asked him to let her know if he came across a handwritten document. She might not have told him why she wanted it, but he wasn't a total idiot.

Was it possible Wesley himself was searching for the third will? If he stood to inherit everything from Kimberly, he wouldn't want a new will showing up giving half to Rachel. Had Kimberly brought the will to Victoria-on-Sea with her and put it someplace in their room without telling him where? Had he been searching for it, and either didn't find it or did find it and tossed the room to make it look as though someone else was after it?

My head spun.

While we waited, Rose called Jean, the weekday housekeeper, and asked what time she'd been in room 202 and if she'd noticed anything amiss. The answer was obviously in the negative, and Rose thanked her and hung up without explaining why she was asking.

"I suppose it's pointless to ask her if she saw anyone in the house today who shouldn't have been here," I said.

"Jean cleaned that room shortly after noon and nothing was out of place. She says no one was in the house when she did the rooms, as is normal on a fine day. Even if she had seen someone in the hallway, she doesn't interact with the guests and has no way of knowing who's a guest and who might be an intruder. As for me, I spent the morning in my office going over the accounts. After lunch, I had a walk and a pleasant chat with Simon about his plans for expanding the rose garden. I was at my post"—meaning the reception desk waiting for check-ins—"between three and five. After the last arrival was settled, I returned to my room, which is where I was when I heard that awful man bellowing for me. I saw no one who's not a guest in the house itself, but random people were wandering in the gardens, as is normal." Our gardens are open to the public. They are, according to Tripadvisor, the number one garden attraction in North Augusta. There is no number two. A good part of the reason Rose can charge as much as she does for a stay at Victoria-on-Sea is the quality of the landscaping on the property.

"Anyone could have come in," I said. The front door's normally kept unlocked during the daytime. "But they would have had to know what room to go to." Rachel? It was entirely possible, likely even, Rachel had been the one searching the room. When Wesley told Rachel where he and Kimberly were staying, he might have mentioned which room they were in.

My phone beeped.

Bernie: **Where are you? We're waiting at Matt's.**

Me: **You'll have to go without me. Something's come up.**

Bernie: **What?**

Me: **Trouble. What else?**

Bernie: **On my way**

Me: **No need**

Bernie:

I put my phone away as the police car turned into the driveway. I went to let them in.

Chapter 12

I wiped my fingers on a paper towel torn off the roll. That had been one good pizza, smothered in mushrooms, onions, and peppers, exactly the way I like it.

Dinner with my friends had turned into takeout pizza in the B & B kitchen, joined by my grandmother.

Bernie, along with Simon and Matt Goodwill, had arrived minutes after the police. They cooled their heels on the veranda while Rose told Redmond and Williams what had happened, and I took them upstairs to have a look at room 202. They were not impressed, to put it mildly, to hear that Wesley decided he had more important things to do than wait until they arrived.

I asked Redmond if they'd been able to locate Rachel, and she gave me a sharp shake of the head. About that, she was clearly also not impressed. Once the police left, I told my friends I wasn't in the mood to change and go out to a restaurant, so Matt ran to his house for beer and a bottle of wine, while Bernie called to order pizza delivery, and I went home to let Éclair out. Simon had gone with Matt and they'd returned with, of all things, a door and a doorhandle and the tools to install it in room 202.

The house where Matt now lives had been his family home for generations. It's as big as, and at one time had been as grand as, Victoria-on-Sea, but it's been unoccupied and ignored for years, allowed to gradually crumble into the rocks and sand. He's doing most of the renovations and repairs himself, as time and money permit. Conveniently, he had doors ready to install.

"Wesley didn't appear to be concerned that anything had been taken," I said, first to the police and then to my friends once we'd gathered in the kitchen. "More upset about the invasion of privacy, more interested in making a scene. He didn't search for anything, or check if anything was missing."

"That seems odd," Bernie said.

"Perhaps not. He'd been in his car, so he would have had his wallet, keys, and phone on him, and he carried a laptop bag. Maybe those are the only things important to him."

"What about his wife's stuff?" Bernie asked. "Her purse? Jewelry?"

"He went into his room before calling for me," Rose said. "I didn't hear him arrive, so I don't know how long he'd been upstairs."

"He could have put anything he wanted into the laptop bag," I said. "Or had a quick search before coming downstairs and found nothing of value missing."

"Jerk," Bernie said.

"You two talk as though you know this guy other than him being a guest here," Matt said.

"A bad memory for Lily," Bernie said.

"Don't ask," I mumbled around a slice of pizza.

Matt and Simon exchanged a shrug. "Okay." Simon took a sip of his beer. "We won't ask. What happens now?"

"About the break and enter, Redmond called Wesley, and she's arranged to meet him in town later. About the other matter, nothing we can do but hope the police get whoever killed Kimberly." As Matt opened the box in search of another slice of pizza, I caught Bernie's eye and gave my head a quick jerk. She nodded.

Simon looked from one of us to the other. I gave him a smile. He didn't return it.

Pizza demolished, beer finished, wine bottle empty, case discussed, and no conclusions reached, Rose said good night. and she and Robbie retired to their rooms. I stifled a yawn, and Bernie said, "Enough excitement for one day for me. I'll walk you home, Lily."

Simon and Matt leapt to their feet. "We'll come with you."

"No need," Bernie said.

"No problem," Matt said.

"Our pleasure," Simon said.

I called for Éclair, locked the kitchen door behind us, and we strolled along the edge of the cliffs toward my cottage. The tide was coming in and below us waves crashed against the rocks.

We reached my gate. "Sorry to ruin your dinner plans," I said.

"I had fun," Matt said. "Your grandmother's a hoot."

"She has her moments."

"Good night, Lily," Simon said.

"Good night."

Simon glanced at Matt and he must have read something in his friend's face before he turned and walked away.

Matt shifted his feet. "Feel like coming over for a nightcap?" he asked Bernie.

She yawned. "Not tonight, thanks. I'm beat. See you tomorrow maybe."

"Okay, tomorrow. Uh . . . your car's at my place."

"So it is. You run along, and I'll follow in a minute."

"Night, then."

"Good night," I said.

He continued along the cliff path, heading for his own house. Éclair began to follow, and I called her back. Bernie let out a long breath. "You owe me big-time, Lily Roberts. I've hurt his feelings, and just when we were starting to get to know each other better."

"Starting? You've been cozying up to each other for weeks."

"These things take time."

"Since when did you ever take time over a relationship?"

"Since I met Matt. He's . . . special. Never mind that now, what's up?"

I let us through the gate and dropped into a chair on my porch. Éclair sniffed around the foundations of the cottage and under bushes, searching for signs of recent intruders.

"I didn't want to talk about it in front of Matt and Simon. You know what men can be like."

Bernie perched on a porch railing. "Wanting to take over. Rush to the rescue and all that."

"Rose too. You know what she can be like."

"Also wanting to take over and rushing to the rescue."

"I'm getting seriously worried about this situation, Bernie. Wesley implied to the cops that I had reason to kill Kimberly."

Her face was a picture of pure shock. "What!"

"On the grounds that I am such a jealous . . . you know what . . . I killed his wife to get him to come back to me."

"Jerk. Surely the cops don't take that seriously?"

"Redmond, not at all, and she told me such. As for Williams . . . I don't trust him not to take the easy route and arrest the most convenient suspect. Meaning me."

"We've never gotten on with Williams, true enough, but I can't see even him doing that, Lily."

"At the moment, no. But these things can escalate. The break-in of Wesley's room? No one is in a better position to do that than me."

"Except you have no reason to have done it."

"If I'd wanted to search his room, I'd take the spare master key off the hook in the kitchen and let myself in, not break down the door. But that's beside the point. I feel threatened by all this, and I want to know more about what happened to Kimberly and what's going on now."

"What do you want me to do?"

"I know you're busy with the book and all—"

"Come on, Lily. This is me, Bernie. What have you got in mind?"

"This all started with the Peter Rabbit tea chest and its hidden contents." I filled Bernie in on the details of what Rachel had told me about her mother's will. Wills.

"So this missing third will was hidden in the tea chest."

"Almost certainly. Kimberly found it in the tearoom and left with it. Where it is now is the question a lot of people seem to want answered. The other question is what people might do to either recover it or ensure it's never seen again."

"Don't you think Kimberly would have destroyed it as soon as she got her hands on it?"

"She didn't open the envelope in front of me, so I'm only speculating as to what was in it based on what Rachel told me. If it was the third will, it's possible Kimberly didn't have time to get rid of it. Burning paper in a guest room might have set off the smoke alarm. Maybe she didn't want to attract attention. Maybe she wanted to keep it for some unknown reason, even if only for a short while. We have to conclude that whoever searched Wesley's room earlier today was after the third will. Whether they found it or not remains unknown."

"What about Wessie himself?"

"He's not a patient man and he has a temper. It was his room, but he might have been frantically trying to find it—if he suspected Kimberly hid it in the room—and only when he finished did he realize the extent of the mess he'd made and then he had to find someone to blame. We have only his word he didn't come back to the house earlier today."

"You need security cameras, Lily. I've told you that before."

"I know. I know. Rose doesn't want the expense, and she considers it an invasion of the privacy of her guests."

"I'd say breaking down a bedroom door constitutes an invasion of privacy, but never mind that now. We'll shelve that conversation for another time. As for now, what's your plan?"

"Rachel mentioned that the housekeeper at her mother's home has been with the family for many years. Rachel's is the only side of their family saga I've heard. I want to meet this housekeeper and see if she can give me any insights into the family and the relationship between the sisters."

"I'm in. When?"

"I hate to take the time off work, but we're most likely to find a housekeeper at work in the morning. If you can give me a hand with the B & B breakfasts, we might be able to get away at nine. It's about forty-five minutes to Chatham."

"I'll be here. In the meantime, I can do more than that. Wesley's mixed up in this, one way or another. He has plans to open two new restaurants with the possibility of a third. That takes money and, without money, investors. Even with money it takes investors and business partners. I'll see what I can dig up on him."

"Thanks."

"You can always count on me, Lily."

And the wonderful thing was, I knew it.

Chapter 13

I can always count on my grandmother, too, but sometimes that's not so wonderful. She came into the B & B kitchen at eight thirty, made-up and dressed and ready for an outing.

"Where are you going?" I said suspiciously.

"Wherever you are, love. Investigating the events surrounding the death of our recent guest, I presume."

I threw Bernie a questioning look.

"I never said a word," she protested.

"You didn't have to," Rose said. "I saw you two exchanging secret glances last night when the men weren't looking. And then Bernie drives up this morning at six thirty? I'll have my tea now, Edna."

"Kettle's over there." Edna grabbed four pieces of toast as they popped out of the toaster, laid them on a plate, and carried a tray with two full breakfasts into the dining room. As soon as she'd arrived, I asked her if the paper had any updates on Kimberly's death, hoping there'd been an arrest and I could stop worrying about it. To my disappointment, she said no. The chief of police had given a press conference yesterday evening at which he said they were pursuing all leads. "That means," Edna said, "they haven't got a clue."

"You'll not be pleased to hear that your . . . friend . . . is staying on," Rose said.

"My friend?" I said. "You don't mean Wesley? Staying on where? Hopefully not here."

"He called me very early this morning to ask if he could stay for two more days. We had a last-minute cancelation last night, so I do have a room free."

I shook my head. "Yesterday he was threatening to sue us."

"He was very polite. Apologized for the fuss and bother and thanked me for replacing the door to his room so quickly and efficiently. He was chatty, and although I didn't ask, he informed me that his business affairs require him to stay in the area longer than he'd initially expected. He then hastened to also ensure I understood that he wants to remain in North Augusta until the police release his, and I quote, 'beloved wife's body.' "

"You could have said no."

"That would not have been a wise business decision, love. We do have an available room, although the cancelation was so last minute, we can keep the deposit. I deduce this is not a man to be inconvenienced or antagonized. Keep your friends close and your enemies closer, don't they say? Stay out of his way, love, and all will be fine."

"I agree with Rose," Bernie said.

"As you usually do," I muttered.

I'm Rose's granddaughter and I look very much like her, but we're opposite in personality, whereas Bernie and Rose have identical characters, which is probably why they've always gotten on so well. They're both impulsive, adventurous, overconfident, and can be counted on to throw caution to the wind and to boldly go where the timid dare not tread. Whereas I, one of the timid, have to consider every angle before I take action. And even then, I've been known to hesitate.

Sometimes I found the two of them more than annoying. But sometimes, like now, I knew I was lucky to have them on my side.

"Rose is right in that it's better to have Wesley here, onsite," Bernie said, "than at another place in North Augusta where we can't keep a watchful eye on him. If he tries to bother you, I'll run interference."

While we were talking, Edna returned to the kitchen. She put a tray of dirty dishes on the counter. "He was in just now. Grabbed a coffee in a take-out cup and a muffin. Told me he has a business breakfast meeting in town. One order of the egg-white omelet and one who's just having cereal and yoghurt, and we're done. You do that omelet, and I'll finish up so you can be on your way."

"Thanks, Edna." I reached for the eggs.

We were on the road at ten after nine. I drove, Rose was in the passenger seat, and Bernie in the back, leaning forward between us. "Ready for my report?"

"Go ahead," I said.

"I have nothing."

"That's your report?"

"Early days yet. No one was in their office last night, but I started putting out some feelers and found what I could online. The Smithfield family is wealthy, compared to you and me, but nowhere near as rich and influential as they were in their heyday. The decline began in the late 1990s, mostly caused by bad business and investment decisions on the part of the late Julian Smithfield, grandson of the company's founder and thus founder of the family fortune."

Rose tut-tutted. "You know what they say, rags to riches

to rags in three generations. The Frockmorton family, mind—"

"Julian was Kimberly's father and Rachel's stepfather," I said before we could get into a discussion of the business practices and genealogy of the owners of Thornecroft Castle.

"The family no longer controls Smithfield Industries," Bernie said, "most of which was broken up and sold off years ago. The son, Stephen, lives in California, where he appears to have settled down after a wild youth. He has a police record around the Lower and Mid Cape for things like public drunkenness, possession, minor vandalism. Nothing more serious than that, and he never spent any time in jail. No doubt it helped that his family had money and influence. Rachel, as we know, is a big name in the restaurant world. Kimberly didn't seem to do much of anything other than go to movie premiers and parties. She was well known in the New York and Boston social scenes. She tried her hand at modeling, but other than a few bra ads for the likes of Wal-Mart flyers, nothing. She's had no work, that I could find, in the last two or three years and is no longer associated with her former modeling agency. She's not been married previously."

"Wesley?"

"As I said, early days yet. From what I can tell his restaurant in Manhattan is doing okay, but no more than okay. Maybe a bit less than okay. I'll try to find out more. That reality TV show he starred in was canceled after one season because of poor ratings, and nothing new came up. He doesn't appear to have any other source of income than his restaurant, so I'd say if he wants to open two, possibly three, new places, he's dependent on finding well-heeled investors. Or a well-heeled wife. Even better, an inheritance from the well-heeled wife."

"How well-heeled was Kimberly herself?" I asked.

"I don't know for certain, but I'd say far less than you'd expect. Most of the money the family has left is in the house."

"Rachel told me Kimberly liked to act as though she had money, although she didn't."

"Rachel is not an impartial observer when it comes to her sister, but in this case I believe she's correct. As for the house itself, it doesn't appear there's a mortgage on it, and it's gotta be in the ten to fifteen million range, maybe a bit more, judging by what I could see of it and its surroundings on Google Earth."

"That's a heck of a lot," I said.

"It is. The house is on a huge piece of oceanfront property, with a private beach, patches of woodland, nice gardens. Big old house, triple garage, pool, outdoor hot tub, the works. But as I said, that seems to be about all the family still has to their name. Their mother required round-the-clock private nursing care over the last year of her life, and that doesn't come cheap."

"You found out a lot more than nothing," Rose said.

"I was hoping to find direct links between Wesley and organized crime." Bernie settled back in her seat and pulled out her phone. "As I said, I have feelers out. Let's see if anything pops up today."

Chapter 14

I had no trouble believing the Smithfield home fell into the monetary range Bernie estimated. The directions on Bernie's phone led us to an oceanfront property just outside the town of Chatham, surrounded by a high wall and closed gates. Over the wall, I could see the tops of tall trees, black and white oaks mostly, with a few red cedars and native pitch pine.

I turned into the long driveway and stopped at the communication panel next to the gates. "This might have been a totally wasted trip."

"I enjoyed the drive," Rose said. "I need to get out more. The Cape's so lovely in summer."

I pressed buttons, and soon a crackly voice said, "Hello?"

Last night, I'd debated how to approach the housekeeper with my questions. I considered pretending to be with the North Augusta police. I considered pretending to be a newspaper reporter wanting to do a puff piece on Kimberly. I considered pretending be a friend of Kimberly not aware of her death. I considered pretending to be a potential investor in Wesley's restaurant venture. In the end, I remembered that I'm not a very good liar, and I decided to simply stick to the truth.

"Good morning. I hope I'm not disturbing you. I was hoping to have a chance to chat to Mrs. Chambers. Is that you?"

"It is. What's this about?"

"My name's Lily Roberts, and I'd like to talk to you about Kimberly Smithfield. She was a guest at my grandmother's B & B, and I'm the person who found her, after her death I mean, and I'm bothered by that . . . I guess I'm hoping knowing more about her will help me."

Silently, the gates swung open.

"Good one," Bernie said from the back. "I was afraid you were going to tell her you were with the police."

"Lily's a terrible liar," Rose said. "Unlike her own mother. Now she is a world-class liar."

I ignored them and drove down the long driveway lined with stately oaks. The lawn was freshly cut, affording a fabulous view of the deep blue sea shimmering in the distance. The flower beds overflowed with lush blooms, and more flowers spilled from urns lining the front steps and the path to the detached three-car garage. Neat gravel paths wound their way through the lawns and along the waterfront. The house itself was made of red brick on a stone foundation with a gray roof. It was multilevel, with a wraparound ground-floor veranda and upper-floor balconies. I counted four chimneys and numerous staircases and entrances. A smaller version of the main house sat to our left: smaller only in comparison to the big house. It was larger than many suburban homes.

"Place looks nicely kept up," I said. "I'd have thought Kimberly'd be the sort to cut corners."

"If the will is still in dispute," Rose said, "the lawyers would likely have instructed that no staffing changes be made until it's resolved."

I parked at the bottom of the main steps, and by the time we got out of the car, the front door had opened and a woman emerged from the house to greet us. She was in her early sixties, with a thin face and strong features, dressed in black yoga pants under a long turquoise shirt. Ballet flats were on her feet, and her gray hair was bound up in a knot at the back of her head. She didn't smile as she watched us approach.

"Thank you for seeing us," I said. "I'm Lily and this is my friend Bernadette and my grandmother, Rose."

"My condolences on your loss," Rose said in her best working-class Yorkshire accent.

The edges of the housekeeper's mouth turned up and she said, "Thank you."

"Have you worked for the family for a long time?" Rose asked.

"More years than I care to remember. I'm Helen Chambers. Please come in."

She stepped back and we walked into the house. The entrance was large and designed to impress: black and white marble tiles on the floor, a sparkling six-point chandelier overhead, huge mirror on one wall, portrait of a lady in a midtwentieth-century evening dress on the other, small glass sculptures in all shades of blue and green arranged on a glass display table. A wide staircase with deep red and gold runners and thick oak banisters curled toward the second floor. There wasn't a speck of dust on anything.

"I don't know that I can help you, Ms. Roberts, ladies," Helen said. "I have to confess that although I'm the housekeeper here, I always felt as though I was more like family. I watched my poor Kimmy grow up." She pulled a tissue out of her bra and blew her nose. "Such a darling little thing she was."

Darling wasn't the word I'd have chosen to describe Kimberly Smithfield, but I hadn't known her as a child, and so I smiled in sympathy. I was pleased to hear Helen considered herself to be almost one of the family. She'd know far more about them than if she'd been recently hired and kept her distance.

"I understand," Rose said. "I myself spent time in what in England we call 'service.' The line between employer and staff can become blurry in this more casual day and age."

"So you understand, then. Kimmy married recently, and she and her new husband were vacationing in North Augusta. She called it a pre-honeymoon. He had business in the Outer Cape. They were planning a proper honeymoon in Paris later in the year. You . . . said you found her?"

"My grandmother and I own the B & B where they were staying. How did you hear what happened?"

"Wesley called me to break the news. That's Kimberly's new husband. Wesley Schumann's his name. Such a nice man." She smiled and a slight twinkle came into her eye. "And a celebrity chef at that. The police came by later, with questions about Kimberly. I . . . I can't believe they think someone might have deliberately done her harm. Were you . . . with her when . . . ?" Her voice trailed off.

"I was close by," I said. "I tried to help, but . . . I'm sorry."

She made no move to invite us to step farther inside, or to offer us refreshments. It wasn't her house, of course, so not her place to welcome visitors. Rose and Bernie took care of that minor inconvenience before I had to decide whether or not to simply come right out and ask what I wanted to know.

"That's a lovely portrait." Rose indicated the one dominating the foyer. "What a beautiful woman. Is the lady a family member?"

"That is Mrs. Karen Smithfield. Mr. Julian's first wife.

She died far too young. Such a tragedy. Mr. Julian was bereft, the poor man. I hadn't been working here for long when she passed. He married again shortly after, too hastily in my opinion, but that's what men do sometimes, isn't it?"

"It can be." My grandmother took a step forward, as though she wanted a closer look at the painting. Her left leg wobbled; she gasped in pain and fear. Bernie's arm shot out and grabbed Rose's. "Careful there, Rose. Are you okay?"

Rose breathed heavily. "One of my dizzy spells. They come over me so suddenly these days. Give me a minute, and I'll be fine." She swayed and let out a restrained, and extremely polite, groan.

Bernie threw me a panicked look.

"May I bother you, Helen," Rose's voice trembled, "for a glass of water? If it isn't too much trouble."

"Of course," the housekeeper said. "Please come in. You need to sit down." She led the way down the hallway. Bernie followed, supporting Rose, and I brought up the rear. Helen showed us into the living room: beige paint, white furniture, glass-topped tables, good landscape paintings, subdued lighting. The French doors looked over the clear waters of a swimming pool surrounded by lush greenery. A gardener was bent over a flower bed, trowel in hand, while another deadheaded geraniums. Lounge chairs were arranged around the pool, but the cushions had been taken in and the sun umbrellas were furled. The sea, dotted by white sails, sparkled in the distance. Rose sank into a plush armchair with a grateful sigh and adjusted the cushions behind her.

"I'll be right back." Helen slipped out of the room, and before Bernie and I could do any more than get our bearings, the housekeeper returned with a glass of water, which she handed to Rose.

Rose gave her a grateful smile and sipped.

"Nice house," Bernie said. "Do Kimberly's parents live here?"

"Mr. Julian Smithfield died some years ago. Such a wonderful man, he was. Kind, loving, generous." Her face filled with sadness. "His second wife, Kimmy's mother, followed very recently," she added, and the trace of sorrow disappeared.

"I'm sorry to hear that," Bernie said.

"What do you suppose will happen to this gorgeous house now?" Rose asked. "I hope you won't be out of a job, love. New owners can be . . . careless in their regard for longtime staff. Do you live in?"

"Live in? No, I don't. As for the house, that's still to be determined. Kimmy left a brother and a half-sister, as well as her new husband."

"That's good, then. So much better to keep it in the family." Only Rose had taken a seat. Bernie wandered around the room, admiring the art. I stood at Rose's shoulder, smiling inanely. Helen wasn't going to stand here chatting for much longer. I needed to find out what I'd come for, but I was rather at a loss as to how to continue.

"I'm sorry but—" she began.

"Kimberly's siblings must be a great comfort to you," Rose said.

Helen's expression changed abruptly and she snorted. "Hardly. Her brother's a salesclerk." The word dripped with scorn. "Of all things. Stephen. He lives in California." More scorn. "A dreadful disappointment to his father, Stephen was. Mr. Julian counted on Stephen, as the only son, to follow in his footsteps and eventually take charge of the family business, as he did for his father and his father did before him. But the boy was weak of mind and personality. He preferred to take drugs and strum tunelessly on his guitar. I blame *her*. Giving in to his demands for music lessons, nothing good ever came of that. She spoiled him rotten."

"Her?" I asked. "You mean his mother?"

"Mr. Julian's second wife. Rosemary was her name. She . . . struggled to find her place in this household." Helen sat down. Ready, as I'd hoped, to forget about her work and settle into a good gossip session.

And we were all ears.

Kimberly, by my estimation, had been in her mid-thirties, and Rachel was probably forty. If Rachel had been three when her father died and her mother married Julian, then Rosemary had lived here for about thirty-six years. A heck of a long time to "struggle" to find her place.

"As did Rosemary's daughter by her first marriage," Helen went on. "Her name's Rachel. Rachel Morrison. She never changed her last name for all Mr. Julian was like a father to her. Rosemary was a widow when she married Mr. Julian. Mr. Julian loved that girl as much as he did his own children, but she was a troubled one. Always up to no good. When she was little, Kimberly adored her older half sister. More than I thought wise, but it wasn't my place to say." She sniffed. "As the years passed, Rachel got angrier and angrier. At everyone and everything. When Kimberly became a teenager, she and Rachel fell out, once and for all. Their fights were something to behold, let me tell you. Very stressful to Rosemary, as I recall. Her nerves were never good, although I thought she enjoyed playing that up more than she should have. Mr. Julian spent a lot of time in his study in those years, with the door firmly shut. The entire family, even her own mother, breathed a sigh of relief when Rachel went off to college and then stayed in New York."

"Have you . . . uh . . . seen Rachel in the last couple of days?" I asked.

"No, and I can tell you the police are looking for her. I had a call from a detective in North Augusta, and then the Chatham police themselves came around. They asked me if I knew where Rachel might be. Make of that what you will. Goodness, where are my manners? Can I get you ladies a coffee or a soft drink?"

I opened my mouth to decline, but Rose beat me to it. "That would be splendid, thank you. Please don't go to any trouble."

"No trouble. Coffee's already made. I was about to take some out to the gardeners." She leapt from her chair and bustled out of the living room.

Bernie jerked her head at me.

"What?" I mouthed.

Another jerk. I finally got the hint. I also bustled out of the living room, calling, "Let me give you a hand."

The kitchen was large and as immaculate as the rest of the house, although slightly dated. Black and white tiles on the floor, glistening white cabinets, some with glass doors, granite island, leather-topped stools, inset microwave and oven, countertop stove, and a large white fridge. The wide windows behind the double farmhouse sink provided a view of the landscaped garden leading into a patch of perfectly maintained woodland.

"You mentioned Rachel lives in New York," I said, hoping I wasn't sounding *too* nosy, "and her brother in California. Do you think they'll want to keep this house?"

"Therein lies a tale." Helen got four mugs out of a cabinet and laid them on a tray, along with a bowl of sugar.

"The children are fighting over Rosemary's will." She took a cream jug out of the cavernous fridge, affording me a quick peek inside. Not much other than beer cans, pizza boxes, and the usual half-full bottles of ketchup and condiments. Unless Helen ordered in pizza for her lunch, someone was living here. "Spoons are in that drawer."

I found the needed items. "How awful. That must be so stressful for everyone."

"It is. Rosemary was ill for a long time before she passed. At the end, her mind was as sharp as it had always been, but she had her good days and her bad days and, I'm sorry to say, Rachel took advantage of that."

"Rachel? What did she do?"

Helen glanced toward the hallway, as if fearing someone was eavesdropping. She lowered her voice. "They're not my children, of course. So I'm allowed to have favorites, right?"

"Sure."

"Rachel was only three when her mother married Mr. Julian, but she was resentful from the moment she arrived in this house. She was rude to Mr. Julian, as hard as he tried to be a good father to her. She resented Kimberly when she was born and then Stephen. Only children can be upset when they think they've been replaced by a new baby, but Rachel never got over it. She always hated Kimberly, and all Kimmy every wanted was to be loved by her big sister. I've always believed it was Rachel who set Stephen on a bad course. He was a boy, and a lot younger than her—eight years difference—so not competition the way the prettier, more popular Kimmy was. It was Rachel who encouraged his music; she told him only losers worked hard at school, and she introduced him to a bad crowd."

"Bad crowd?"

"You know what I mean. Drugs and the like. Petty theft, just for the fun of it. More than once Mr. Julian had to go down to the police station and bail that boy out."

"That's what you meant by a dispute over the will, then? They're fighting over it?"

"Oh, yes. When Mr. Julian died he left everything to Rosemary, as he should have. Her will originally left everything to her children, again as was proper. Rachel was in Europe when her mother took ill. Couldn't be bothered to cut short her vacation to come home when her mother needed her the most. And then she continued to stay away under the pretext of pressure of work.

"With Rachel not bothering to visit her dying mother, Stephen galivanting in California, only Kimberly at her side, Rosemary changed her mind and rewrote her will, leaving the bulk of the estate to Kimberly."

"I can see that would have upset Rachel and Stephen."

"Naturally. Then Rachel showed up. All sweetness and light, playing loving daughter once again, and Rosemary had a change of heart."

"She wrote another will?"

"I blame myself."

"For what?"

"I should have advised her against it, but I try not to intervene in the family's affairs." Helen glanced to one side and patted her hair. "This was in Rosemary's final days, you understand. She asked me to call her lawyer. I did so, but he was away on vacation, and she declared she couldn't wait and she'd do it on her own. She was ill and on drugs, but her mind was still good, as anyone could tell you. She asked me to find her two witnesses. I did so, and we gathered in her room to watch her write a new will in her own hand. It was duly signed and sealed and returned to her."

"You did what you were asked to do. Nothing wrong with that. It sounds aboveboard to me."

"I foolishly told Rachel about the new will. A few days later, Rosemary died."

"You're not implying . . ."

"That Rachel killed her mother? I have no proof of that. Nothing but my knowledge of the girl's character. I tried telling the police what I suspect, but they dismissed me. And now, dear Kimmy . . ."

Chapter 15

Helen carried the coffee things into the living room, and while she arranged the contents of the tray on the low table, I gave Bernie and Rose a quick nod, telling them to drink up—I'd learned what I needed to know.

"How are you feeling?" Helen asked Rose.

"Feeling?"

"After your dizzy spell?"

"Oh, that." Rose waved her hand in the air. "Perfectly fine. These things come and go. More come than go when you get to be my age. As you young things will discover soon enough." She added a splash of cream and a hefty spoonful of sugar to her coffee.

"Is there a chance that Kimberly's husband will inherit a share of the house in her place?" I asked Helen.

"Now that would be a wonderful turn of events." Helen's polite smile turned radiant, and a touch of color came into her cheeks. "Such a darling man. And absolutely gorgeous to boot. I was thrilled when Kimberly and he married. It was a quick marriage, but coming so soon after her mother's death she didn't want a fuss or any sort of formal affair. It was Rachel who introduced them. Isn't that ironic? The one nice thing Rachel ever did for her younger sister. He's wanting to open a chain of restaurants here on Cape Cod. I hope he doesn't abandon those plans in his grief."

"No chance of that," Bernie muttered.

I threw her a sharp look, but Helen's attention had been caught by the sound of the front door opening and then slamming shut.

"Helen! Whose car's that? Do you have company?" A man came into the living room. I knew immediately this must be Stephen Smithfield. He looked very much like Kimberly, short and slim, with a small chin and widely spaced brown eyes. He glanced around the room, taking in the coffee things, the seated housekeeper, the three smiling guests. "Looks like you're entertaining, Helen. I didn't realize you'd moved in."

Helen stood up. "I have not moved in. These ladies knew your sister and are paying a condolence call."

"Hello," I said.

"Hi," Bernie said.

"I'm sorry for your loss," Rose said.

His lip curled up. "Thanks, but you might be mistaken, ladies. This woman isn't my mother. She's nothing but my housekeeper. I know you don't have a lot of work to do these days, Helen, so if you're finished for the day, you can be going. I won't need you any more today."

Regardless of the circumstances, it was a shockingly rude thing to say. Color flooded Helen's face, and her hands clenched at her sides.

Bernie leapt to her feet, and I followed. Rose rested her own hands on the top of her cane. "Mrs. Chambers was explaining to us how like family you've always been to her." Rose's tone was sharp. "Is that not true, young man?"

This time it was Stephen's turn to flush. He gave Rose a small bow. "Helen's worked for my family for a long time.

She came here not long after my father married his first wife. I suppose some allowances can be made for so many years of . . . occasionally loyal service. Nevertheless, work is what she does, and she's always been paid well in exchange. She's not paid to throw a coffee party in my living room."

"Speaking of work," Bernie said. "What do you do?"

"Me? A bit of this. A bit of that." He gave her a long, appraising look. Judging by the expression on his face, he liked what he saw, despite the fact that she was a good foot taller than him.

She tilted her chin down and blinked from under her lashes. "Sounds intriguing."

"I've been living in California for a couple of years, but I might be moving back here. If things pan out. My mother died not long ago, and her affairs . . . have to be settled."

"I'm sorry to hear that. And then the death of your sister so soon after." Bernie's green eyes were wide, overflowing with sympathy.

"Thanks. It was tough, losing my mom. As for Kimmy . . . I can't say we were close, not over the last few years, anyway, but it's been a hard blow."

Helen scoffed.

He turned to her. "Sorry, what was that? I missed it."

She began collecting cups and putting them on the tray. I hadn't finished my coffee yet, but I wasn't about to protest.

"Thank you for coming," Helen said. "It was kind of you. Stephen, I'll leave you to show our guests out. If you can find your way to the front door." Helen left the room. Bernie gave Rose an arm to help her to her feet.

"Sorry about that," Stephen said. "Miserable old bat. There's going to be some changes around here, and soon."

Rose gave him a furious glare. "Your housekeeper has

been employed by your family for many years. Are you suggesting you're going to toss her into the street?"

Stephen lifted his hands in protest. "Whoa! Don't be so quick to jump to her defense. She's never approved of me, and I never much cared. Her future, and that of this house, isn't up to me. All I mean is, my mom's dead, one sister's dead, the other's goodness knows where and not answering her phone. My mother never cared for my lifestyle, and she might have been right about that. I was written out of the will a long time ago, and I've gotten over it. If my father's house goes to my late sister's slimy husband, I'll get over that, too." He grinned at Bernie. "I've always been an optimist. I hope I run into you again someday."

"Maybe," she said.

"It seems to me," I said once we were on the road heading north toward North Augusta, "that I read about that family somewhere."

"You mean in the paper?" Bernie asked.

"No, it reminds me of *Rebecca*, the novel by Daphne du Maurier."

She fell back laughing. "Oh, yeah. I can see it. I haven't read the book, but I've seen a couple of movie versions. The loyal housekeeper, the constant haunting memory of the late first wife, divided loyalties. Did you notice how Helen kept calling Stephen and Kimberly's father Mr. Julian, but their mother was just plain Rosemary. And wow, does Helen have some opinions on the kids in that family."

"Not fond of Stephen to put it mildly."

"No, and as for Stephen . . . There's something really off with him," Bernie said.

"Other than being an obnoxious jerk?"

"That was about the most ham-handed attempt at flirting I've ever encountered and, as you well know, I spent a good part of my college years participating in the Manhattan club scene. It was as though he was onstage, and not doing a very good job of it. Playing a part, but he didn't have his heart in it."

"It's been many a long year since any young man attempted to flirt with me," Rose said. "So long, I've completely forgotten what it's like, but I'll take your word for it. One day you must tell me about this Manhattan club scene, Bernadette. Perhaps Stephen's behavior was a part of his dominance display over Helen."

"Could be," I said. "She's got no love lost for Rachel, either. Kimberly was clearly her favorite, whether that was deserved or not we'll never know." I told them what I'd learned in the kitchen. "Much the same story as Rachel told me about the third will, although Helen put an entirely different slant on it, implying Rachel manipulated her dying mother into rewriting the will, yet again."

"I don't suppose she happened to mention where this third will is now?" Rose asked.

"Unfortunately not."

"Stephen said he didn't care what happens to the family estate," Bernie said. "Can we believe him?"

"In that, I detected a note of sincerity, for what that's worth," I replied. "He's been away from the family for a long time. Did you notice he called Wesley slimy? Makes me think he's a good judge of character."

"Helen was impressed by him. Wes, I mean."

"Exactly. Which makes me wonder about the value of her judgment. She implied, strongly, without coming out and saying so, that Rachel killed her mother, or at least contributed to her death, once Rosemary had rewritten the will."

"That's a heck of a thing to say." Bernie leaned farther forward. "Do you think it has any merit?"

"I don't know. The police didn't, according to Helen, give it much consideration."

"They don't always say out loud what they're thinking."

"As we well know." I had a sudden thought, and I pulled off to the side of the road. I turned in my seat so I could face Rose and Bernie. "I'm curious about the tea chest. The one that contained the will. Didn't that antique dealer tell us she has a store in Chatham? As long as we're here, I'd like to pay a call on her. Bernie, can you look her up and see what the store hours are? D. McIntosh, Fine Antiques, her sign said, as I recall."

"On it." Bernie pushed buttons and scrolled. "Got it. Address isn't far from here, and as it's a Wednesday, she should be open."

I pulled back into traffic. Bernie read the directions off her phone, and we arrived in less than five minutes. The antique shop occupied space in a tired-looking strip mall. A dollar store at one end, a fast-food joint at the other, nail bars and convenience stores in between. Not many cars were in the parking lot, but the sign in the window of D. McIntosh, Fine Antiques was turned to OPEN.

The chimes over the door tinkled cheerfully when we went in. The woman we'd met at the antique fair was behind the sales counter, flicking idly through a magazine. When she heard the bells, she looked up with a smile of anticipation.

The shop put me in mind of a scene out of Dickens. Small, dark, dusty nooks and crannies stuffed with long-forgotten items, cobwebs clinging to the corners. Almost every inch of space was filled with what to my eye looked like nothing but junk. Wooden furniture badly in need of refurbishing, chairs and sofas covered with fabric so sun-faded it was impossible to tell what color they'd originally been. Wobbly-legged tables piled high with yellowing magazines and posters, torn and broken toys, rusting watering cans, milk-glass jugs and dishes, ancient toasters, rotary dial black telephones, tarnished and dusty military and service medals. A tallboy, one of the few pieces of furniture that had received a proper dusting and a layer of furniture polish, displayed a nice arrangement of good china and silver. A Wedgwood tea service caught my eye, and I took a step in that direction. Bernie grabbed my arm and said, "Concentrate."

"Hello," Ms. McIntosh said. "Welcome. We've met before, haven't we? Sorry, I don't remember where."

"We were at the North Augusta community hall a week ago," Bernie said.

She broke into a huge smile and hurried out from behind the counter. "I remember. The people from the tearoom. You were interested in tea settings." She indicated the tallboy. "I've got a few more items in since then. Feel free to have a look."

"Thanks." My eyes wandered back to the Wedgwood. It was a gorgeous set, in the classic Wedgwood blue pattern with cream-colored grapes around the edges and footed cups. Eight cups and matching saucers for three hundred dollars. A steal!

"We're not here to buy," Bernie said quickly. "Sorry, but we want to ask you about something that happened at that event."

"Shoot. What do you what to know?"

I dragged my attention back to the matter at hand. "I bought a Peter Rabbit children's set in a wicker box. Do you remember the piece I mean?"

"I sure do remember that one. And not just because it was nice." She chuckled. "I wish I had more of them. It turned out to be pretty popular."

"Popular?"

"A couple of people have been looking for it."

"A couple? Can you describe them?"

"Two women, but they didn't come together. The first came to the show a couple of days after you. It was Saturday, probably in the afternoon as the hall was absolutely packed. It was a successful show. She was looking for that box in particular and described it perfectly. You gave me your card, so I told her where to find you. I hope I didn't cause you any problems?"

That was an understatement, but I said, "That's fine. No harm done. She did track me down. Thanks."

"The second woman came in the next day. I didn't say anything about the first woman, but I told her I'd sold the set. She was upset and asked if I remembered who'd bought it. As I'd already given the first one your info, I did the same for the second."

"Had you seen either of these women before?" Bernie asked.

"Not that I remember. And I probably would have. The first one was a stuck-up little thing. She demanded to know where the box was and then turned outright rude when I said I'd sold it. I probably should have phoned you to ask if I could send her on to you, but I didn't think of it. Sorry. Like I said, we were busy, and I had customers waiting. Maybe I hoped she'd return the favor by buying something. No such luck. I gave her the name of your tearoom and she stalked out without bothering to say thank you. I watched her go. She didn't visit any of the other booths; she marched straight out of there like a woman on a mission."

"Which she was," I said. "What about the second woman?"

"She came in the next day, Sunday, not long after opening. She was also looking for that tea set in particular. She was few years older than the first one. Taller, with long black hair. A heck of a lot politer." Rachel. "I gave her the name of your restaurant, too. I'd given it to the rude one, so I figured I might as well tell the polite one."

"I'm confused," I said. "You said you'd never seen either of them before. But didn't the first woman sell it to you in the first place?" Rachel told me Kimberly sold their mother's things without first asking if Rachel wanted any of it.

"I see a heck of a lot of people in this job. I'm sure you do, too, in your business. Much of the stuff I buy and sell is the same as all the rest. Silver cutlery and tea sets. Dinner dishes no one wants. Old medals from long-forgotten ancestors. But I do remember buying that tea chest because it was particularly nice. A man brought it in."

"Can you describe him?" I asked.

"Early to midthirties, maybe. Skinny, on the short side for a man. Long, thin, twitchy fingers. The nervous type." This had to be Stephen, Kimberly and Rachel's brother. "He had a box of other stuff, too, good quality most of it. Silver photo frames that are worth something, a couple of vintage rings and a nice broach."

"Jewelry?"

She laughed. "Not the valuable stuff, no. I don't handle that." She indicated a display case on the sales counter. Rhinestones and sequins and colored glass shimmered in the light above the counter. "Midcentury costume jewelry is hugely popular these days, so I do a nice business in it. And, yes, before you ask, I can recognize costume jewelry from the real thing. If he had good jewelry, I would have sent him to a jeweler who gives me a finder's fee."

"Did the women tell you why they wanted the Peter Rabbit set?" Bernie asked.

"They both said it belonged to their late mother and had great sentimental value, but it had been sold to me by another family member by mistake. I've heard that story more times than you'd believe, and I might have had some sympathy, except that the first one didn't seem all that emotional about it. I wondered if that story was even true. The second woman was upset when I said I didn't have it, yes, but she poked around a bit before leaving. She recognized a broach as one that had been in the lot the young man sold me, so she bought it. She seemed happy to have it. What happened to the set? Did one of them buy it off you?"

"They ended up not wanting it after all."

"Weird. But no weirder than a lot of things I see in this business. You would not believe some of the things people will fight over."

The chimes tinkled and Darlene called, "Feel free to browse." She then said to us, "If that's all . . ."

"Thank you, you've been very helpful. Let's go, Rose. Rose?"

My grandmother was admiring the items in the tallboy. "This is a lovely collection of Wedgwood. Reminds me of preparing tea in the kitchens at Thornecroft Castle when Lady Frockmorton was entertaining special guests." Rose leaned over and peered at the price tag. "How much is it, dear?"

"I'm asking three hundred dollars," Darlene said, "but because I apologize if I caused any trouble by sending those women after you, I'll give it to you for two hundred and fifty."

"That's rather a lot," Bernie said as Rose opened her purse.

"My Christmas present to you," Rose said as I loaded the box of Wedgwood into the trunk.

"Thanks, but it was too much to spend for items for the tearoom."

"You spent a hundred and sixty on the children's set," Bernie said.

"And wasn't that a mistake. Look at the trouble that caused us."

"Ms. McIntosh broadly hinted that Kimberly was rude because she didn't buy something in exchange for information." Rose settled herself into her seat and fastened her seat belt. "I don't want her bad-mouthing us to the next person who comes calling."

"I hope no one will come calling on her or anyone else with questions about us," I said.

"Reputation is important. As Lady Frockmorton pointed out to Mr. Cairncross, the butler they employed for all of two weeks before he was caught rifling through the drawers in a guest bedroom. It turns out he forged his letter of recommendation and . . ."

"A story for another day," I said. "Looks like it was Stephen, not Kimberly, who sold the Peter Rabbit tea chest. Then Kimberly tried to get it back."

"Do you think it matters who sold it?" Bernie asked.

"Probably not. But I was curious. It's another piece of the puzzle. Kimberly would have been furious at him when she found out what he'd done."

"What next, love?" Rose asked once we were under way.

"Tearoom and a day's work for me. I don't know what we achieved this morning, but I'm glad we came, even though it seems to have done nothing more than muddy the waters still further."

"The water is always muddiest before the clearing. Or something like that," Bernie said. "I'll see what else I can dig up regarding the affairs of the Smithfield family, as well as Wesley's financial situation. Speaking of Wesley, I have an assignment for you, Rose."

Rose clapped her hands. "Excellent. What can I do? Scale the outside of the house to access his room in the dead of night? Tie him to a chair and hold him at gunpoint until he confesses? Use my feminine wiles to convince him to run away with me?"

"That's painting a picture I don't want to see," I said.

"You're closer than you know," Bernie said. "He thinks himself a charmer. Stereotypically, no one can be charmed faster than little old ladies. Invite him for a drink on the veranda. Tell him you're *soooo* interested in hearing all about his new restaurant venture. Maybe suggest a partnership—you'll recommend his place to your guests in return for certain favors."

"Definitely not a picture I want to see," I said.

"Not that sort of favor," Bernie said. "All I'm saying is, give him a chance to talk about himself and see what spills out."

Rose chuckled. "Mata Hari had nothing on me."

"That might be a nice angle for the book," Bernie said. "I could introduce a *femme fatale*–type spy character to act as a nemesis to Rose and Tessa."

"No," I said.

I hadn't missed too much work time in my expedition to Chatham, and I dove straight back into it after dropping Rose and Bernie at the house.

I was getting started on a batch of shortbread when, of all people, Rachel Morrison strolled into my kitchen. "You've done a good job decorating this place, Lil, but it could use a few discreet modernizations. I'm thinking Art Deco–style paintings of members of the royal family. Something to ground us firmly in the twenty-first century amidst the tradition of afternoon tea itself."

"I don't want my tearoom to be grounded in the twenty-first century, thank you very much."

"Everything okay?" Cheryl asked. "I told this lady I'd see if you had time to talk to her but—"

"Not a problem," Rachel said. "I know my way. How about a consultation? Say an hour? I'll do it for free to apologize for the trouble certain members of my family have caused you." Her attitude today was bubbly and cheerful, and she'd dressed in plain, but nice, white jeans and a fresh bright yellow summer blouse. Her makeup was subdued, and her hair cascaded in sleek waves down her back. Something had happened to improve her mood since she'd been in here yesterday, when she'd been "on the lam," so to speak.

I added flour, cornstarch, and icing sugar to the butter in the mixer, switched it on, and spoke over the roar of the small motor. "It's okay, Cheryl, thanks. How's it looking out there?"

"Full house on the patio, three quarters of the indoor seats taken. A couple of groups declined to sit inside and are wandering through the gardens, waiting for an outdoor table to come free."

"Sounds good. Why are you here, Rachel?"

"To offer my professional services? No, I'll admit that came as an afterthought. I wanted to let you know I showed my smiling face at the police station this morning and had a nice chat with your detectives."

I turned the mixer off and scraped down the sides of the bowl. "You obviously haven't been arrested."

"They were a mite touchy at first, demanding to know why I never returned their calls. 'Calls?' I said sweetly, 'Have you been calling me? I was so overcome by the news of my beloved little sister's tragic and unexpected death, I turned my phone off.' They calmed down eventually. That is to say, he did, the fat, old cop. I don't think she lets anything ruffle her hair, does she? Oh, sorry, am I in your way?" She stepped to one side to let Cheryl pass with her tray containing two teapots. The smokey scent of Lapsang souchong filled the air. "You need a larger kitchen, Lily.

That will be difficult, with the limited space you have and these old stone walls." Rachel rapped her knuckles on the wall next to the back door. "Too bad. I was hoping this might be a façade, but nope, solid stone. You could reduce some of the area where you display that stuff for sale and knock out part of that wall. Open kitchens are all the rage these days. Maybe stop selling that kitsch all together. You probably don't sell much, if any, of it."

I had not the slightest intention of ever working in an open kitchen. Never mind that we made a nice bit of extra income from the sale of fine teas, individual teacups and pots, and locally made preserves. Speaking of which, I might try to unload the Wedgwood set Rose had bought, which I hadn't yet taken out of the car. I switched the mixer back on. "I'm pleased they didn't arrest you, Rachel. Now, if you don't mind, I have work to do."

"They didn't arrest me because I have an alibi."

Despite myself, I switched off the mixer. "You do?"

"Thanks to you, Lily, the time of Kimberly's death is pretty much fixed. At that particular time, I was in a charming bar in your charming town, drinking away my sorrows. I spent most of my time chatting to a nice young man and, in case you're interested, chatting is all we did. When we left, he gave me his number. Which I had no intention of ever following up on, but that's irrelevant to the present situation. Fortunately, I didn't simply toss the paper with his number in the nearest trash can. I wanted to talk to him before reporting to the police, to make sure he'd tell them he was with me. The bar was crowded, and I wasn't sure the bartender would remember me or notice what time I left. Tracking the guy down took most of yesterday—he has a charter fishing boat and doesn't switch his personal phone on when he's out with clients. He agreed to come to the police station with me this morning. Wasn't that nice?" She studied the desserts, ready to be arranged on stands for our guests, and helped herself to a hazelnut macaron. "Very nice."

"Thanks for letting me know. Were you here yesterday afternoon?"

"No."

"At the B & B maybe?"

"Funny you should ask that. The police did as well. I told them a slightly different version of what I'll tell you. I was not, considering I was in hiding pending my interview with the forces of law and order. I prefer to do those things on my own terms. Did something happen here?" Rachel smiled at me around the macaron. "As good as anything I had in Paris."

"Thanks." Had she been in the B & B yesterday while Wesley was out? Had she tossed his room, searching for the will? Had she found it? I might as well come right out and ask. "Have you located your mother's third will?"

Her face fell. "No, I'm beginning to fear it's long gone. If Kimberly didn't destroy it, Wesley would have."

"If she showed it to him. She might not have."

"True. Somewhere deep inside, she had to have known he only married her for her money. The money she thought she had."

"Does Kimberly have a will?"

"I don't know. I called our family lawyer, and he says he didn't prepare one for her. No reason she wouldn't have gone to someone else. I'd certainly never let him handle my affairs."

"Why not?"

"I can't stand him, and I never fully trusted him. My stepfather made some massively poor investment decisions in his later years, and I suspect his lawyer was the one who advised him on that. I didn't want him handling any of our legal affairs after Julian died, and I told Mom so, but she seemed to think she should have some loyalty to him and his firm as they'd been the Smithfield lawyers for generations."

"I don't know anything about the laws of inheritance," I said. No one in my family has ever had enough for any of us to worry about. "If Kimberly died without a will, won't her husband get it all?"

"He'll get whatever's hers. He will not get what I can prove is mine. If I can prove it. Which is why I need to find that will. If it still exists."

"Royal tea for six. Full afternoon tea for two," Marybeth called. All the while Rachel and I had been talking, Marybeth and Cheryl were in and out of the kitchen, going about their tasks. Trying, that is, to go about their tasks.

"Good luck," I said. "What will you do now?"

"I truly do not know, Lily. Helen Chambers, that's our family's longtime housekeeper, as much a mother to me sometimes as my own mother, called me last night. She left a message, so I returned the call when I switched on the phone after leaving the police station. We had a nice, long chat. I missed her in the short time I was persona non grata in Kimberly's house. Now that it's not Kimberly's house any longer, I'm welcome to come and stay as long as I like. My brother's decided not to go back to California yet and has parked himself there."

I dumped handfuls of shortbread dough onto the counter and began rolling it out prior to slicing and baking. I probably should tell Rachel I'd been at the house earlier today, but for some reason I held my tongue. What Rachel was telling me about Helen was a sharp contrast to what Helen had said to me about her. I didn't say that, either.

"However," she continued, "I'm reluctant to leave here

until I know for sure that my mother's last will is lost, or I finally give up all hope. I don't suppose you have any spare rooms in your grandmother's B & B?"

"Sorry, no. Fully booked. One came free, but Wesley took it."

"He's staying on?"

"He seems," I chose my words carefully, "to be more concerned about his business venture than preparing for his wife's funeral."

Cheryl heard that last comment as she came into the kitchen. "No surprise there. For some of them, money's the most important thing there is. It's none of my business, and I don't know you," she said to Rachel, "but you are standing there, directly in my path, talking about your personal affairs, so I'll give you a piece of advice for free. Let it go. Nothing good comes out of a family fighting over money."

"You wouldn't fight for what's rightfully yours?" Rachel asked her.

"I wouldn't destroy my family over it. No matter if we didn't get along. Family's still family."

"And my mom," Marybeth said, "knows all about feuding families. Right, Mom?"

"Enough lollygagging," Cheryl said. "We have a full house out there, a lineup's forming at the gate, and I don't see anyone else making those cookies. Marybeth, dishwasher's finished its cycle."

"I can take a hint," Rachel said. "I'll get out of your hair."

"'Bout time," Cheryl mumbled.

"I want to hear the story about this feuding family of yours," I said as the door closed behind Rachel, "but now is not the time. Whatever you do, don't tell Bernie. She'll get it into her head that she needs conflict—more conflict—among her characters' relatives, and then she'll be off on another tangent."

Cheryl laughed. Marybeth unloaded the dishwasher.

Shortbread in the oven, I turned my attention to preparing the pastry for fruit tarts. As I measured flour and sugar, weighed butter, and judged the correct amount of ice water, I thought about Rachel and her alibi. If her alibi, this charter boat captain she supposedly met in a bar, was good enough for the police, it had to be good enough for me.

Meaning, Rachel Morrison had not murdered her half sister.

Is that the end of that? Perhaps not. Considering the animosity between the sisters and the ongoing fight over the inheritance, Rachel had to know she'd be the prime suspect in Kimberly's death. Killers can be hired. Friends convinced to do the deed in exchange for favors. I tried to remember what I'd overheard of the argument outside my window Monday night. Kimberly had said she wasn't going to agree to . . . something.

Had Rachel asked, or paid, someone to approach Kimberly on her behalf, to suggest they come to an agreement about the will, and had things escalated until they were out of control? Or had the conversation about . . . whatever it was . . . merely been a ruse to get her out of the house? A nice walk, a private chat, and then . . .

Chapter 16

I pushed aside all thoughts of feuding families, lost wills, and murder most foul for the remainder of the day and got on with trying to make a living. I stayed late to catch up on my baking and prepare for another busy day tomorrow, and the sun was dipping into the bay when I locked up and headed home. I hadn't heard from the police today, and that was definitely a good thing. Redmond must have been able to convince Williams that Wesley's accusations against me had no merit.

I'd like to learn more about what had been going on. I'd like to keep digging. But I did have a restaurant to run and no time to open a detective agency as a side business.

A car passed me as I strolled up the driveway, enjoying the quiet of the evening. It was a Cadillac Escalade, black paint gleaming. A silver-haired man gave me a casual glance as he drove by. I didn't recognize him, and I assumed he was a B & B guest, arriving late. He parked the car, climbed out, and headed directly for the house. He was alone, dressed in a dark suit, carrying only a briefcase. Unlikely to be a guest, then.

I didn't turn off toward my cottage but followed him

onto the veranda. No one was sitting out tonight, having a drink after dinner and relaxing from a busy day before turning in, so he'd rung the bell.

"Good evening," I said. "Can I help you? Are you looking for a room for the night?"

He turned. He was around seventy. Short gray hair above a high forehead, light tan, thick glasses, teeth so white and straight they had to be dentures, manicured hands. "Do you work here?"

"I'm the granddaughter of the owner."

At that moment the door opened to reveal Wesley Schumann. "Hi, Martin, thanks for coming. Lily, what's up?"

"I was asking this gentleman if he needed anything."

"I've got this, thanks. He's here to talk to me."

"If you have business to discuss," I said helpfully, "you'd be more comfortable in the drawing room, if it's not in use. Do you want me to check?"

"Good idea," Martin said. "I hate doing business in hotel rooms." I led him inside, and he looked around. "Nice house, this. How long has your grandmother owned it?"

"About three years."

"She do okay out of it?"

"Well enough."

He passed me a square of thick paper. "My card. If you need any legal advice, happy to help."

"We don't, but . . . thank you."

The drawing room serves as a common room for guests. A place where people can gather if it's a rainy day or if they don't want to read alone in their room. We stock it with board games and well-thumbed paperbacks. Tonight, it was empty, and I gestured to Wesley and his visitor to come in.

Wesley gave me a sideways glance as he passed. "Thanks, Lily."

I began to shut the door. I assumed this was one of the people Wesley was trying to interest in his new restaurant venture, and I was going to leave them to it, when Martin said, "As the Smithfield family's longtime lawyer, I—"

I shut the door and took stock of my surroundings. No one was in the hallway, no footsteps sounded on the stairs or drifted down from the second-floor landing. No voices out on the veranda. I opened the door to the linen closet and stepped quickly inside, pulling the door shut after me.

What can I say? Wesley had involved me in his business by telling the police I might have killed his wife. In return, I had no qualms about eavesdropping on his conversation with his lawyer.

I piled linens on the floor and pulled the lever concealed beneath the second from the bottom shelf. The shelves slid silently aside, revealing a person-sized gap low to the floor. I crouched down and waddled into the secret room. The wall separating this space and the drawing room was not only exceedingly thin, but small holes had been drilled through them and covered with an oil painting in a heavy, ornate frame.

My grandmother and I don't make a habit of hiding in the secret room behind the linen cupboard eavesdropping on our guests, but we have found it handy when the police have commandeered the drawing room to interrogate suspects.

". . . lack of a will complicates things, but not unduly," Martin was saying. "Under the laws of Massachusetts a spouse is automatically entitled to the entirely of the estate if the husband or wife dies intestate, providing there are no other potential heirs, such as children or grandchildren."

"But . . ." Wesley said. "It's because of the but in this case I wanted to talk it over with you personally. I apologize for the late hour, but I had business meetings all day. Very promising meetings, I might add."

"Glad to hear it. I trust you're aware your late wife's sister maintains their mother had written another will, and she has witnesses to confirm it."

"Kimmy told me all about it. She also told me their mother changed her mind, once again, and destroyed the will. Rachel's chasing shadows. Sorry, I can't offer you a drink. I'd call the staff and ask what they have, but . . . let's say the lady you met earlier is not inclined to do me any favors these days."

Got that one right, Wessie.

"Why are you staying here, then?"

"Why not? It's a nice place."

"If you have personal complications with the owners, I'd advise you not to draw them out."

"Complications is the word. Let it go. Back to the will. Wills. Tell me what you know about all that."

"Rachel Morrison claims her mother's last will specified that her estate was to be divided equally between the two sisters, following provisions made for their brother, Stephen, and various household staff. That will cannot be located. If it is located, Mr. Schumann, it will take precedence over the one Mrs. Smithfield filed with me, the one leaving the entirety of the estate, minus minor provisions, to Kimberly alone. Do you understand?"

"How long does Rachel have to locate the new will and turn it over to the court?"

"She has forever. As long as she lives."

Wesley swore. I heard footsteps as he paced up and down. "Meaning it will hang over my head as long as she lives."

"Her and any heirs she herself might have."

More swearing.

"If the new will is found, it will have to pass legal scrutiny, and there's no guarantee of success. A handwritten will is perfectly legal, but strict conditions have to be met.

Properly witnessed, signed, and dated, for example. The signer must have been in full possession of her wits and fully aware of what she was doing, without being unduly influenced."

"You can testify Mrs. Smithfield wasn't of sound mind. If the will shows up, that is."

"I cannot say that, Mr. Schumann. Because it is not true."

"I'd . . . ensure you were properly renumerated."

"I'll ignore that suggestion, but even if I was inclined to accept, Mrs. Smithfield's doctor and her private nurse would contradict me. As would her housekeeper, Mrs. Chambers."

"Just a thought."

"My advice to you, young man, is to let things fall where they may. The will is lost. Almost certainly Mrs. Smithfield had another change of heart and threw out the handwritten will. There would be no reason for her to write yet another will superseding it, as her earlier will was filed with my office and remains valid in the lack of a later one. Her husband was a close friend of mine, and through that relationship I knew her well. My wife and I dined often at their house and they at ours, although I've seen little of Mrs. Smithfield, and nothing outside of business, since Julian's death. My wife wanted to continue the friendship, but Rosemary cut her off. Rosemary was a woman of strong opinions, particularly about people, and quick to express them. I might have admired that, except she changed those strong opinions for the slightest of reasons and sometimes for no reason at all. No reason I could see at any rate. In my opinion, she threw away the handwritten will, probably before the ink was dry."

"I can count on that?"

"No, you cannot. You should not. Rachel is looking for

it. It might yet be found and be determined to be valid. I trust you're aware that the fortunes of the Smithfield family have declined steadily over the past years. Julian Smithfield was my good friend, and I advised him strongly against some of his more perilous investments, when I could. But he was not one to take advice, no matter how sincerely meant."

Rachel told me the lawyer had given that poor financial advice to her stepfather. Interesting, but probably irrelevant. The man wouldn't confess to it, and Rachel wouldn't have had insights into her stepfather's financial affairs.

"What are you saying?" Wesley asked.

"The majority of the inheritance is in the house. There isn't much in the way of cash, and little of value in stocks and mutual funds. Julian sold most of his stock in Smithfield Industries to make the aforementioned bad investments."

"Is the house mortgaged?"

"No."

"It's got to be worth a lot."

"It is."

There was a long silence as Wesley digested the news. "Can I sell it?" he said at last.

"If Rachel continues to contest the will, the matter will be drawn out. Eventually, if the other will fails to materialize, yes. It will be yours to sell."

"I can't wait for a long, drawn-out legal matter to be resolved. I need . . . funds now."

Martin said nothing.

"Okay," Wesley said. "I guess that sounds bad, put like that. Let's be honest here. Kimberly told me the fight with her sister concerning a new will was over, and she planned to sell the house. She intended to invest much of the proceeds in my restaurant venture. She figured she'd get upwards of twenty million for the house."

I whistled under my breath. Twenty million bucks would build a lot of restaurants.

"Even if the inheritance is quickly settled in your favor with no further complications, my advice would be to not rush things. Houses of that size and cost can take considerable time to find the right buyer, one who is prepared to pay full value. In order to get that full value . . . The house has, shall we say, been in need of structural improvements for a while. Extensive structural improvements."

"I'll cross that bridge when I get to it."

"You could come to an agreement with Rachel," Martin said. "It's to discuss that possibility I've come all this way to talk to you. As I said, Rosemary was a woman of changing opinions. She removed Rachel from her will because Rachel went to Europe. She then decided to put her back. If you agree to divide Kimberly's inheritance with Rachel, you can put all the uncertainty behind you."

If Wesley did have to share the estate with Rachel, and they sold the house, he'd get something slightly under ten million dollars. Less if it was a rushed sale without doing the "structural improvements" needed. Whatever he ended up with, it would provide him with a nice lifestyle. I didn't think he had much to complain about. But, I remembered, Wesley could always find something to complain about.

"What about Stephen, the black sheep brother? Suppose he wants a cut, too?"

"He is entitled to, as you put it, a cut, under both—all—of Rosemary's wills. That's a set amount."

"Not to mention a pack of servants." Wesley continued to pace.

Martin cleared his throat. "My advice to you is to talk this over with Rachel. And with Stephen. Lay all the cards on the table. Rachel might agree to a smaller share in order avoid the trouble of continuing to dispute the will. However . . ." His voice faded away.

"What now?" Wesley snapped.

"Rachel might not agree to sell the house."

"What does that mean?"

"What I said."

"This whole thing gets worse and worse. Look, I don't want anything I'm not entitled to."

Liar.

"But my wife has died and her property is now mine." Wesley's voice got stronger as he approached the wall behind which I sat. He spoke directly to the painting in a voice so low, Martin might not have been able to hear. But I could. "She told me she'd inherited her mother's entire estate; we'd sell the house and put the money into my restaurants. And now I find out all I'm likely to get is years of legal bills and a half share in an old house I don't want." He swore again.

He turned and spoke to Martin. "I have a lot of irons in the fire right now. I've got plans to open two restaurants and possibly a third. I told my potential partners I've got enough cash on hand to settle the debts in my Manhattan place plus fund the initial investment. What am I going to say now?"

"What you tell them," Martin said, "is entirely up to you."

Chapter 17

Every time I decided I didn't need to be involved in this case, something happened to draw me back in.

After what I'd overheard in the drawing room, I had to consider that Wesley himself might have killed Kimberly. If he married her expecting her to give him the money he needed for his restaurants, had he decided he didn't need her anymore? Had she been getting cold feet and starting to balk at the idea of handing over a substantial chunk of her inheritance?

If Wesley had killed his wife, all the more reason for him to try to pin the crime on someone else. That someone else might still be me.

What about Rachel? If Wesley killed Kimberly for the Smithfield estate, would he decide he now had to get rid of Rachel, so as not to have to share with her if the new will ever did come to light?

Martin said it was time he was on his way, and Wesley showed him to the door. I waited until I heard Wesley climbing the stairs before slipping out of the linen closet.

A line of light shone from beneath the door to Rose's

suite. I knocked and announced myself, and she called for me to come in.

She was dressed in her long white cotton nightgown, a cup of tea on the table beside her. One part of Rose's sitting room serves as the B & B office—desk, ergonomic chair, computer, corkboard covered in notes, filing cabinet—the rest is her own living room. The table next to her was covered with silver frames containing family portraits dating all the way from Rose's own wedding to her latest great-grandchild. Bookcases were stuffed to overflowing with the English mysteries she loved, and a big-screen TV hung on the far wall. Robbie was curled up in her lap, and the TV was showing a costume drama. The cat opened one eye, saw it was only me, and closed it again.

"Cuppa, love?" Rose said. "The pot's still warm."

"No, thanks."

She picked up the remote and pressed a button. The TV went dark. "Something wrong?"

"Wesley had a visit from the Smithfield family lawyer. Essentially what he said is that Wes will inherit everything that had been Kimberly's, but if Rachel can find the third will and it's legally valid, he'll have to share with her. Wesley doesn't like to share. He wants to sell the house as fast as he can. In the meantime, Rachel's likely to throw up legal roadblocks, insisting she needs time to find the missing will."

"Families." Rose stroked Robbie. "Aren't you glad your grandfather and I weren't rich, love? Your mother and her brothers have nothing to fight over."

I decided not to think about what would happen to Victoria-on-Sea, and thus Tea by the Sea, which sat on the property, when Rose went to her reward. "Wesley has never been a patient man, and he's juggling lots of balls trying to work out negotiations for these restaurant plans of his. He's got to be getting desperate. I'm worried—"

"That he might decide to eliminate Rachel's potential complications."

"The thought did cross my mind. That's if he killed Kimberly, and we have absolutely no reason to believe he was responsible for that."

My grandmother studied my face. "I regret to say I failed in my assigned mission."

"Mission? What mission?"

"Of allowing Wesley to charm me and thus spilling all his secrets. I invited him to join me on the veranda, with the aim of engaging him in an intimate chat, but he brushed me off. You know this man, Lily. What do you think? Is he capable of murder? Of killing a wife on their honeymoon?"

I thought for a long time before answering. "I suppose anyone's capable of killing given the right circumstances. Wesley has a temper, as I well know, and he likes to have his own way, no matter the cost to someone else. He acts without thinking through the consequences. Yes, he might have lashed out and killed Kimberly, but I don't think he'd have the self-control to stay here playing the innocent. He'd run for the hills, which in his case is Manhattan. But that's only my opinion, and I might be wrong. Wesley's full of storm and thunder. High drama. He likes to play the bad-boy chef in all his glorious rage. Some people still think temper's the sign of a good chef. I think it's the sign of a spoiled brat, but never mind that now. I find it entirely possible to believe Wesley could get into an argument, a serious argument, with his wife, and for things to get way out of hand. But the voices I heard outside my window Monday night were not of a serious argument between two people. Kimberly was angry, and she was yelling. The person she had been with had not been yelling. It wasn't

Wesley. Again, I could be wrong. He didn't kill her in a sudden flash of temper, but if he'd planned ahead of time to get rid of her, he might have suggested a walk, let her rant and rave and blow off steam, and then . . ."

"And then . . ." Rose said. "Money truly is the root of all evil. Wasn't Bernadette going to look further into this horrid man's financial affairs?"

I dropped into a chair and pulled out my phone. "I do believe she was." I put the phone on speaker so Rose could listen in, and I made the call.

"I was going to give you my report in the morning," Bernie said. "I had some luck. Earlier I said he seemed to be doing okay. Not quite right. Wesley Schumann is, essentially, underwater."

"Meaning?"

"He's more than broke, Lily. From what I can find, which isn't always fully conclusive, he has substantial debts he can't pay."

"I know he isn't rich, but I didn't know things were that bad. West Steak House is doing well, isn't it?"

"Have you been keeping up with the gossip in the Manhattan restaurant world, Lily?"

"No. I made some calls when that reality TV show was filming here, but no one I spoke to said anything about Wesley. I didn't ask. I didn't want to know. I still don't want to know, but it looks as though I need to."

"Do you know the name Luis Rodrigues?"

"Sure. He's the head chef at West when Wesley's not around. Wesley owns the place, his name's on the sign, and he designed the menus and all, but he doesn't work there full time. Particularly not now that he's trying to open more restaurants."

"Luis quit about six months ago, not long after you left, Lily, and everyone says the food has gone steadily downhill since then. Word is Wesley was coasting on both Luis and you. Luis with the meals, and you as the pastry chef. And now that you're both gone, West Steak House doesn't cut it anymore. Hey, I made a pun. Get it?"

"I get it. One of my friends told me she had lunch there not long ago, and she wasn't impressed. The filling in her chocolate pie was too sweet and too runny. I thought she was being nice, thinking she was making me feel better about leaving by telling me the new pastry chef wasn't doing a good job."

"Reservations are down by more than half in the past six months. Staff, both front of house and kitchen, are quitting in droves, and Wesley's paying bottom dollar for their replacements."

"Meaning he's giving his customers bottom-dollar service."

"Yup. On top of that, a major new restaurant opened less than a block away, serving the same sort of food, and it's getting glowing reviews from basically everyone."

"Thanks, Bernie."

"I had to do a bit of digging into the finer details, but none of this is a terribly well-kept secret," Bernie said. "Any people Wesley might approach to invest in his new venture are going to have all this info. And more."

"Let me think it over, and we can talk tomorrow."

"Night, Lily. Night, Rose."

"Good night," my grandmother and I said.

"Is all that significant, do you think, in the matter of the death of Kimberly?" Rose asked once I'd disconnected.

"It might well be. If Wesley's reputation is on a downward trajectory, no respectable businesspeople will be willing to hand over piles of money for his restaurant venture. Anyone who still wants to invest will expect Wesley to put a heck of a lot of his own money into it, or no go. He needs that inheritance. Which puts him firmly in the frame as preplanning Kimberly's death."

"It also means, love," Rose said, "that he might have to make deals with less than respectable businesspeople. The sort of people who might have decided to . . . shall we say . . . help him secure that inheritance."

Armed with what I'd learned last night, I called Amy Redmond once breakfast service was finished in the B & B, and Éclair and I had retreated to the privacy of our porch with a welcome mug of coffee, a slice of coffee cake, and a dog biscuit.

I've suspected, more than once, that on occasion Bernie goes places on the Internet she isn't supposed to go. It could be tricky, telling the police what we'd learned, without coming right out and telling them how we know. In this case, it was easy. All I was doing was speculating, and I'd invite the detective to speculate also.

"How's the investigating going?" I asked.

"Well enough. Have you learned something I need to know?" She got straight to the point, as always.

"I might have. You might know this, or you might not, but . . ."

"Go ahead."

"I have a lot of contacts in the Manhattan restaurant world. I asked a few questions of my friends." Okay, that wasn't entirely true, but no need to complicate things. "I learned that, basically, West Steak House, Wesley Schumann's flagship restaurant, is failing. It would appear," I added with a touch of pride, "it started down the slippery slope shortly after I left." Honesty forced me to add, "Probably more because the acting head chef left around the same time, but never mind. My point is that restaurant provides Wesley's main income, as far as I know. I dated him for a while, and I didn't see any other sources of funds. Believe me, if he had money to splash around, he would have. He had a TV gig for a short while, but it ended prematurely and nothing else came up."

"We've been investigating the financial situation of all the people in this matter, Lily. Why are you telling me this?"

"I suspect you don't know a lot about the restaurant biz."

"That's true."

"In some ways it's unique, in others it runs like any other business. At the Manhattan Michelin-star level, the head chef *is* the restaurant. Even if he has a chain of places and is the star of a reality TV show or runs a culinary school and is rarely, if ever, to be found with his sleeves up working in front of the ovens. If West Steak House fails, it will fall squarely on Wesley Schumann. *He* will have failed, and no one, no matter what sort of business we're talking about, will pour money into a failing venture. Or give money to a man seen as a failure."

"Yet he's still running around the Cape making deals to open new restaurants. Trying to make deals, I should say."

"Therefore, I have to conclude that his potential business partners either believe he's about to come into enough money to fund the majority of the venture himself, or those partners are the sort who don't worry a great deal about reputations. If you get my drift."

"I believe I do, Lily. We have the NYPD making some inquiries into Mr. Schumann and his affairs. At the moment that's all I can say."

"Okay. Can I ask one quick question?"

"Only one?"

"Does Wesley have an alibi for the time of his wife's murder?"

She was silent for such a long time I thought she wasn't going to answer, but eventually she said, "No. He had dinner in Orleans with a couple of Hyannis businessmen.

They arrived at the restaurant separately and left separately at eight fifteen. One of the men is positive about the time because he received a phone call from his daughter away at college as they were on the sidewalk saying good night. It's about a half-hour drive from Orleans to Victoria-on-Sea, faster in a fancy sports car for someone who doesn't worry too much about accumulating speeding tickets. Mr. Schumann could have arrived at your place as early as twenty to nine."

"I heard Kimberly outside my cottage at nine. You and I saw him drive up around, what, nine forty-five, ten? Any possibility the man with the college-age daughter is lying about the time?"

"The other man they had dinner with agrees with the time frame, and the waiter at the restaurant confirms it. He remembers them well—big spenders, small tippers. Schumann himself doesn't dispute it. He says he had a lot to think about and went for a drive before returning to his B & B. He says the prospects of the deal going through were not looking good, and he had to decide what he was going to tell his wife. Like a lot of men who are too full of themselves, too anxious to impress to think things through before speaking, he hastened to assure me that if one deal fell through he had plenty more irons in the fire. Which might mean less respectable businessmen, as you call them, Lily." A small chuckle came down the line. "Sometimes being a young woman is an unexpected benefit in this job."

I rolled my eyes, although only Éclair was here to see me. Wesley had tried flirting with Amy Redmond. Did the man have no common sense?

I answered my own question: *No.*

"Before you go, Lily, I'll tell you one more thing. The NYPD spoke to the staff at West about possible enemies their boss might have had. No one told them about a former employee slash girlfriend stalking him or otherwise causing trouble."

I started to say, "So?" when I realized the police had been asking about me.

"The staff has turned over almost entirely since you worked there, but one busboy remembered the incident you told us about which occurred between Wesley and you the night you quit, and he backed up your version of events. That person went on to tell us Wesley badmouthed you every chance he got for a long time."

"Thanks for checking," I said.

"Did you doubt we would?"

"No."

"As you are no longer a suspect, Lily—not that in my mind you ever were a very good one—I'll thank you to keep yourself out of my investigation."

"'Bye," I said. *Easier said than done.* Under normal circumstances, I'd be more than happy to go back to work and forget all about what had happened, but Bernie was like a bloodhound on the trail, and once Rose's curiosity had been unleashed, there was no controlling it.

As for me: Rachel and Kimberly and, most of all, Wesley had involved me in their domestic affairs. I wasn't going to drop it that easily.

Chapter 18

I might want to continue investigating, but not being a detective, I didn't know what to do next. I had no leads to follow.

So I finished my coffee and headed into work.

And leads followed me.

As I was crossing the lawn next to the rose garden, heading for Tea by the Sea, a gray Audi pulled up. I expected a distinguished-looking older couple to step out, but to my surprise the man who emerged was Stephen Smithfield, and I remembered Kimberly had also been driving an Audi. Her car had been taken away by the police following her death. It must have been returned to the family, and Stephen was now using it.

He was dressed in ragged-hemmed jeans worn in the knees in what I suspected was not a fashion statement and an AC/DC T-shirt that had seen better days. The untied laces on his right sneaker dragged along the ground behind him. They appeared to be dragged regularly, and the shoe had a hole in the side. His hair was disheveled and he hadn't bothered to shave this morning. Again, not a fashion statement, just neglect or a lack of concern about his appearance.

He walked toward me and gave me a nod of greeting.

"Stephen. Good morning," I said.

"Morning. You're Lily, right? We met at my house in Chatham yesterday."

"I remember. Can I help you?"

"Help me? No, not really. I wanted to . . . have a look around." He indicated Victoria-on-Sea shining in the morning sun.

"Are you interested in gardening?"

"Gardening? No, why do you ask?"

"Our gardens are open to the public and they're considered to be very good. Garden clubs come a long way to see them. You're welcome to tour them, but the house is private."

He rubbed his jaw. A man and a woman—him in garish plaid trousers and orange golf shirt, her in a short white skirt, sleeveless pink top, and pink sun visor—came down the steps.

"Good morning," she called to me. "What a great day to hit the links." They got into their car and drove away.

"My father golfed," Stephen said to me.

"Is that so?"

"He was keen I take it up. In my mind golf must be just about the most boring sport there is. He said it didn't matter if I liked the game or not; if I wanted to be a successful businessman, I had to golf. I told him I didn't want to be a successful businessman, I wanted to be a successful musician. Turns out, I was neither. I'm sorry I wasn't nicer to you and your friends yesterday, when you came to the house."

"You don't have to apologize. This must be a difficult

time for you." He wasn't, in fact, rude to us, but to Helen, and that was not a relationship I wanted to concern myself with.

"No more difficult than any other. Thing is, Helen Chambers has always gotten under my skin. She doted on me when I was little, but as soon as I became a teenager and my father and I started having our differences, she turned on me. She could be more vicious to me than my dad. Always under the pretext of speaking her mind and only wanting what was best for me. She didn't get on all that well with my mother, either, but Mother was too kind to get rid of her. Now that . . . Mother's gone, Helen's enjoying having the house to herself. I sometimes suspect she pretends to herself it's her house."

He grimaced and said, "Sorry. All that's not your problem, is it? I don't quite know why I'm here. I wanted to see where my sister died, I guess."

"Were you two close?"

"Not really. My parents were unemotional people, and my sisters and I were raised to be the same. I was the youngest, and a boy, so my father had different expectations for me than he did for the girls. All water under the bridge now. Can I see it?"

"See what?"

"Where Kimmy died."

I hesitated. I didn't want crime-scene groupies poking around, but Stephen was Kimberly's brother. "I . . . I don't know where exactly, but it happened at the back of the house. Near the cliffs. If you want to have a look around, that should be okay."

"Thanks."

"Have you spoken to Rachel since Kimberly's death?" I asked.

"Yeah, she called me yesterday afternoon. I told her the cops were looking for her, and she said she's spoken to them and has been cleared. I don't know why she's hanging around. Still imagining she's going to find some secret will my mother wrote on her deathbed, I guess."

"You think she's imagining that?"

"The will existed, but it's long gone now. Rachel can't let it go. She's always been like that. If Rachel wants something, she wants it, and no one can tell her she can't have it."

He started to walk away, heading for the back of the house. I wasn't sure what to do. I got the feeling Stephen Smithfield wasn't entirely emotionally stable.

The door to the house opened and Wesley came out. His laptop bag was thrown over his shoulder, and he was dressed in ironed beige slacks and a white shirt. He stopped when he saw me. Or, I realized, he stopped when he saw whom I was with.

The edge of his mouth curled up and he gave his head a shake.

The two men stared at each other for a moment, and then Wesley slowly crossed the veranda and came down the steps. "Looking for me?"

"No," Stephen said. "I'm here to see the place where my sister died. Where you killed her."

I sucked in a breath, but Wesley didn't seem all that concerned at the accusation. "If you've got something to say, kid, spit it out."

Stephen shrugged. "Whether you killed her or not, the result's the same, isn't it? You get her money. Which is all you really ever wanted."

Wesley sneered. "I hear you've moved into the house. Into what's now my house. I'll give you to the end of the week to pack up and get lost."

"My mother's will hasn't been settled yet. In the meantime, I'm fine where I am, thanks."

Wesley's face tightened. A vein began to pulse at the side of his neck. I recognized the signs and wanted to get out of there, fast. "Let's go, Stephen. I'll walk with you."

Stephen and I walked away. I felt Wesley's eyes following us.

"You don't get on with your sister's husband?" I said once we'd rounded the corner and the open waters of the bay appeared before us. Behind us, Wesley's car roared up the driveway, going far too fast.

"I only met him twice. At Mom's funeral and then at his and Kimmy's wedding. He'd just started going out with Kimmy when Mom died. I couldn't stand him on sight. He's supposedly some big hot shot in the restaurant world. Ironically, they met through Rachel at some fancy art gallery opening or something. We had a small reception at the house after Mom's funeral. The moment that guy saw the house, I could see the dollar signs dancing behind his eyes. He married Kimmy in a rush, certainly not the big, splashy society wedding of her dreams, supposedly out of respect for my mother's passing. More to get it done as fast as possible, I say. He expected her to inherit my father's family fortune. Turns out there's not much of a fortune left and what scraps there are, Kimmy and Rachel were fighting over."

"Do you think he killed her?"

"I don't know. I said it because he was looking at me in that way he has of thinking I'm something stuck to the bottom of his shoe. Kimmy and I never got on, but she was my sister and she deserved better than she got. Better than a self-centered gold digger like him. Better than"—he choked—"an early death." He turned his head away from me and wiped angrily at his eyes. He wandered toward the railing and stood there, staring out over the calm waters of the bay.

"If you need anything," I said at last, "I'll be in the tearoom at the top of the driveway by the road."

He didn't reply, and I left him to his thoughts.

It was shortly after one and I was making icing to decorate the coconut cupcakes, when Rachel barged into my kitchen once again, followed by Cheryl, who made "What can I do?" gestures.

"It's okay," I said to Cheryl. "What do you want now?" I said to Rachel.

"A moment of your time."

"I am rather busy."

"You're a baker. You can bake and listen while I talk." She leaned against the butcher block and gave me a crooked smile. She was nicely dressed in a cheerful summer dress, her makeup was fresh, her hair twisted behind her head in a loose, perfectly arranged chignon, and she'd had a manicure since I'd last seen her. "I need some advice, Lily."

"Advice? From me?"

"From you. I don't have anyone else to talk to. I called Stephen a short while ago, and we had a good long talk, but he's not in a position to hear about my dilemma."

"Okay. Advice about what? I find it helpful to keep your hands busy when you're wrestling with a decision, so here's the piping bag. Those cupcakes need icing. Put a swirl on each, please."

She took the bag out of my hands. "I might not be a cook, and I'm definitely not a baker, but after all these years I do know my way around a kitchen. Wesley called me late last night, asking for a meeting this morning."

"Did you go?"

"Yes, we had coffee at a bakery in town at ten."

That would explain the trouble she'd gone to over her appearance. She needed to look like a woman in control of herself. "As you're asking my advice, Rachel, I'll give you some information in exchange. Your family lawyer got here around nine last night. He and Wesley were in the B & B drawing room for a long time. I . . . uh . . . don't know what it was about."

"I figured as much. Wes wants to come to a deal. Settle the dispute about Mom's will. He'll give me two million bucks after the house is sold if I agree to drop my claim."

"What do you think about that?"

"The house is worth around twenty mil. Say a couple mil to fix it up to get the best possible price. So fifteen mil, minimum, after renovations, agents' fees, taxes, etcetera, etcetera. I was good at math in school, and from what I remember, half of fifteen is not two."

"No, but two is also not nothing. Which is what you'll get if the new will cannot be found."

"Thus I have a decision to make. What would you do?"

I began chopping chocolate prior to blending it with butter for the start of an Earl Grey chocolate tart before turning to face her. "I've never had to consider sums like that. To me, two million bucks is beyond imagining. Maybe it's not to you."

"It's a lot for me, too, Lily. My stepfather paid for my education, so I never had to worry about student loans, but I never had a trust fund or anything like that. I worked hard to make it as a designer and decorator, and I make my living the same as you do—I work hard. So yeah, two million bucks in my bank account would allow me to do some of the things I'd like to do—travel more, take risks with my career. But that wasn't my mother's intention. My mother left the house to Kimberly and me, equally. End of story."

"Rachel, you've asked me for my advice. I'm not going to give it to you, because I don't have any to give, but I will point out that your mother could have given the new will to her lawyers, even to her nurse or the housekeeper for safekeeping. Or to you, with a copy to Kimberly. Instead, she put it in a child's Peter Rabbit tea chest."

"I told you how important that tea set was to her."

"You did. And because you're talking about the intentions of people I don't know, I can't advise you."

Marybeth was behind Rachel, preparing curried egg sandwich fillings. She gave me an exaggerated wink and made the universal sign for money, rubbing the thumb of her right hand and first two fingers together. I pretended not to notice. Marybeth was indicating that Rachel should take the money and run. If it were my decision, I'd probably do the same. How long did Rachel think she could keep searching for the lost will? She couldn't abandon her career for much longer. Apart from her needing the income, restaurant designers, like celebrity chefs, fall in and out of fashion. If she disappeared, even temporarily, she'd risk being forgotten.

It might be one thing if Rachel knew for certain the will still existed, but assuming that's what was in the envelope hidden in the tea set, Kimberly'd had it. She had the opportunity to destroy it, and no reason not to do so. Rachel also had to consider who might have searched room 202. Had that person found the will and destroyed it? Had that person been Rachel herself, and she was playing a game of her own with Wesley? Was she talking to me in an attempt to deflect any suspicions I might have about her?

"You know Wes better than I do." Rachel kept her head

down and her eyes on her task as she moved down the row of cupcakes, adding a decorative swirl of buttercream to each. "What do you think he'll do if I play coy? Will he up the amount?"

"It turns out I don't know Wesley as well as I thought I did, but at a guess, I'd say yes. He wants this to be over as much as you do, Rachel." Probably more, if he was going to be able to save his grandiose restaurant plans.

"I'll go in with seven million. I'm prepared to haggle down to five. Maybe as low as four if he begs enough. Thanks, Lily. You've been a doll. That's that done." She put aside the piping bag with a smile. The cupcakes looked gorgeous.

"Anytime," I said.

"One more thing. Can you squeeze me and a guest in for tea for two this afternoon? Say three o'clock?"

"Marybeth, do we have space then?" I asked.

"Two people shouldn't be a problem."

"See you then." Rachel skipped happily out of the kitchen.

"I'd like to have that decision to make," Marybeth said once Rachel was gone. "Whether to take two million or hold out for half of fifteen."

"Or end up with nothing," I said.

"Money doesn't buy happiness, but it makes being miserable a heck of a lot better."

I laughed and returned my attention to the tower of grated chocolate.

"In case you want to know," Marybeth said promptly at three o'clock, "your friend's here, and I seated her and her guest on the patio."

"You mean Rachel?"

"Yup. They've ordered the royal tea and a pot of English breakfast and one of Lapsang souchong." She got down the canisters of loose-leaf tea.

"Go all out, will you, please?" I asked. "Use my personal china." For my sixteenth birthday, my Campbell grandparents gave me a full set of Royal Doulton Winthrop china. I brought it out in the tearoom for the most special of special guests. "Make sure they get the prettiest desserts and the best-looking scones."

"All your desserts are pretty and your scones all look the same, Lily."

"Not to me. And they won't to him, either." If Wesley Schumann was going to have afternoon tea at my place, I'd make sure he had nothing to complain about.

"Him?" Marybeth said. "What him?"

"Rachel's guest. It's not a man?" I'd assumed Rachel and Wesley were meeting over afternoon tea to continue haggling about the dispersal of the Smithfield estate. It would be like Rachel, I thought, to want the perfect backdrop for negotiations.

"It's an older woman. I've never seen her before."

Once I had macarons out of the oven, a fresh batch of fruit tarts in, and a moment to grab a break, I took off my apron and hairnet, retied my hair, and slipped out of the kitchen. I was curious as to whom Rachel had invited to tea.

As always, when I can grab a moment in the day to check what's happening out front, I was glad I did. It's one thing to work in the kitchen all day, every day, cooking and baking and cleaning up, and then starting all over again, quite another to observe your happy customers. Sometimes I forget the sheer pleasure of seeing how much people enjoy the fruit of my labors. Several tables had been pushed together to make a table for twelve in the main room. A couple who were likely in their nineties, if not more, sat at either end, resplendent in their best clothes. An assortment of children, grandchildren, great-grandchildren, and maybe even a great-great-grandchild, in the person of a baby in a highchair, were gathered around them, everyone also done to the nines. The baby had a pink bow stuck to her bald head. I'd had a request in the reservations book for flowers to mark an anniversary, and I asked Simon to put together the best bouquet he could. Red roses filled a glass vase. A hand-painted banner had been placed in the arrangement: *Happy 75th Anniversary, Gran and Gramps.*

Seventy-five years married. Imagine that.

The food at their table was almost all gone, and the teacups empty. I detoured to greet them. "Good afternoon. I'm Lily Roberts, the cook here, and I want to take the opportunity to extend my congratulations."

The baby burped. She held a piece of cupcake in her chubby hand. The rest of the cupcake was smeared across her face and down the front of her suit. The young man next to her wiped a touch of drool off her face.

The elderly lady beamed at me. "Thank you so much. Hard to believe anyone could keep up with that old coot all these years, but I managed. Nothing better to do with my time, I suppose."

The family laughed. The elderly man at the other end of the table gave the old woman a smile so full of affection my heart turned over. I carried on my way with a spring to my step.

My parents' marriage hadn't lasted much longer than it took for me to arrive, and my own relationship history isn't anything to brag about. That might have made me cynical, except I've always known how much my grandparents had adored each other, to the day of my grandfather's death. And after. Rose kept their wedding picture prominently displayed in her sitting room. Seeing the happy faces of the seventy-fifth anniversary couple reminded me that love did exist and it could last through all the ups and downs life had to throw at it.

Every seat on the patio was taken. Cracked teacups tinkled cheerfully in the light breeze, and colorful umbrellas protected diners from the hot sun. People laughed and chatted, cutlery and china clinked as tea was poured and milk and sugar stirred in. The scent in the air was a delightful mix of the sea, tea, fresh baking, and flowers. On the other side of the low stone wall marking off the Tea by the Sea patio, a few people wandered through the rose garden, admiring the plants. Simon was pulling weeds out of a perennial border.

Rachel and her guest had been given a table for two in a corner, tucked next to the drystone half wall. Brilliant green moss and tiny purple and white flowers spilled between the stones. Rachel was leaning forward, emphasizing a point to her guest. The other woman laughed and Rachel fell back, smiling broadly. Rachel lifted one of the teapots and filled her own cup. The other woman glanced around. She saw me and raised a hand in greeting.

It was Helen Chambers, housekeeper to the Smithfields, dressed for the occasion in a lime green blouse and long white skirt with green trim. Her bare feet were in sandals, and gold hoops were in her ears.

She said something to Rachel, and Rachel turned her head. "Lily! Get over here. Helen was just saying these are the best scones she's ever had. Weren't you, Helen?"

"I was. Everything's been good."

"Thank you. I'm pleased you like it. Can I ask the waitress to refill your teapot?"

"I've had more than enough," Helen said. "Although I hate to see this last treat go to waste. It looks like a perfect little jewel." She reached for the remaining lemon square.

Rachel smiled at me. She looked relaxed, content if not actually happy, cradling the last few drops in her prosecco flute.

"Enjoy the rest of your day." I left them, intending to scurry back to my kitchen.

At the far end of the patio, near the gate, Cheryl was approaching a table of recent arrivals, bearing a tray with a large teapot, milk jug, and sugar bowl. The moment she reached the table, one of the guests let out a roar of laughter and flung her arms in the air, striking the edge of the tray. The woman's friends yelled; the miscreant leapt to her feet, screeching her apologies, grabbing for the teapot, and hindering Cheryl's attempts to keep not only her balance but everything in place on the tray. I crossed the patio at a run and grabbed the teapot before it could hit the ground.

"I am so sorry," the customer said. "Are you all right, hon? I can be so dreadfully clumsy sometimes."

"I'm fine." Cheryl gave her a bright smile. She'd been waitressing for a lot of years and not much phased her. "Don't give it another thought. Ms. Roberts saved the day."

I put the pot on the table and attempted to match Cheryl's smile. "Enjoy your tea, ladies."

As I turned away from them, I caught a flash of movement as something slipped out of the sunlight to blend into the shadows at the side of the building.

I opened the gate and went through. Stephen Smithfield stepped forward. "Hi. Thanks for letting me have a look around." His face was red, and as I studied him he flushed more.

"Have you been here all this time?" I asked.

"No, I left." He kept his eyes on the ground at his feet. "I had some . . . shopping to do. Then I . . . uh . . . decided to come back and say a last good-bye to Kimmy before going home."

"Rachel's here. Are you looking for her?"

He lifted his head and looked directly into my eyes. "Rachel? Here? I'd love to say hi, but I don't have the time. Bye." He walked as fast as he was able without breaking into a panicked run.

I glanced toward Rachel's table as I headed back inside. They'd finished their meal. Rachel was pulling out her credit card, while Helen drank the last of the tea. Their body language indicated they were relaxed in each other's company.

When Rose, Bernie, and I had been at their house, Helen had almost accused Rachel of murdering not only her half sister but her mother as well. And now she was here, relaxing in the sunshine, enjoying tea with the supposed murderer?

Should I tell Rachel what Helen said to me about her?

As for Stephen . . . he was a dreadful liar. Not only had he known his half sister was here, enjoying the best of afternoon tea at Tea by the Sea, he'd been watching her table, and doing so while trying to remain unobserved. The word that came to mind was *spying*. The question was, had he been watching Rachel or Helen Chambers? Or both? He'd not had anything good to say about the family's housekeeper and he'd been outright rude to her when Rose, Bernie, and I visited the house.

It was a complicated family, and I didn't want to get any more involved in their problems than I already was. Hopefully Rachel would soon come to a deal with Wesley, and they'd both be on their way. The police would continue searching for the killer of Kimberly Smithfield, but I didn't want any more to do with it.

Rachel and Helen finished their tea without saying good-bye to me. Marybeth told me Rachel had paid and had left a substantial tip. I didn't see Stephen's car leave, but when I peeked outside after closing, the Audi was not in the driveway.

That, I decided, was a good thing. The sooner I saw the back of the entire family, the better. Now all I had to do was get rid of Wesley, who was still staying at Victoria-on-Sea. I feared I knew why. B & Bs run by elderly ladies and frequented by middle-aged couples on vacation were not the sort of accommodation Wesley Schumann preferred. He might have stayed here initially because Kimberly liked it, but now that he was on his own, I'd have expected him to flee. Wesley preferred high-end hotel chains with spacious lobby bars, twenty-four-hour room service, good restaurants, and a substantial wine list. It couldn't even be argued he was economizing, as Victoria-on-Sea was more expensive than many nice hotels.

He had to be staying because of me. Whether he wanted to be near me or because he was keeping an eye on me with the intention of causing me more trouble, I didn't know. Maybe Wesley himself didn't even know.

I was putting the last batch of the day's scones into the freezer, when Bernie texted: **How about having that dinner in town we missed the other night? Matt's idea. Simon's in.**

Me: **Sure. Can I have half an hour?**

Bernie: **Matt'll pick you up.**

At seven thirty I was standing on the veranda waiting for my lift. Rose had taken her customary chair and was enjoying her nightly gin and tonic. Her book rested on her lap, and Robert the Bruce rested on top of the book. Four people had pulled chairs up to a table at the far end of the veranda, and a pack of cards had been produced. Bottles of wine and bags of chips and nuts had also been produced.

"I don't dare hope Wesley said he's leaving tomorrow?" I asked my grandmother. Today was Thursday.

"He has the room until Sunday morning. We're fully booked for the next two weeks, so he'll have to leave as planned."

"I can't help wondering what he's up to. I assume there've been no more incidents of his room being broken into."

"You assume correctly. Have you considered, love, that all he's up to is trying to get his business plans going? He always has that computer bag with him when he goes out, and he's never dressed as though he's heading for the beach. More like what I believe they call business casual these days."

"He could move into the Smithfield house if he wanted. In theory it's now his house, partially, anyway, but I'll admit even Wesley has the occasional sense of propriety and might realize that isn't entirely appropriate. Not yet, anyway. Have the police been around to talk to him again?"

"Not that I saw, but them coming here shouldn't be necessary. If they have something to discuss, he can go to the police station as easily as them coming out here."

"I guess. Here comes Matt now." The top was down on my neighbor's shiny red two-seater BMW convertible as it navigated the sand- and weed-choked driveway of the house next to us and turned into our neat flower bed– and bush-lined lane.

"I'm thinking of inviting Petunia for a visit," Rose said.

I paused at the top of the stairs. "Mom? Why, and why now?"

"It's been a while since I've seen her."

I never had any doubt that my mother loved her mother deeply, and the feeling was returned. But their relationship worked best when they kept a healthy distance. Both of them were headstrong to the point of stubborn. From what I heard from my uncles, my mother's teenage years had been dramatic, to say the least. She'd left Grand Lake, Iowa, for the bright lights of New York City before the ink was dry on her high school diploma, and the only time she'd gone back had been for her father's funeral. It had been up to Rose and my grandfather to keep the family together, and over the years I was growing up, they regularly traveled to New York City to visit.

Rose and her three sisters all had flower names, and following family tradition, Rose named her only daughter Petunia. Mom loathed that name and went by Tina. Rose pretended not to know that.

"Seeing the strife and the animosity in your friend's family," Rose said slowly, "has reminded me of the importance of family ties. Your mother and I have had our differences, but she is my beloved daughter. Perhaps Christine could come at the same time."

"I'd like that," I said. Christine was my half sister by my mom's second husband, and she and I had always been close. She, notably, did not have a flower name.

"I'll call them tonight, then." Rose wiggled her book out from under Robbie. He glared at me as though the disruption was my fault.

My friends and I had dinner at a burger joint near the pier in North Augusta before heading for the ice cream stand on the boardwalk. The night was warm, the air soft, and the pier and boardwalk were crowded with townspeople out for a stroll and tourists enjoying their holiday. Over our burgers and fries, I'd updated my friends on the goings-on of the Smithfield/Morrison clan.

"Sounds exactly like the type of family that provides me with my living," Matt said. "When I've finished the project I'm working on now, if this thing you're telling us about is over, I might see what I can dig up." Matt was a hugely successful true-crime writer. He used the pseudonym of Lincoln Badwell, believing Goodwill didn't exactly suit the type of books he wrote.

"Has anyone considered that the death of Kimberly Smithfield might not have anything to do with her family?" Simon asked. "Families fight over wills all the time without killing each other."

"Until they do," Matt said. "It happens. Often in families in which there isn't even much money, if any, to be divided. The real reason isn't the money itself. It's the old resentments stirred up when one child isn't given what they think they're entitled to."

"A lot of resentments are swirling around that family, all right," I said. "Every one of them interprets things differently. Helen Chambers told me Julian tried to be a father to Rachel, and Rachel told me he never liked her. Rachel never accepted her mother's new marriage, that's for sure. But never mind all that, I heard what Simon said, and I don't want to. If Kimberly wasn't killed by someone in her family, the possibility that a random killer was wandering around our property—outside my own front door—in the dead of night, doesn't bear thinking about."

Simon popped a fry into his mouth. "I didn't mean random. I meant someone from another part of her life. Nothing to do with the sister and the will and the greedy new husband."

"It's possible," Bernie said, "but that would be way too much of a coincidence, considering she'd only just located the secret will she'd been hunting for. The one that restored her sister's inheritance."

"Don't discount it." Matt sipped from his beer mug. "Coincidences happen."

"If I put a coincidence like that in my book," Bernie said, "no one would believe it."

He'd grinned at her and lifted his glass in a toast. "Which is why I prefer to write non-fiction. Truth really is stranger."

Ice cream cones in hand, we strolled down the boardwalk heading for the pier. Matt and Bernie walked ahead of us, and Simon kept pace with me on my right side.

"When's Rose's birthday?" he asked.

I licked at my French vanilla cone. Simon had ordered the triple-size triple-chocolate blast. "January 26. Why do you ask?"

He frowned. "That won't work. We're talking about expanding the rose garden, and I had the idea of getting something special, without her knowing, and making a big deal of planting it on her birthday."

"That's very thoughtful of you," I said. "I love the idea, but maybe not the idea of standing on a bare patch of ground in a winter storm trying to shelter a fragile new plant. My grandparents' wedding anniversary is in August."

"That might work. Your grandfather was of Scottish heritage, right? Campbell. I'll see what I can find out about the history of roses in Scotland."

I began to smile at him. That was such a Simon idea.

The smile died when someone bumped my left arm. I opened my mouth to extend my apologizes, but the words never came.

"I thought I recognized you," the bumper sneered. "Can't you watch where you're going?"

"I believe," I said, "the sidewalk's wide enough for both of us."

She bared her teeth in a move that reminded me of Éclair the time Robbie swooped in and snatched a slice of dropped sausage out from under the dog's nose.

"Allegra," Simon said calmly. "Nice evening, isn't it?"

Her eyes flicked toward him and then returned to me. "Folks are saying you had another death at your place, Lily. I'm surprised the police haven't shut you down yet. I suppose bribery goes a long way."

Simon placed his hand lightly on my shoulder. I kept my breathing steady and licked my cone. I didn't have to say anything to her in reply, but I couldn't help myself. "Guests stay with us and they bring their problems with them. Happens in any hotel. You weren't poking around Victoria-on-Sea on Monday night, were you?"

Her face tightened. Allegra Griffin was the owner and head baker at North Augusta Bakery. She could dish it, but she couldn't take it. She and I weren't in competition; our places offered vastly different food and experiences, but we'd been pitted against each other in an ill-fated reality TV show called *America Bakes!* Ill-fated because the show was canceled before our segment finished filming. Allegra had been counting on winning the grand prize and, with the money that went with it and the publicity the program generated, being able to sell the bakery and leave North Augusta permanently. She blamed me because she hadn't won, because she and her bakery hadn't even made it to TV. I had nothing to do with it, except that a person who was involved with the show had been killed at Tea by the Sea.

"I have no need to sneak around your so-called restaurant or any other place." Allegra lifted her chin. "I'm known for being straightforward. If I have something to say I say it."

Bernie and Matt had become aware Simon and I were no longer behind them and turned back to stand with us.

"Why don't you say it now, then?" Bernie said.

Allegra ignored her. We were blocking the sidewalk, and people gave us curious looks as they circled our little group. "Quite the heroine, weren't you, Lily? Fighting off the crazed killer, capturing them single-handedly? I saw your picture in the paper."

I hadn't actually captured anyone, and I hadn't been any sort of a heroine. Nor had my bedraggled self looked all that impressive in the picture that made it into the *North Augusta Times*.

"Lily did what she had to do on that occasion," Simon said. "I'm sorry the TV show didn't work out for you, but it didn't work out for Lily, either. I didn't even get my moment of fame." Simon had been filmed showing one of the stars around the gardens. "I was looking forward to me mum seeing me on the telly."

Allegra took a step toward him. Simon stepped back. He lifted his hands and held them up, palms out. Bernie and Matt exchanged worried glances. Allegra was a short, plump, middle-aged woman, not a match for the combined forces of Bernie, Matt, and Simon if it came to that. My friends and I most definitely did not want it to "come to that." She was a fabulous baker, and her place did very well because of it, but her reputation in town was of a rude, angry, ill-disposed woman. She hated North Augusta, and she hated the bakery her mother had saddled her with. She spat her words at Simon. "The publicity around the arrest didn't do the reputation of her silly little tearoom any harm, did it? Or her fancy grandmother's B & B with the la-di-da name."

"Please, let's go." The taste of vanilla had turned sour in

my mouth. Melting ice cream dripped off the cone and ran down my fingers. "I've done nothing to you, Allegra, and I don't know why you don't like me, but so be it. Good night."

I marched away. Simon followed me, and then Bernie and Matt.

"Matthew Goodwill," Allegra called after us. "You write about crime. Maybe you should think about writing a book about people who get a kick out of killing because they're hooked on the publicity."

Chapter 19

"Don't let her get to you." Bernie licked at her tower of bubble gum–flavored ice cream, her tongue tinged a lurid pink.

"Easier said than done." I'd tossed my unfinished cone into the nearest trash bin, and now I wiped ice cream off my fingers with a napkin. I'd been afraid Allegra would follow us, shouting accusations, but she hadn't. We walked onto the pier to watch the seals playing in the cool waters below, but the mood of the evening had been ruined and we soon left. I knew I should feel sorry for Allegra—she was an unhappy woman, angry at life, angry at everyone and everything—but I found it hard to drum up any sympathy for her.

I firmly believe that in a small community like North Augusta, totally dependent on the summer tourist trade, it's in everyone's interest to work together for the good of the town. If people came to Tea by the Sea and we couldn't accommodate them, or if they decided the menu or our prices weren't to their liking, we were happy to suggest they try North Augusta Bakery. I'd foolishly hoped the bakery would return the favor. No chance of that.

No one liked or respected Allegra, so I shouldn't have to worry she'd poison my reputation among the townspeople, but still . . . people did love listening to gossip, even if they didn't like the gossiper.

I eventually fell asleep, determined not to think about her again. As I drifted off, I wondered if she'd encountered us on the boardwalk by accident, or if she might have been following me. Spying on me. That was a thought I found hard to dismiss.

I was woken by the ringing of my phone. I groaned and rolled over. Surely it wasn't time to get up already. I slapped at the alarm trying to find the snooze button. Finally, my befuddled brain realized that no sunlight was leaking through the curtains; it was my phone that was ringing, not the alarm, and Éclair stood at the window, barking into the night. I heard someone shout and then the terrifying scream of sirens coming closer.

I grabbed my phone and shouted into it, "What's happening?"

"Come quickly, love," Rose said, her voice high and breathless. "There's a fire."

That got my attention. I leapt out of bed, stuffed my bare feet into flip-flops, and headed for the door, phone still in hand. Éclair charged after me, and I momentarily hesitated. I couldn't leave the dog inside. If the main house was on fire, the flames might leap to my cottage. I called to her to come and hoped she'd stay close by me.

The sirens were getting closer, turning off the main road and tearing down our driveway. Flashing blue and red lights broke the night, doors slammed, voices called, and others answered. To my infinite relief, I couldn't see flames from my front porch, although I detected a trace of smoke drifting on the wind. Across the roof of the house, a red and orange glow rose into the night sky: too far away to be coming from the house itself and in the wrong direction to be the tearoom. That came as an enormous relief. In my panicked mind, I'd seen the house reduced to ashes, Rose homeless, my livelihood destroyed.

People dressed in an assortment of nightwear lined the veranda of the big house; heads popped out of upstairs windows. Fire trucks and police vehicles were parked every which way on the driveway and across the lawn, and firefighters unrolled hoses and shouted instructions to one another. Rose stood on the veranda, one hand holding her phone and the other gripping the railing so tightly her knuckles were white. She gave me a wave when she saw me, and my heart settled into a slightly more normal rhythm. Rose was safe, the house wasn't burning, and nothing else really mattered.

A couple stood next to my grandmother, the woman's hand on her arm, offering her emotional and physical support. My eyes swept across the watching faces. Wesley was also on the veranda, dressed in nothing but loose pajama trousers, held up by a string tied low over his slim hips. I pulled my eyes away.

Éclair began to gallop toward the firefighters, eager to play with the newcomers in the wonderful-smelling clothes. I called her back, and she came, although reluctantly. I bent down and gave her a pat and words of praise. She would have preferred a dog biscuit, but I didn't happen to have any of those on hand at the moment.

Our garden shed sat on the far side of the lawn, near the south end of the property. Flames chewed through the roof even as I watched. Fortunately, no other structures were located near the shed, and the gardens were well watered, so they wouldn't provide a source of tinder. Simon's motorcycle was not in its regular place next to the shed. He keeps his hand tools, potting soil, bags of mulch and fertilizer, empty pots and urns, hoses in there. The heavy equipment, such as the lawnmower and the rototiller, are stored in the garage.

I stood at the edge of the driveway, my heart in my mouth, watching the garden shed being rapidly consumed. The night sky was streaked red and orange. Éclair sat by my side, occasionally letting out a soft whine. I reached down and rubbed the top of her head once again, giving and taking comfort. The roof of the shed collapsed in a shower of sparks, and fresh flames leapt high, but they had no more fuel, nowhere to go, and the hoses did their work. It wasn't long before the shed was nothing but smoldering wood and wet ashes, and the only light came from the headlights of the firetrucks, flashlights, lamps over the veranda, and shining from the bedrooms.

"It's over, Lily," Matt Goodwill said. He'd come to stand next to me and put his arm lightly around my shoulders. I hadn't even realized he was there.

"Are you the owner?" a second voice asked us.

"My grandmother is," I replied. The firefighter was an older guy, and I took him to be the captain. "You can talk to me. I . . . I have no idea what happened here."

"I called it in." A woman joined us. Her pajamas were a deep blue satin, her feet stuffed into beach sandals. "My name's Joy Eastland. I often have trouble sleeping and tonight was no exception. I was reading in bed, using only the light from my e-reader because my husband was asleep. Our window faces in this direction." She pointed to the south, toward the ruined garden shed. "I saw the light out the window change, and then I smelled smoke, so

I got up to have a look. I called nine-one-one and then alerted Mrs. Campbell." She bent down and greeted Éclair with a hearty pat. The dog thumped her tail in return.

"Mrs. Campbell's the owner?" the fire captain asked.

"Yes," I said.

Two firefighters approached the smoldering ruin. They kicked aside debris and stepped cautiously into what remained of the building. I held my breath for a moment, dreadfully afraid of what they might find in there. But no one came running out, no one shouted for an ambulance or the coroner, and I relaxed with an enormous amount of relief. Matt must have been thinking the same; he squeezed my shoulder and gave me a soft smile.

"I'm going to have a closer look," the fire captain said to me. "If you take a seat on the porch, I'll join you in a bit."

"Do you know what happened?" I asked. "We don't keep anything flammable in there. I mean, I don't think we do. I guess I don't really know. You can ask our gardener."

"Is she around now?"

"It's a he, and no, he doesn't live on the premises. Do you want me to call him?"

"Let me have a look first."

"We use store-bought fertilizer in our gardens. Does that ever self-combust?" I half turned at the roar of a motorcycle tearing down the driveway. "No need to call. Here he is now. He might be able to tell you more about what is . . . was kept in there."

Simon leapt off his bike and sprinted across the lawn, pulling off his helmet as he ran. "Thanks for the call, mate," he said to Matt. "What happened here? Was there someone . . . in there?"

"No one harmed, thank goodness. You didn't light a

candle or leave anything burning, did you?" I asked Simon.

"Nothing like that. Can't have been caused by bad wiring. The shed's not electrified. No need for it to be—I don't use it after dark."

"When we've confirmed it's safe, I'll need you to have a look. See if you can spot anything out of place," the fire captain said.

"Sure."

The captain called to one of his crew, and they headed for the shed.

"That wasn't caused by any unattended burning candle." Matt pointed to the smoldering ruin. "One of my earliest books was about a serial arsonist, so I know more than a small amount about how that stuff works. I'd be willing to bet an accelerant was used here, poured on the floor and the walls, most likely, and then a match tossed after it. Gasoline, probably. You can still smell traces of it."

"Nasty business," Simon growled.

"Who would do such a thing?" I asked.

"That's the question," Matt said. "Far as I know there've been no reports of arsonists in this area lately. . . ." His voice trailed off. "Although they have to start somewhere."

"I'm going to suggest Rose and the guests go back to bed," I told the men.

"I'll try and get closer," Matt said. "Hear what they're saying."

I called to Éclair to follow, and Simon walked with us toward the house. I was suddenly and embarrassingly aware I was wearing my shortie pajamas, the blue ones with cute cartoon characters on them. My grandmother had taken a chair, and someone kindly brought her a glass of water. Her short hair stood out in all directions, the skin on her cheeks and chin formed dark furrows, and her eyes were heavy with fatigue and worry. I expected to have to argue to get her to return to her bed, but she gave me a nod and allowed Simon to help her up.

"No one hurt," I said, "and no harm done to anything but an old shed and some garden tools. Oh, gosh. You didn't have anything valuable in there, did you, Simon?"

"Nothing of my own. Rakes and secateurs can be replaced easy enough."

"All's well that ends well, Mrs. Campbell," one of the guests said. "Your granddaughter will be needed here for a while yet. Can we escort you to your room?"

"Thank you," Rose said. "How very kind of you." She took the offered arm and they went into the house.

The guests began to disperse. Some returned to their beds, some wandered over to the firetrucks to watch them rolling up hoses and preparing to leave. Matt had reached the shed without being ordered to leave, and he was studying something on the ground. Excitement over, Éclair snuffled across the veranda, visiting everyone in turn, sniffing at feet and receiving pats and praise.

I became aware that Wesley was watching me. I caught his eye and rather than turn away, he gave me a slow, lazy wink. *Flirtatious? Threatening?* I couldn't tell. I ducked my head.

"Never a dull moment when you're around, Lily Roberts," he said.

"Through no fault of mine," I replied.

Simon caught the frost in my voice, and he gave Wesley a sideways look. Wesley stuck out his hand. "Wesley Schumann. Don't think we've met."

"We did, when you were making a scene at breakfast the other morning. Simon McCracken. I'm the gardener here."

The edges of Wesley's mouth turned up. "The gardener, right. I remember you now." He reached out and gave my head an affectionate pat, much like the lingering guests were doing to Éclair. I pulled sharply away. "Lily and I go back, way back," Wesley continued. "I'm hoping she'll soon get tired of living in this tourist backwater and come back to the city, where she belongs. She's squandering a hard-earned reputation as a top-ranked pastry chef out here in the boonies. The long winters can be tough on a tourist-based business, I'd expect."

Simon said nothing.

"Then again, maybe this place has other attractions." Wesley looked directly at Simon. "That won't last."

"Excitement's over." Simon's English accent was sharp. "You can go back to bed now, sunshine."

"I'll do that." Wesley pointed across the lawn, toward the dark, ruined garden shed. "You're lucky, Lily. This time. Nasty things happen out in the countryside. Or so I've been told. Good night." He kissed me on the cheek before I could pull away, and went inside.

"Charming bloke," Simon said. "Ex-boyfriend?"

"Unfortunately, yes. A mistake on my part. Pay him no mind."

"I'm not sure I can do that. Sounded to me like a threat, Lily."

It had to me, too. Had Wesley set the fire? For what possible aim? I was hardly going to suddenly decide North Augusta wasn't safe and flee back to Manhattan.

"Here they come," Simon said. "Let's join them."

Police officers were stringing yellow tape around the south end of the property. The unpleasant scent of smoke and ash and burned wood hung heavily on the night air.

Éclair began to head for the shed to do some investigating of her own. I called her back. She hesitated. I called again and snapped my fingers, and she returned, reluctantly I thought, to my side. She'd been very good up to now, but the temptation of nosing (literally) around a fire scene might prove more powerful than her training to obey me. The scents must be intoxicating to her powerful senses, and she was a curious dog. I scooped her up. She licked my face, and I laughed.

We met Matt and the fire captain in the driveway. "I'll have an arson investigator here first thing," the older man said.

"You think it was deliberately set?" I asked.

"Not much doubt about it, ma'am. We'll be opening a full investigation in conjunction with the North Augusta police. In the meantime, stay away from that area and make sure your guests do, too." He rubbed Éclair's ear. "And this dog."

"You didn't see any indication of who might have started the fire?" Simon asked. "Like a dropped driver's license, or something?"

"No such luck." The firefighter gave me a nod. "Go back to bed, folks. Ms. Roberts, we'll talk in the morning."

"Thank you," I said.

Simon, Matt, and I watched him head back to his vehicle. Éclair wiggled in my arms, asking to be let down. I held on firmly.

A car sped down the driveway, swerved to avoid the firetrucks and police cars, and screeched to a halt. Bernie had arrived.

"Okay," I said. "Who called her?"

"Not me," Matt said.

"Nor me," Simon said.

My friend ran toward us, red hair streaming behind her. She'd pulled on black yoga pants and a pale-green workout shirt. She stretched out her arms and enveloped me and Éclair in a ferocious hug. When she finally let us go, she gazed deeply into my eyes. "Lily, are you okay? You look okay. Tell me you're okay."

"I'm fine. We're all fine. Why are you here?"

At that moment my phone rang, and I recognized the tune indicating it was Rose calling, so I answered, trying to balance the phone and the squirming dog at the same time.

"Meeting. Kitchen. Five minutes." She hung up.

"Rose called you," I said to Bernie.

"Of course she did. Did you doubt it?"

"No." I should also not have expected my grandmother to meekly toddle off to bed. My phone rang again, and I shoved Éclair into Bernie's arms.

"Lily, I assumed you'd still be up," Amy Redmond said.

"As I am."

"I've been notified of an incident at your house. A fire. No one harmed and no property damage, other than to an outbuilding and its contents."

"That's right."

"Do you have reason to believe this might be connected to the death of Kimberly Smithfield?"

"Detective, I have no reason to think it can be anything else. The fire chief seems confident the blaze was deliberately set."

Bernie's eyebrows rose, and she exchanged a worried glance with Matt.

"I have no enemies—" The words died in my throat.

"What?" Redmond asked.

"I had a minor, and I mean minor, altercation with Allegra Griffin in town earlier tonight. I can't say she made threats against me, but she was . . . *hostile* might be the word."

"Do you need me to come around tonight?"

"No, we're fine here. I'm heading back to bed." I looked at my circle of friends, all of them watching me, and shrugged.

"I doubt that very much, but I'll be around in the morning to talk to the arson investigator. If anything else happens, let me know."

"I will." I hung up.

Chapter 20

We were a motley group gathered in the B & B kitchen that night. Rose and I in our nightwear (although I'd found a ratty old sweater in the front closet and thrown it on in a poor attempt at preserving my modesty), and Bernie, Matt, and Simon in whatever clothes they'd grabbed (probably off the floor or out of the laundry basket) in their rush. Robbie settled himself comfortably on Rose's lap, and Éclair assumed her usual place under the table, where she could keep an eye on me, her muzzle resting between her front paws. I was not in the mood to make coffee and tea, but I offered refreshment out of habit. Everyone refused hot drinks, but Bernie ventured into the fridge and brought out jugs of juice while Simon found glasses.

Before sitting down, Rose had produced a pad of paper and a pen from the depths of her housecoat pockets. She flourished the pen now. "The first order of business is to draw up a suspect list."

I groaned.

"We have to assume this incident is related to the Smithfield killing," Matt said.

"Actually, we don't," Bernie said. "Top of the list, Rose, write down 'Allegra Griffin.' We ran into her earlier tonight. Or rather she ran into us. She's obsessed with blaming Lily for her losing her chance to be on *America Bakes!*"

"That happened weeks ago," I said. "Why would she strike tonight?"

"Seeing you in town reminded her," Bernie said.

"I don't buy it. It's too much of a coincidence, happening so soon after Kimberly's murder."

"We talked about coincidences earlier," Bernie said. "We agreed they can happen."

"Before settling on suspects," Matt said, "let's consider the details of the fire itself. The intent was obviously to do no serious damage."

"Destroyed my best secateurs," Simon growled.

"Might not have even done that," Matt said. "If they're made of metal. The fire moved fast, but it was put out soon."

"It was only by chance a woman was awake and in a bedroom facing the direction of the shed at the right time," I said. "She saw the fire and raised the alarm."

Matt nodded. "That's true, but we still have to bear in mind that the shed's a good distance from any other buildings, with no trees immediately surrounding it, and the lawn and plants are well watered. Not much chance of the fire spreading."

"In the grand scheme of things, the condition of Simon's preferred pruning instrument is of little consequence," Rose pointed out. "I'll call my insurance broker in the morning; we should be fully covered. Simon, mark a shopping expedition in your calendar for later this week."

" 'It's an ill wind . . .' " he said.

Bernie cleared her throat. "If we may continue. Matt's point is that if this person or persons unknown wanted to cause real damage, they could have. An old house full of sleeping people. Lily alone in her cottage. Guest cars in the driveway. Rose's car and heavy garden equipment in the garage. If it was Allegra, wouldn't she have been more likely to try to burn down Lily's tearoom?"

"One thing I've learned," Matt said, "is not to spend too much time trying to understand the motives of anyone who'd do such a thing. Their motives are totally understandable to them, but they might make no sense whatsoever to anyone else. However, in this case, I'd say the fire was set to send a message, and nothing more."

"What, then, is the message?" Rose asked.

The table fell silent.

"A warning," Bernie said.

"What are we being warned against?" I asked.

"Interfering in the investigation into the death of Kimberly Smithfield."

"I'm not interfering."

"But you were . . . we were."

"You were?" Matt said. "Why would you do that? Leave it to the police."

"Lily gets curious," Bernie said.

"Me!"

"Okay. We get curious. I get curious."

"I can be curious," Rose added.

"To say the least," I muttered.

"More to the point," Bernie said, "we're involved despite ourselves. Lily had possession of the tea chest which contained the envelope which supposedly contained the last will and testament of Rosemary Morrison Smithfield. Kimberly Smithfield died steps from Lily's cottage. Rachel Morrison, also in search of the lost will, has been to the tearoom asking for Lily's help. The dead woman and her husband were staying here, at Rose's B & B. The husband's still here, and he and Lily have a history."

"Nasty bloke, that one," Simon said. "Passive aggressive in the worst way."

"Sounds like Wesley," Bernie said. "He's conflicted, to say the least, about how he feels about Lily. I wouldn't put it past him to have set the fire in the hope that she'll seek solace in his manly arms."

I snorted.

"Precisely." Rose wrote his name on her list beneath Allegra's with a flourish.

"Catch me up with your not-investigating," Simon said. "Who do you suspect of killing Kimberly? That person must be the one who set the fire."

"We have, sorry to say, nothing but suspects," Bernie admitted. "It's all a jumble. The greedy husband, the jealous brother, the resentful sister."

Rose scribbled down names.

"As well as people outside the direct family," I said. "I've heard opposing things about the family lawyer, including a suggestion he contributed to Kimberly's late father losing a great deal of money. Maybe Kimberly learned something about that and threatened to take him to court."

"The housekeeper doesn't like Rachel," Bernie said. "Although that doesn't explain why she'd kill Kimberly, and not Rachel."

"And that's another complication. Helen Chambers, the Smithfield housekeeper, took tea today with Rachel. They were, as far as I could tell, getting on perfectly well."

Bernie threw up her hands. "I give up."

"Which is exactly what I'd decided to do," I said. "Until someone set a fire on my grandmother's property and thus made it very much my business. Our business."

"Okay," Bernie said. "What do we do now?"

"I haven't a clue," I said.

"The fire department will be here at first light tomorrow," Matt said. "They can learn a surprising amount from a burnt-out building. Amateur criminals are never, ever as smart as they think they are, and they usually leave a whole bunch of clues trailing along behind them. Call me when they get here, and I'll pop over."

"Of all those suspects' names Rose is carefully recording," Simon said, "only one is staying here. In this house. You need to give him the boot. Tomorrow. I'll escort him off the property myself."

"I don't—" I began.

"I do," Bernie said. "I'm with Simon on this one. I'm sick and tired of the great Wesley Schumann passively aggressively, or outright aggressively, threatening Lily. You have reason to ask him to leave and legal grounds to do so."

Robbie stood up, stretched every fiber of his substantial being, and opened his mouth in an enormous yawn. That broke the tension, and we all laughed.

"Nothing more we can do tonight," Simon said. "I'll spend the rest of the night in the drawing room."

"You don't—" I began.

"I do," he said. "Our intruder might come back. He"—he looked pointedly at me—"might not have left."

"I'll be on call," Matt said.

"Me too," Bernie said.

Éclair barked.

I didn't think Wesley would agree to go quietly, and I wasn't wrong.

Simon came into the kitchen shortly after six as I was starting breakfast prep. Éclair leapt to her feet to accept a rub behind the ears.

"How'd you sleep?" I asked Simon. His sandy hair was

tousled, his eyes bleary, the trace of stubble dark on his jaw, and his clothes rumpled.

He smothered a yawn. "Not well. Those sofas are not meant to serve as beds."

"I'm sorry about that. It was nice of you to stay."

He turned his attention from the dog and smiled at me. "Other duties as assigned."

We looked at each other for a long time. He broke away first and helped himself to coffee, while Éclair settled herself back down under the table. "I was thinking about your problem guest, and I don't think Rose should be the one to tell him he's being given the boot. He might not take it well."

"He's not going to attack an old woman. It is her property, after all."

"She isn't usually up before breakfast is over, and I'd like to see the back of him as soon as possible. I'll knock him up at seven."

"You'll do what?"

He laughed. "Sorry, English expression. I gather it means something quite different in America. I'll knock on his door and tell him to pack his bags."

"I'll come with you," I said.

"Best not."

"Probably, but I will, anyway. He'll think you're acting on our instructions, so I need to be there."

"In the meantime, I'm going to have a look at what remains of the shed. I won't go past the line of tape, but maybe I can have enough of a look 'round to see if anything's salvageable. As long as I wasn't able to sleep, I did some checking into garden sheds. That shed was an old one, handcrafted of good wood, nicely made. Unless Rose wants a custom-built replacement, we can order a prefab thing from the hardware store and they'll deliver."

"I'll let her decide that. Custom built will be expensive, but the old one added a good deal of charm to that section of the property. The decision might depend on what her insurance company has to say."

I got the baking started and put together an egg-white frittata, and then I laid out eggs and sausages for those wanting the traditional English breakfast. When Edna arrived, I told her I had an errand to do at seven, but it shouldn't take more than a few minutes, and I'd start the cooking when I got back.

"I heard what happened last night," she said. "No harm done? Other than to that outbuilding?"

"It gave us all a heck of a fright, but there wasn't any real danger. When was the last time an arsonist was at work in North Augusta?"

"Never," she said. "Kids on vacation or celebrating the end of school have been known to set trash cans on fire, and things can get out of control causing a great deal of fuss and bother. Teenagers sneaking around, quiet, alone in the dark? Nope."

"That's what I was afraid of."

Simon came in, smelling of smoke, his hands and face dusted with ash and gray and black dust. "Mornin', Edna."

"You went past the keep-out tape," I scolded as he scrubbed his hands at the sink.

"Couldn't help meself. I didn't go inside the shed, though. What remains of the shed, that is, and it's not much. Almost everything's gone."

Coulda been worse, I reminded myself. Far worse.

"Ready?" he said.

Voices drifted in from the dining room, the first of the guests arriving for breakfast. I took my apron off, shook out my hair, and gathered my courage around me. "Ready. Be right back, Edna."

Simon and I went into the hallway. "Room two-oh-two," I said. "He didn't change rooms after his wife died."

"He's kept the same room?"

"Yes."

"Doesn't that seem a mite . . . weird to you, Lily?"

"Weird, yes. I get the feeling he's not exactly in deep mourning. Then again, we all grieve in our own way."

"Or not at all. He's been mighty fast to put the moves on you, Lily."

When we reached the top of the stairs, Simon stopped. He took my right hand and cradled it in his. "You're too kindhearted. That's usually a good thing, except when you can't recognize trouble in other people."

My heart thudded in my chest. Simon's hands were large, rough, and heavily calloused, as befitted a man who made his living working with trees and plants and stone and earth. His eyes were a deep blue, the color of Cape Cod Bay on a warm summer's day.

Farther down the hallway a door opened, and Simon and I moved apart.

"Good morning," the guests said as they passed.

"Good morning," we replied.

I waited until they'd disappeared and then knocked firmly on the door of room 202.

The door opened almost immediately. Wesley was freshly shaven, his hair damp from the shower, dressed for a day of meetings in pressed slacks and a golf shirt. His face broke into an enormous grin when he saw me. Then he caught sight of Simon, standing silently behind me, and the expression turned wary. "What's up?"

"I'm sorry, Wesley," I said, "but I'm going to have to ask you to check out early."

"How early?"

"Today," Simon said. "Like now."

"Any particular reason?" Wesley spoke to Simon.

"As you're well aware, *sir*, there was some trouble here last night."

"Nothing to do with me." Over his shoulder, I could see that someone—unlikely to have been Wesley—had made an attempt to tidy up after the intruder. The pictures had been straightened and the furniture returned to its place.

"Maybe not," Simon said, "but your behavior toward Lily can be considered threatening, and we think it's best you were on your way."

"You do, do you? What are you again, the gardener? Isn't there a rose or a weed out there in need of your attention?"

"Having you here, Wesley, is not working out," I said. "I'm truly sorry about Kimberly's death, but . . ." My voice trailed off. Maybe Simon was right. I was too tenderhearted. I should have kicked Wesley to the curb the moment he told the police I had a reason to kill his wife.

"I have meetings this morning," he said. "Important meetings. I haven't got time to pack."

"Make time," Simon said. "You don't have much. This is a hotel room, not your house."

"You're trying to impress Lily by acting the tough guy, are you?" A vein began to pulse in Wesley's forehead.

"Not trying to impress anyone, mate," Simon replied calmly. "Just making a simple request."

Wesley turned to me. His eyes were dark with anger, and I tensed. "You're kicking me out."

"Yes, Wesley, I guess I am."

"I offered you a job. I offered you the chance to get your life back."

"I have a life, and I don't want your job."

His eyes flicked to Simon. "What do you want, Lily? A *gardener*?"

"That's enough," Simon said. "We're not here to argue

about it. Lily has to get back to the kitchen; guests are arriving for breakfast. I'll wait for you at the bottom of the stairs. I assume you gave Mrs. Campbell your credit card info when you checked in. No need to disturb her. She'll send you the receipt."

Kimberly had checked in before Wesley arrived. She would have paid with her credit card, and it might not be valid anymore. I'd worry about that when the time came, but right now I wasn't going to get into the details of payment for a six-night stay in one of our best suites.

Wesley looked at Simon for a long time. Next to me, Simon's body was tense, braced to move suddenly if he had to. Wesley gave him a final sneer and turned to me. "Okay, Lily. You win. For now. You will come to regret this." He took one step backward and slammed the door with such force the walls trembled.

I let out a long breath. Simon circled his shoulders to release some of the tension.

"He doesn't like to lose, that one," Simon said.

"No."

"I'll wait at the reception desk. If he isn't down and gone in half an hour, I'd like your permission to call the police."

"It won't come to that. He said he'd leave, so he will."

"We'll see."

Wesley left without kicking up a fuss about it. I sincerely hoped that once he was gone, he'd forget about me. He did have a short attention span and more important things on his mind these days.

The police and the arson investigators arrived shortly after Wesley's car roared down the driveway, kicking up gravel and spewing it in every direction. Simon phoned Matt, and the two men met the authorities at the shed, while I continued making the breakfasts.

Simon came in as I was flipping the last of today's sausages and poured himself a cup of coffee.

"What did they say?" Edna and I asked at the same time.

"Much mumbling and making notes and taking pictures, followed by more mumbling. You'll receive a copy of the report to submit to your insurance company. Essentially, there's no doubt about it. The fire was set. Petrol was poured around the exterior of the shed and ignited. Would have gone up with a whoosh."

"Petrol. You mean gasoline."

"Yup. What you can get at any station in town to fill your lawnmower or put into a can for an extra supply for your car. Amy Redmond joined us, and she said no one reported to a nearby hospital with burns last night, the sort of thing that might happen if they misjudged the distance between themselves and the conflagration they were about to set. She and the arson investigator put their heads together, but Matt and I weren't party to that chat."

"No clues as to who was on our property last night, such as the proverbial dropped driver's license?"

He sipped his coffee. "They took images of footprints on the ground and measured mine for comparison. But it hasn't rained for a couple of days, and a lot of people wander around our gardens. Including near the shed. Some visitors want to talk to me about plants and growing techniques and the like, and it's part of my job, as Rose explained to me when I started here, to engage with them." He lifted his mug in a salute. "Speaking of my job, I'd better get to it. I'm preparing a list of what I have to replace and then I'm off to the hardware shop to get it all. Need anything in town?"

"No, thanks."

* * *

We had a full house in the tearoom, both inside and out. The arson in our shed was reported by the online paper, and a few people discussed it on Twitter, but the general agreement was that the incident had been caused by out-of-control teenage visitors making trouble. A handful of longtime residents of North Augusta complained, as they always did when anything at all unpleasant happened, that tourists were destroying the peace and safety of the area. I didn't add my own opinion, which is that a small wooden shed at the rear of a private garden ten miles outside of town was an unlikely spot to be hit by drunken teenagers or college kids on vacation. Not to mention that the supposed out-of-control young tourists both arrived quietly and then slipped silently into the night once the deed was done.

As I baked and filled the orders Marybeth and Cheryl brought to the kitchen, I thought. I came to no conclusions, but I was inclining toward suspecting Allegra. Yes, it was a coincidence this happened when the police investigation was still ongoing regarding the death of Kimberly Smithfield, but it wasn't as much a coincidence as might appear. We'd run into her in town only a few hours prior to the setting of the fire. Had encountering my friends and me refocused all of Allegra's bitterness in my direction, and she impulsively decided to act?

Our neighbors, the owners of other businesses, the head of the North Augusta Business Bureau, even the mayor herself, called either me or Rose to express their sympathy and extend an offer of help if we needed anything.

Not a word from Allegra, and I wouldn't have expected to hear anything from her. Unless she'd caused the fire in the first place. If she had been responsible, she'd be quick to show up here to gloat. She'd make a big deal of how the burnt-out hulk of our garden shed ruined the view from the tearoom. Which it did, I had to admit. Simon told me he had to wait for the arson investigation to be concluded before he could start tearing down the remains of the structure and installing a new shed.

It was coming up to three o'clock when my phone announced Rose was calling.

"If you have a moment, love, can you come up to the house?"

"Is it important? We're busy here."

"Important. Yes, it might be. I don't need assistance, but I have something you'll want to see."

"On my way." I washed my hands at the sink and spoke to Marybeth. "I'm needed up at the house. How's it looking out there?"

"Patio's full. A couple of tables free inside, but people said they'll wait to get a place outside."

"Can you manage? We should be okay food-wise until closing if I don't get back right away."

"We'll be fine. No special orders in the reservation book for the rest of the day."

"Call me if you need anything."

I trotted up the driveway thinking, *What now?*

Rose hadn't sounded concerned or worried about anything. She said she had something for me to see. I couldn't imagine she'd been poking around the arson scene, sorting through scraps of burned wood and warped garden tools with the edge of her cane in the manner of an elderly Sherlock Holmes, but with my grandmother you never knew. She might well have been doing exactly that.

I found Rose seated behind the reception desk. Jean, our weekday housekeeper, was with her. The house was quiet, a pleasant breeze blowing through the French doors of the dining room and into the foyer.

"Jean found something she thought we'd be interested

in, love," Rose said. "I suggested we wait for you before we open it."

"Found what?"

"This." Jean pulled an envelope out of the pocket of her dress.

I sucked in a breath. A plain white letter-size envelope, unaddressed, no stamp. "That looks a heck of a lot like the one Kimberly Smithfield found in the Peter Rabbit box."

"As I suspected," Rose said.

Jean handed me the envelope, her round face alight with curiosity.

"Where did you find it?" I asked.

"Room two-oh-two. My daily instructions said the guest had checked out early, so I was giving the room the thorough going over we do when preparing for new arrivals. I'd like to say I found it because of my diligent cleaning or sharp detecting instincts, but that wasn't it. I tripped on a scrunched-up edge of the rug and dropped the basket containing tea bags, sugar, and creamer. The little containers flew everywhere, so I had to get down on my hands and knees to gather them up. In crawling around the floor, I felt a bump beneath my knee, under the rug, close to the bed. I lifted it and found this. Do you suppose it's what whoever searched that room the other day was looking for?"

"Yes," I said. "I do. It must be."

When Kimberly found the envelope in the tea chest it had been sealed. The flap was now torn, but it felt as though something was still inside.

"Shall I call the police?" Rose asked.

"Let's wait to see what we have. Might be a shopping list."

It wasn't.

I took out two pieces of paper and unfolded them. The

handwriting was large, the penmanship clear, although a bit shaky. Across the top, printed in large black letters, it said: *Last Will and Testament.*

While Rose called Detective Redmond, I lay the two pages side by side on the desk and snapped pictures with my phone. The edge of one lifted in the breeze, and Jean put a pen on top to keep it down. My fingerprints would be on the paper, and mine and Jean's on the envelope, but that couldn't be helped. We, after all, had found it. Jean had, anyway. Redmond would scold me for opening it and reading the contents, but how could I not?

It was, as expected, the will of Rosemary Jane Ireland Morrison Smithfield. The language was simple and clear. This document was to replace all previous wills. In it she made a bequest of twenty thousand dollars to Albert Reeves, the gardener, and another twenty thousand to Helen Chambers, the housekeeper; she put two hundred thousand dollars into a trust fund for one of her children; and stipulated that the house was to be sold and the proceeds, along with the remainder of her estate, were to be divided between her other two children.

The will was drawn up as I'd been led to believe. Except for the names attached to the bequests.

Chapter 21

"You shouldn't have opened this, Lily," Amy Redmond said.

I gave her a sheepish grin and said nothing. After taking the pictures—for nothing but my own curiosity—I'd slipped the two pages back into the envelope, and Rose, Jean, and I waited for the police to arrive.

We hadn't had to wait for long.

Redmond and Williams came together. They had serious expressions as they slipped on gloves prior to taking the will out of the envelope and reading quickly. Williams let out a low whistle, while Redmond said, "So Kimberly's been disinherited. No wonder she wanted to get her hands on this will."

"Not cut out entirely," Williams said. "She got two hundred thou."

"A pittance compared to half the value of the house and the rest, which is what she'd been expecting."

He nodded.

"I haven't seen the previous wills," I said. "So all I can tell you about them is what Rachel told me. The first will, the one Mrs. Smithfield drew up a few years ago following her husband's death, left the bulk of the estate to Kimberly and Rachel equally. A provision was made for an income for the son, Stephen, and some minor bequests to the long-time servants, although I wasn't told the details of that. Rosemary Smithfield called in her lawyers after she fell ill and drew up a second will. This happened while Rachel was working in Paris. In that will Rosemary left almost everything to Kimberly, cutting out not only Rachel but the aforementioned staff, although Stephen was still provided with a small amount. . . ."

"I don't consider two hundred thousand to be a small amount," Jean said.

"Neither do I," I replied. "But compared to an equal share of the full estate, it is. He wasn't to get the money in a lump sum, but as an allowance. When I spoke to him about it, he seemed blasé, but it has to have stung. Basically, his mother said she didn't trust him. Rachel, however, got even more of an insult in the second will. She got nothing. Not a red cent."

"Yet here," Rose said, "in the third will, Rachel gets half along with Stephen and it's Kimberly who's given nothing but the moderate allowance."

"Rachel was open and up front about that all along," I said. "She made no secret that she was after the third will only because she would inherit from it. What I find particularly interesting is that, instead of sharing the estate with Kimberly, according to this will, Rachel will be sharing it with Stephen. The black sheep of the family. Who was only given the aforementioned two hundred thousand in the earlier will." I thought back over all the discussions Rachel and I had about her mother's final intentions. "I don't think Rachel knew that. I think she assumed all along Kimberly would get a share and Stephen the allowance."

"You found this under a rug in a guest room?" Redmond asked Jean.

"Yes, and only because I dropped something and had to crawl around after it. If not for that . . . I might not have found it for months. We don't regularly lift the rugs."

"Someone searched that room thoroughly," Williams said. "But they didn't check under the rug?"

"They were likely in a hurry," I said. "Only had time to look in the obvious places. Kimberly wanted to keep this hidden, even from her husband. I wonder why she didn't destroy it as soon as she had her hands on it. The envelope was sealed when she found it, and someone opened it, almost certainly her. She read the contents and realized what it all meant." Had Wesley known where it had been hidden? Unlikely, or he would have gotten rid of it or taken it with him. If Kimberly hadn't wanted, for whatever reason, to destroy her mother's final will, Wesley would have had absolutely no compunctions about doing so. Had Kimberly been hiding the will from Wesley? Entirely possible, if she feared he wouldn't stay with her once he realized she wasn't going to come into a couple of million bucks. I felt a touch of sympathy for Kimberly. She must have been devastated when she learned that her mother had largely disinherited her, but still she held on to the will. For sentimental reasons? Torn between taking what she thought she deserved and honoring her mother's last wishes?

We'd probably never know.

She probably didn't know.

"I think a chat with Stephen Smithfield is called for," Williams said.

"Did you ask him where he was at the time of his sister's death?" I asked.

"We did. No alibi, but that means little. He was at home all evening, alone. So he said. The housekeeper,

Mrs. Chambers, left at five, which is her regular time, and she confirmed Stephen was in the house when she left. Doesn't mean he didn't go out later. We'll start digging deeper into his whereabouts."

Redmond nodded. "You've been a big help, Lily." She slipped the envelope into an evidence bag. "Thanks. Looks like we won't need your help any longer."

"I'm glad to hear that," I said.

I walked the police to the door. "You think Stephen's responsible?"

"I think nothing," Redmond said. "But we will be taking a great deal more interest in his recent movements and activities than we have been. He had an enormous amount to gain from locating this will."

"Your pal Rachel's not entirely in the clear, either," Williams said. "She has an alibi, but alibis can be faked."

"And people can work in conjunction for a common end," Redmond said.

"What happens if one or the other of them is found to have murdered Kimberly?" I asked. "What happens to the estate, I mean? Would the other get it all?"

"I'm not as well up on the intricacies of inheritance law as I might be," Detective Redmond said. "A person can't financially benefit from a crime they committed, so the killer, if convicted, would unlikely be allowed to inherit. We're assuming that this will"—she lifted the evidence bag—"is valid. It might not be. That's for the lawyers to sort out."

I watched them drive away, and then I went back inside to check on Rose. Jean had returned to her tasks, and the roar of the vacuum cleaner sounded over our heads.

"So it was Stephen after all," Rose said.

"That's not proven, but it's likely. If he knew the third will gave him a proper share of the estate, he'd be desperate to get his hands on it. He might have confronted Kimberly, demanding she hand it over, and killed her in a flash of anger when she refused. Maybe Rachel put the idea in his head to get rid of Kimberly, or he came up with it all on his own. Kimberly would likely have contested this third will, and she probably had grounds as her mother was in her final days when she wrote it. Stephen, and perhaps Rachel herself, might have not wanted to go through all that fuss and bother. Never mind the expense of a drawn-out legal case. Regardless, it's no longer our problem."

I was sorry the way things had turned out. When Stephen came here, to Victoria-on-Sea, to visit the spot where his sister died, I'd believed him to be sincere, genuinely grieving. He seemed to have accepted that his background as a wild young man meant his family didn't trust him with money.

Goes to show what a good judge of character I am.

Not.

"Nasty piece of work that Stephen chap," Rose said. "I disliked him the moment I set eyes on him. I should have told the police right away."

I smiled at her. "I'm sure they would have taken your judgment into account."

Robbie curled his lip up at me and Rose sniffed. I hid a grin. They did have identical expressions sometimes. "So they should," my grandmother said. "Observations made as a result of a lifetime of experience dealing with people shouldn't be so easily dismissed as an old lady's fancy. I have to say, I was shocked at the way Helen Chambers allowed that young man to talk to her in front of us. Mrs. McNamara was the housekeeper when I was at Thornecroft. She'd been with the family more than thirty years, her mother before her, and I can tell you none of the children, adult or not, would have been permitted to speak to her the way that young man did in our presence, regardless of whether or not Lady Frockmorton was there to hear it. She ensured her children were property trained and respectful of the people who provided the comforts of life they relied upon."

"Next, Rose, you're going to say standards are slipping in the colonies, and young people these days. . . ."

She winked at me. Robbie yawned. "Perhaps I am. Privilege of old age. Not that I'm old yet, love. But because I hope to be old one day, I'm glad that's all over. I wonder how that awful young man you once fancied is going to take it when he finds out his late wife isn't inheriting several million after all."

"I have no idea, and I hope to never know. The legal complications are going to be interesting, and it's going to take a long time to sort it all out, particularly if the police find the evidence to arrest and charge Stephen. Enough chat. I have to get back to work. I'll phone Bernie on my way to the tearoom and fill her in."

Bernie was, she told me when I called, writing up a storm with a *fabulous* new idea for a subplot involving a lost will and murderous relatives, so she didn't have time to chat about anything happening in real life.

I worked late into the night, enjoying the silence of my kitchen and the feel of pastry and dough beneath my hands. It wasn't over, not for the Smithfield family, not by a long shot, but it was over for me. And I was glad of it.

It was full dark outside, and I was putting away the last of the night's work when Rachel called me. "The police are looking for my brother," she said.

"I know. I'm sorry."

"They can't possibly believe Stephen killed Kimberly. Come on. Stephen doesn't have a mean bone in his body.

When he was a teenager, I sometimes wished he would show some backbone. His father bullied him terribly. Poor Stephen didn't meet Julian's ideals of what a man should be."

"How did your mother react to that?"

"The way she reacted to a lot of things in Julian Smithfield's house: by pretending not to notice. Maybe it would have helped if I'd been there for Stephen, but I'm eight years older than him, and what college girl or twenty-something woman making her way in Manhattan wants to concern herself with the troubles of her wayward teenage brother? I figured Helen would look after him, if my parents wouldn't."

"You don't think he did it?"

"Killed Kimberly? No, I do not. He absolutely doesn't have it in him. Detective Redmond told me they found Mom's handwritten will, but she didn't say where."

"So I heard."

"Do you know where it was?"

I saw no reason not to tell her, so I did. "Underneath a rug in what had been Kimberly's room at the B & B. She must have wanted the will to be kept safe and . . ."

"Hidden from me. I wanted to search that room. The first place I would have looked was under a rug. That's where she kept her diary when she was a kid. Thinking I'd be snooping. As if I cared what she got up to. As I recall, you wouldn't let me into the room, Lily. If I found it, it would have saved us all a lot of trouble, and Kimberly would still be alive."

My hackles rose. After all the fuss and bother Rachel and her family had caused me. "Don't you dare put any blame on me, Rachel. Letting you into that room to search it would have been a serious threat to our reputation, not to mention illegal."

"Yeah, okay. Sorry. You did what you had to do, and I guess I can respect that."

Not that I much cared if I had Rachel's respect or not. "You didn't come back to the house later, after Kimberly's death, and search for the envelope when Wesley was out, did you?"

"I will admit, Lily, the thought crossed my mind, but I decided against it. My break-and-enter skills aren't up to much, and if I was caught, let's say the cops here aren't all that favorably inclined toward me at the moment."

I didn't know if I believed her, but I let it go. All water under the bridge—the will had been located.

"I have an appointment at the police station tomorrow to see the document. I suspect they also have more questions for me about where I was when Kimmy died. They've been checking further into my alibi. Unfortunately, the bartender at the place I was at isn't sure if he remembers me or not, so all I have to rely on is the charter boat captain. Thank heavens I didn't shrug his attentions off outright, or who knows what he'd try to do to get back at me. This whole awful thing seems never-ending, but I suppose that's the way the law works."

"Where are you now?" I asked.

"At the Chatham house. It seems so empty. Mom . . . gone. Kimberly . . . gone. Stephen . . . wherever Stephen is. Helen finished for the day. I guess it's my house now, if the will says what Detective Redmond told me it says. I have the house, or the prospect of having it, but I don't want it. I want to go back to Manhattan. I want to design restaurants. That's all I've ever wanted to do. I have a good shot at getting the commission for the brasserie in a historic hotel near Gramercy Square that's being completely redesigned, and I have to get to work on my proposal if I have a chance of landing the contract." She sighed heavily. "Is Wesley still hanging around?"

"No. He . . . left prematurely."

"Just as well. He's going to be in a rage when he finds out he's not inheriting enough from Kimberly to buy him as much as a full set of kitchen appliances for the high-end restaurant of his dreams."

I refrained from saying, once again, that two hundred thousand was a lot of money. What was the point? Wesley would be in a rage. Who knows when, or even if, he'll see that money?

"Keep in touch, Lily. I'll be popping back and forth between New York and the Cape for a long time to come, I fear, and I'd like to see you again. Maybe we can grab a drink one night."

"I'd like that," I said, not meaning it. I had nothing against Rachel, but I didn't want any more reminders of the trouble she and her family had caused me.

But, once again, the Morrison-Smithfield family wasn't finished with me. I checked the ovens were off, turned out the lights, locked the door of Tea by the Sea behind me, and headed home. Clouds were scudding across the sky and the wind was high. We might, I thought, get some rain tonight. Waves crashed against the shore. Light spilled from the windows of the B & B, and the laughter of people enjoying a nightcap on the veranda drifted toward me. I knew my way well enough that I could light my way home with nothing but the weak glow from the flashlight on my phone. As I walked, I glanced to my left, toward the ruined garden shed, but I could see nothing in the dark. I rounded the house, noticing that Rose's lights had been switched off.

A shape stepped out of the darkness. I let out a muffled scream and staggered back.

"Sorry if I scared you," Stephen Smithfield said.

I gripped my phone. "What are you doing here? Do you know the police are looking for you?"

His face genuinely looked baffled. "Me? Why?"

"I don't know." My heart was pounding in my chest. I edged away, retreating toward the lights and the laughter on the veranda. "Questions about your sister's death, I'd guess."

"Questions. More questions. Always questions. I have questions of my own, and no one to answer them." He took his phone out of his pocket. No light came on when he touched it. "I turned this off earlier, not wanting to be disturbed." He shrugged. "They'll find me if they want me, soon enough." He put the phone away and stuffed his hands into his pocket.

"What are you doing here? And at this time of night?"

"I can't really say. I was out wandering, thinking. Thinking about Kimmy and our parents, and how short life can be. Whether or not I want to go back to California. I haven't got much to go back for. They're holding my job for me, and I like it well enough, but Massachusetts has stores, too, right? If I want to stay in retail, which I haven't decided. I don't have much here, either, come to think of it, except for Rachel. Family matters, doesn't it? But I suppose she'll be heading to New York the moment she can."

I should have been frightened, but I wasn't. I sensed no threat or hostility from this sad, lonely man, but I've been called naive more than once, so I wasn't going to take any chances. Keeping half an eye on Stephen, I retreated, going past Rose's side window and rounding the house, stepping into the light from the veranda where two couples were playing cards. "I hope you're having a nice evening," I called.

They waved cards and glasses at me.

"Where's your car?" I said to Stephen.

"My car? Oh, you mean the Audi. Not my car. Not exactly my style, but you need wheels around here, don't you? That was Mom's car, and no one's bothered to sell it yet. I parked it on the road. Wanted to have a walk. Think things over."

"Come to any conclusions?"

"No."

I lifted my own phone. "I'd like to call Detective Redmond. Tell her you're here. Is that okay?"

"Sure."

I kept my eyes on him as I pushed buttons. It was late, but Amy Redmond would recognize my number, and I hoped she'd pick up. She did. "Lily? What's up?"

"I'm having a chat with Stephen Smithfield. Here at the B & B."

"Are you in any danger?"

"Not in the least. Just having a pleasant conversation on a nice evening."

"I'm on my way."

"Best to come quietly," I said. "I wouldn't want you to . . . upset our guests."

"Understood."

"This is a nice place," Stephen said when I'd disconnected the call.

"We like it. We had a commotion here last night. Did you hear about that?"

"No. What sort of commotion?" The shadows were deep across his face, but what I could see remained impassive, not terribly interested, not at all concerned that the police were aware of his location.

"Our garden shed caught fire."

"That's too bad. Anyone hurt?"

"No."

"That's good, then." He turned and started to walk back toward the edge of the bluffs.

"Would you like to see the rose garden?" I asked.

"I'm not much of one for flowers, but I guess. Okay."

We walked together across the grass. I'd chosen the rose garden because it was within easy screaming distance of the card players, and light from the veranda reached it. I didn't know where Amy Redmond lived, but I hoped it wasn't too far. At this time of night it would take about ten minutes to get here from North Augusta. Keeping to the speed limit, that is, and she might not do that.

"I don't know why I've come here tonight," Stephen said. "Feeling sorry for myself, I guess. I didn't get on all that well with my parents, to put it mildly, and I put myself as far away from them as I could get as soon as I could, but there's something about knowing they're gone, Mom, anyway, and we'll never have a chance to make amends."

He was being talkative, so I decided I might as well learn what I could, while I could. "The terms of your mother's will didn't bother you?"

"You mean giving me a small allowance, rather than outright cash? Sure, it bothered me. But that's the same conditions as the will Dad had drawn up for them both. Mom kept the template and moved some names around." He chuckled.

"Names?"

"She cut Rachel out all together and left everything to Kimmy. Then, according to—" He stopped abruptly and took a breath before continuing. "According to Rachel, she changed her mind and wrote Rachel back in. My mother was . . . I think the word is *indecisive*. She married my dad for his money, and found she couldn't handle all the baggage that went with it."

"You know that for sure?"

"I don't know what she was thinking at the time of their marriage, no. She never said, but it was always obvious she wasn't a happy woman. My dad was not a nice man."

"What sort of baggage?" The first warm raindrop fell on my head.

"Doesn't matter now." He squinted up into the night sky.

A few more raindrops fell.

The card players, dry in the shelter of the veranda, laughed, and a woman said, "Any more in that bottle, hon?"

"It's raining," Stephen said. "I'm not going to stand around and get wet. That cop can call me tomorrow if she still wants to talk. I'll turn my phone on in the morning."

"We can take seats on the porch," I suggested as a few raindrops rapidly became many more. "It's sheltered there."

"Nah, it's late. Time I was going."

He started to walk away, heading toward the road, as the rain fell around him. I didn't believe Stephen was a killer, but what I believed didn't matter. The police had a lot of questions for him, and he wasn't willing to wait for them, but there wasn't much I could do to stop him from leaving. I couldn't run after him, wrestle him to the ground, and hold him down until the police arrived.

"For what it's worth," he said as he passed out of the lights from the house into the curtain of rain. "I'm sorry about Kimmy. I wouldn't have agreed . . ." His voice faded away.

I called Redmond as I ran for shelter. "Stephen's left. Sorry, I couldn't keep him here. If you hurry you might catch him. He said he parked on the road."

"I've been delayed. A multicar accident on the highway

and then a call about a robbery in progress and no one else to take it. He won't get far." I could hear a siren in the background. "Did you see what car he's in?"

"His mother's Audi."

"Okay. Thanks, Lily. I'll run those plates and put a BOLO on him." Redmond hung up.

Chapter 22

Bernie arrived at Victoria-on-Sea shortly before I was finished with the B & B breakfasts the following morning. Her writing, she told me, had gone well, and she was eager to discuss the newest developments in the "case of the lost will," as she referred to it. Before I put her to work unloading the dishwasher, I showed her the photos I'd taken of Rosemary Smithfield's third will.

She studied the pictures in great detail before handing my phone back to me. "Seems pretty straightforward. I don't suppose you turned the paper over to see if there's anything written on the back?"

"No, I didn't think to."

She tsked in disappointment, sounding much like Robert the Bruce when I did something he disapproved of. Which happened regularly. "We have an original will, properly drawn up in a lawyers' office, a second will hastily organized in the dying woman's sick room, then a third will handwritten and concealed in a children's tea set. Who's to say there isn't a fourth will scribbled on the back of that one, or also secreted away. The possibilities are endless. However, I have to say, as far as I can tell, that last will appears to be perfectly legal. The writing's legible, no obvious signs of erasure or tampering with. Dated and properly witnessed. I don't recognize the names of the witnesses, but I assume they're legit."

"That's the last of them." Edna dumped a load of dirty dishes on the counter. "Another lot of happy people fed." She wiggled her shoulders and gave her back a good stretch. I threw down my dishtowel and called to Éclair. I had time to grab a coffee and relax for half an hour before heading up the driveway to start my second shift.

Edna's phone rang. "I have to get this. It's Frank. He knows not to call me before nine thirty, so this might be important. Hi, honey, is everything okay?" As she listened, she waggled her eyebrows at me. I edged closer.

"Thanks, hon." She put her phone away. "The police arrested Stephen Smithfield last night for the murder of Kimberly Smithfield."

"Wow," Bernie said. "That's quite a thing. Killing a sister for money."

"Allegedly," Edna said.

"He must have set the fire to your shed," Bernie said. "I wonder why he did that?"

"Maybe for no reason at all," Edna said. "Because he could."

"He was here Thursday morning," I said. "He told me he wanted to see where his sister died."

"Returning to the scene of the crime." Bernie nodded sagely.

"And then, later that afternoon, I caught him spying on Rachel and Helen Chambers while they had tea."

I said nothing about his third visit last night. I hadn't slept well, going over and over that conversation in my mind. I didn't see Stephen as a killer, and particularly not of his sister, but if I said so, Bernie would remind me that I have a rosy outlook on people. People can kill in anger, lash out in a rage, and it's possible Stephen had been the person I'd heard Kimberly arguing with in the moments before she died and he ran in fright. Although, if that's what happened, I would have expected him to break down and tearfully confess.

Then again, I'd never met the man before this week.

"You don't suppose he and Rachel were in it together, do you?" Bernie asked. "According to the new will, they share the estate, after all."

"None of this sits well with me," I said. "Edna, will you let me know if the paper hears of any new developments?"

"Sure."

"What doesn't sit well with you?" Bernie asked as we walked along the cliff top toward my cottage.

Sunlight sparkled on the clear blue waters of the bay. A fully laden whale-watching boat passed us, heading for the open ocean at the top of the Cape. Éclair sniffed through the grass and around the fence posts, her stubby tail wagging in delight at all the marvelous fresh scents she was finding.

I stopped and leaned on the railing. I wanted to take a moment to enjoy the view, but the beauty of my surroundings couldn't distract my dark thoughts. "I simply can't see Stephen as a killer. He seemed to me to be a gentle sort. Rachel told me his father tried to bully him into being more manly."

Bernie scoffed. "Like Wesley, who I heard was evicted from the premises, and not a moment too soon. If I may be blunt . . ."

"Whyever would you stop now?"

"You're too kind for your own good, Lily Roberts. I've told you that before. People can surprise you, in many different ways."

"I know. It's just . . ." My voice trailed off. I didn't know what I thought. "Maybe Stephen did come here that night to demand Kimberly produce the third will, and they got into an argument over it. He's the one who sold the tea chest, and thus the will, to the antique dealer, remember. He was likely carrying around a lot of anger toward himself for doing that. Mix self-loathing with long-simmering family resentments, and the result can be a toxic brew. He lashed out. Maybe he killed her without meaning to and ran. Okay, I can buy that. But why set the shed on fire?"

"To send a message. Stop interfering or next time it'll be your house. With you in it."

"That's why I don't think Stephen did it," I said. "Maybe my naiveté is acting up again, but my take is he doesn't have the guile. I also have to question if Stephen even knew he was back in the will. Rachel thought it was all going to her and Kimberly, and she was there, with her mother, around the time. Stephen was in California when his mother was dying, but I suppose she could have phoned and told him."

"If you're right about his character, and I have my doubts, we're back to Rachel as prime suspect, and she, according to the cops, has an alibi. Her plus Wesley, who doesn't have an alibi. Is it possible they worked together?"

"Rachel doesn't have a lot of time for Wesley."

"That's a point in her favor," Bernie said.

"I can't see her putting her life in his hands in that way. Plotting a murder with another person must make you mighty dependent on their continuing good will."

"Not necessarily. Both parties would need to keep the secret. Hang together or hang separately, as the saying goes."

"I'll buy that."

"Are you sure they don't get on? People can pretend to have emotions they don't feel, you know. Wesley married Rachel's sister, and apparently in a heck of a rush. That play might have been cooked up between the two of them as a way of getting the money."

I thought about that and eventually shook my head. "Rachel's known Wesley for a number of years. They've worked together in the past, and closely. If anything romantic was going to blossom, it would have by now. She wouldn't have been able to just stand by when he declared his, supposed, everlasting love for me."

"Why would Rachel know that happened? She wasn't a witness to it. If she suspected something along those lines, he could have told her he was playing a role to confuse things."

"Good point. I still don't see it, though. Most of all, because Rachel wanted the will found and Wesley didn't. Why would Wesley kill Kimberly?"

"Maybe she told him she'd destroyed the will. Thinking her inheritance was therefore guaranteed, and his in turn as her widower, he killed her."

"Possible. Anything's possible. What's not possible, Bernie, is for me to put this to rest. Something Rose said has been bothering me a great deal."

"What?"

"Let me think about it. I got the tearoom well stocked last night, so I have time to go for a drive. Wanna come?"

"Have I ever been known to turn down one of your scones?"

"What does that mean? I'm not planning on bringing a picnic lunch."

"It means your question was rhetorical. Of course I want to come."

I sent a text to Cheryl, telling her I'd be late, but to go ahead and open on time. Then I called to Éclair, put her in the house, ensured she had sufficient water until Mrs. Zagorsky, the weekend housekeeper, came to check on her, and Bernie and I set off. We have two sets of keys for Rose's car. One set is kept in her rooms and the spare in the B & B kitchen on a hook next to the aprons.

The kitchen hook was empty. I groaned. "If I have to go in search of the keys, Rose will want to know why I need the car when I should be hard at work in the tearoom."

"Tell her you have an emergency shopping errand to attend to."

I shook my head. "Rose can always tell when I'm lying. It's her superpower. One of many. Did you bring your car?"

"Nope. Biked over. I've been putting in long hours slaving over my computer, so I figured I could use the exercise this morning. Do you need me to go and get it?"

"I don't want to wait. Nothing for it, but I'll have to ask Rose where the keys are."

"Whereupon she'll insist on coming with us."

"Which, I'm sure, is why she hid the spare key."

To my surprise, when we reached the foyer, Detective Redmond was on her way out of the house.

"Detective, good morning," I said. "Are you looking for something? Can I help you?"

"Thanks, Lily, but no. I had a couple of minor loose ends to tidy up."

I had no idea what she meant by that, but I said, "I heard Stephen has been arrested for the murder."

"Not arrested at this time. Brought in for questioning."

"Do you think he did it?"

"I can't, and won't, comment on that. The investigation is ongoing. Have a nice day."

"Did you catch the suspect in that robbery you were called to last night?"

She frowned. "Total and complete waste of time. The homeowner misplaced his glasses and called nine-one-one. He made the situation sound considerably more urgent than it turned out to be." The door shut behind her. She hadn't once looked at my face.

"Did that seem odd to you?" Bernie said. "She was surprisingly cagey."

"I find it odd that she was wandering around this house by herself. It is a private home, although we have paying guests. Whatever, she must have rung the bell and no one answered."

Bernie and I found my grandmother in her suite, fully made up, hair done, dressed for the day in sneakers, a wide pink skirt with cavernous pockets, and a long-sleeved yellow blouse buttoned to the neck. All ready for an outing.

"Amy Redmond was here just now," I said. "Did she come to talk to you?"

Rose waved her hand in the air. "A quick question about Stephen Smithfield, which I couldn't answer. I've never met the man, and I told her so."

"She couldn't phone to ask you that?"

"Who knows the mysterious workings of the NAPD?"

"True enough. I can't find the keys to the car."

"Sorry, love. I decided they weren't safe in the kitchen where anyone might wander in and take them."

"No one, ever, wanders into the kitchen."

"I do," Bernie said.

"Except for you."

"And Edna."

"Edna works there."

"Simon and Matt."

"I get the point, Bernie! No one who is planning on stealing Rose's car will wander into the kitchen hoping we left the keys in plain sight so they can grab them and go for a joy ride in a Ford Focus."

"Fortunately." Rose produced the keys with a flourish. "I have them here. How convenient. Where are we going?"

"Why do you suppose we're going anywhere?"

"You want the car keys, for one thing. For another, Edna called me a short while ago to say the paper's reporting that the police have made an arrest in the killing of our guest."

"Not an arrest," Bernie said, "but taken in for questioning."

"A legal nicety. I assumed you two would not be content with secondhand developments and would want to follow up. As I am also the curious sort, I decided to come with you." Her blue eyes danced.

I snatched the keys from her hand and marched out the door. Bernie and a chuckling Rose followed me.

Chapter 23

As I drove, I explained my thought process to Rose and Bernie. Bernie mumbled, and Rose said only, "I have to point out, love, that my days in service were a long time ago. Things have changed."

"To some extent, perhaps, but I believe your fundamental point is still valid."

Traffic was light and we arrived in Chatham in good time. The gates to the Smithfield home were closed. I pressed the button on the intercom and waited. I waited some more. I pressed again.

Finally, a burst of static, and Helen Chambers said, "May I help you?"

"Hi, Helen. It's Lily Roberts here. I've come to see Rachel. Is she in?"

"Is she expecting you?"

"Not really. This is sort of an impromptu call. If she's not in, I've . . . uh . . . got something to drop off for her."

"Come up." The intercom buzzed, and the gates swung silently open.

"Easy peasy," I said.

"Don't get too far ahead of yourself," Bernie said. "The

life of a housebreaker doesn't suit you. You announced your name. I thought we were going to park down the street and climb over the walls."

"I might have suggested that," I said. "But we have a woman not in the prime of youth with us who would insist on joining in."

"I can climb over walls," Rose said. "With assistance and a sturdy ladder."

Rachel Morrison was waiting for us at the top of the steps, standing in front of the open door. I gave her a cheerful wave as I parked the car. Rose, Bernie, and I got out.

"This is an unexpected visit," Rachel said in a warm, welcoming voice. "What brings you all here?"

"I'm hoping we might be able to clear up some loose ends regarding the death of your sister," I said.

Her sculpted eyebrows rose. "Why is it up to you to clear anything up? You're not with the cops."

"I don't want to bother them with my unformed ideas. Not yet, anyway. Can we come in?"

"Sure." Rachel stepped back and we entered the house. She led the way to the living room and invited us to sit. "Coffee? Tea?"

Rose started to say, "Tea, please," but I cut her off. "Nothing thanks. Are you here by yourself? Other than Helen?"

"Yes. No one left, is there? Have you heard Stephen's been detained?"

"I did."

"I don't have too long to chat, Lily. My lawyer and I have an appointment at the police station in North Augusta at noon to see the will, and I hope to be able to see Stephen."

"What happens now?" Bernie asked. "Regarding the will?"

"Assuming it is my mother's will, my lawyer will do what he has to do to get it into court and declared valid," Rachel said. "Once that's over, then . . . that depends on what happens to Stephen. I can't believe the cops think he killed Kimberly." She shook her head. "Not Stephen. Not my little brother."

"You're very fond of him," I said.

"He's my baby brother. I told you that. I should have done more to protect him, all those years ago. I didn't, and that's on me, but it's water under the bridge. I'll do what I have to do for him now, and to that end, I've hired a criminal defense lawyer."

"What lawyer are you using?" I asked. "For the will and the murder case? Martin . . . uh . . . something."

"I wouldn't trust Martin to handle the sale of my car, Lily. He caused Julian to lose a substantial amount of money. More recently he conspired with Wesley behind my back, after Kimberly died. I have no reason to have any loyalty to the old family firm. Quite the contrary."

"Speaking of Wesley . . . Is he still around?"

"Oh, yes. I got a call from good old Wes. He heard through the grapevine that my mother's will's been found—" She stopped abruptly. Her eyes narrowed. "Did you tell him?"

I threw up my hands. "Not me. I haven't spoken to him since he left the B & B yesterday morning, and even if I had, I wouldn't have told him anything."

"He didn't seem to be aware of the contents, though." She chuckled. "He knows he needs to be nice to me, hoping he and I can sell the house and share the proceeds without fuss and bother. He's going to be in for a heck of a shock, isn't he?"

"How do you feel about shocking him?" Bernie asked.

"I can't say I care. I'd rather share my family's money with my brother than my late sister's odious husband."

"If Stephen goes to jail for killing Kimberly," I said, "you won't have to share with anyone."

Her eyes narrowed. The warmth of her earlier greeting had disappeared. "My sister—half sister—died on your property and you found her, Lily. I suppose you think that gives you some rights to stick your nose in my family's affairs, but the way I see it, it doesn't. Your participation is over." She stood up. "Thanks for calling."

Bernie threw me a questioning look. Rose had folded her hands across the top of her cane and was looking around the room, studying the furniture and the art, for all intents and purposes paying no attention to the conversation.

I stayed where I was. "You got a good lawyer to defend Stephen?"

"The best I could find. He doesn't come cheap, but I don't intend to help Stephen on the cheap. I have my savings, and eventually, I hope, I can sell this dump of a house."

"If it makes you feel better toward me," I said, "I don't think Stephen killed Kimberly, either. But someone did and—if it wasn't Stephen—then that person is still out there."

Rachel slowly sat back down. "I am aware of that, Lily. As long as we're talking about Wesley, my money's on him."

"Mine's not," I said. "I know him. Knew him, I mean. He might have married Kimberly in a rush because he wanted to get his hands on her inheritance, but on her part the rose was not yet off that bloom—"

"I think you mean, love, the bloom was not off the rose," said my grandmother.

"Thank you, that is what I mean. Which is to say, he may not have been in love with her, but she was still in love with him. She was more than happy to give him whatever he needed for his Cape Cod restaurant ventures. Eventually, someday, she might come to regret that, but not yet."

Rachel nodded. "Who else, then? And I hope you're not thinking it was me."

"We're agreed Stephen didn't kill Kimberly, and it's unlikely Wesley did. You don't trust your family lawyer, but I'd say killing a client in cold blood takes malpractice to an entirely different level. If he did encourage your stepfather to make bad investments, that was a long time ago, and he didn't—far as I know—hold a gun to the man's head."

"What you're saying, Lily, if I understand you properly, is I killed Kimberly in order to get possession of the third will." Rachel held out her arms. "But, as we all know, I didn't find it. It's only luck Kimberly didn't destroy it and it turned up."

"Someone searched her hotel room after her death," Bernie said. "It's obvious whoever it was had been looking for the will. That they didn't find it is immaterial. It was only happenstance the housekeeper found it."

"It would have shown up eventually," Rose said. "We do lift our rugs to give them a good cleaning every few years or so."

"The killing might have been a random thing," Rachel said. "The police dismissed the idea, but probably not entirely. Such things do happen."

"Kimberly wasn't arguing with a random stranger outside my cottage that night," I said. "She was murdered by someone she knew, and knew well enough to say she wasn't going to agree to . . . whatever that person had suggested. I might have admitted the possibility that the argument and her subsequent death had nothing to do with you and your family and your mother's will, but then someone set fire to my grandmother's garden shed, and no random serial killer would return days later to the scene of the crime to commit a minor act of arson."

"An expert in the behavior of random serial killers, are you?"

"Lily's not," Bernie said. "But I know a thing or two. In my previous job I worked mostly tracking down financial fraud and tax evasion, but on occasion a killer tries to cheat on his, or her, taxes, too."

"If you're going to ask me to prove I didn't set your blasted garden shed on fire," Rachel said, "I can't. But I'll remind you I have an alibi for the time of Kimmy's death. Now, I'm going to insist that you leave. Your accusations are getting insulting."

"I know you didn't do it," I said. "Either the fire or the murder."

"What are you getting at, then? You're talking in riddles."

"In the manner of the best housekeepers," Rose said, "yours is listening at keyholes. I think it's time we invite Mrs. Chambers to join us, don't you all agree?"

Helen Chambers stepped into the living room. "I wouldn't say listening at keyholes, but sound does travel in this house. Shall I call security, Rachel? If these *ladies* won't leave willingly, they might need to be shown the door."

"I'm glad you've joined us, Helen," I said. "What did Stephen promise you? Half his share?"

She studied my face and said nothing.

Rachel stood up. "Surely you're not accusing—"

"I am," I said. "My grandmother figured it out."

"Not entirely." Rose stood up, made some adjustments to her blouse, and crossed the room to take a chair closer to Helen. She patted her chest modestly. "But I did provide the spark."

"We paid a call here on Wednesday," I said. "Stephen was shockingly rude to you, Helen. So much so that when I spoke to him later and he presented a different side of his personality to me, I wasn't sure I correctly remembered what had happened. But I had, and Bernie remembered it that way, too."

"He always was a spoiled little brat," Helen spat. She eyed me warily and did not take a seat.

"What are you talking about?" Rachel said. "You always adored Stephen."

The look of fury Helen threw at Rachel confirmed all my suspicions. I hadn't been sure of my reasoning, not at all. Vague impressions of people I didn't know well. Random misgivings. Scraps of conversation. My grandmother's memories of what relationships were like long ago between servants and employers.

"Stephen would not have been raised to be permitted to speak to the staff like that," I said. "More to the point, he wouldn't have wanted to, would he? Rachel told me that when she left this house to move to New York, she abandoned Stephen to his father's bullying, because she believed you, Helen, would step in to look after him. Not something she'd have done if you didn't like the boy. When we visited you the first time, you convinced him to play an act in front of us, to make us believe you and he didn't get on."

"Why would she do that?" Rachel asked.

"For the same reason Helen told me she suspected you of killing not only Kimberly, but your mother."

Rachel laughed. "You have got to be kidding me. That's ridiculous. Helen, do you have anything to say to that?"

Helen simply stared at me.

"You invited her to tea at my restaurant," I said to Rachel. "I don't normally come out of the back, but my waitress told me you'd arrived, and I thought I'd pop out and be friendly. I was surprised, to say the least, to see how well you two were getting on. Considering that, according to what Helen told me, she thought you were a cold-blooded killer."

"That makes no sense," Rachel said.

"It makes perfect sense, I believe, to Helen. She knows I have some sort of a rapport with the North Augusta police. She might even think my opinions carry weight with them."

"Which they don't," Bernie said. "More like the opposite. But never mind that now."

"I'm sorry to say this, Rachel, but Helen wouldn't have been entirely unhappy to see you charged with the murder of Kimberly."

Rachel dropped into a chair with a groan.

"Under the terms of the new will, and with you and Kimberly both out of the way, Stephen would inherit the bulk of the estate. Shortly before she died, Mrs. Smithfield decided to rewrite her will. She must have realized she'd acted in haste in disinheriting Rachel, and she regretted that. She intended to simply go back to the terms of the original will, which divided the estate between Kimberly and Rachel and left an allowance for Stephen. I believe Helen managed to convince your mother that Kimberly didn't deserve it, and it was time Stephen was forgiven. Stephen, according to the deal I believe he worked out at Helen's suggestion, agreed to give a substantial part of his inheritance to her if she helped him get back into the will. He went along with what she said, as I suspect he'd done for much of his life. Later, whether Stephen realized Helen had killed Kimberly, or suspected, or simply didn't want to know, I can't say, although I think he suspected. I wonder what he's telling the police right now, Helen. Are you worried about that?"

"Not in the least," Helen said. "You have a highly active imagination, Lily. You should save it for decorating your cupcakes. I was too polite to say so at the time, but I found them too dry and the frosting excessively sweet."

"I'll look into fixing that right away. I notice you haven't denied anything I said."

"I prefer not to honor your fantasies with argument."

"Helen's been the housekeeper for my family for many years," Rachel said. "I have trouble believing what you're saying, Lily."

"For many years, yes. What did Rosemary Smithfield give you in reward for those years of service, Helen? Twenty thousand dollars. The same as the gardener."

"I was not party to the contents of her will," Helen said.

"That's my entire point. You were. You were in the room when Rosemary Smithfield wrote the third will. You told her what to say. You convinced her to fully include Stephen, and possibly to cut Kimberly out, although that might have been her own idea. People have said she was mercurial. You might have suggested she give you a bit more, or maybe not if you knew she wouldn't agree."

I had a sudden realization. "You weren't even mentioned in the second will, were you?"

If looks could kill . . .

I turned to Rachel. "You told me provisions were made for staff in the original and the second wills. I assumed, that word again, Helen was included. But she couldn't have been, not if she witnessed the will. As for the third will, the handwritten one, Helen wasn't a signing witness. She was mentioned in the will, although not given a substantial amount. For some reason Rosemary decided to remember Helen in the third will, although in a minor way. Perhaps your mother was angry with Helen at the time she wrote the second will, or when it came to the third, she simply decided to let bygones be bygones. Helen didn't witness the final will, but she was in that room, persuading Rosemary to forgive Stephen. She might have tried to suggest she leave Rachel out, as well as Kimberly, but that didn't work."

"It was an insult." Helen bit off the words. "Twenty thousand dollars in thanks for a life's work. I raised her children. I wiped Stephen's tears after his father yelled at him to be a man. I took the brunt of Kimberly's teenage temper tantrums. She always was a spoiled little miss, far too sure of her own importance in this life."

"My mother treated you well," Rachel said. "Is this how you repaid her, exerting influence on her when she was dying?"

Rose was perched on the end of her chair, turned toward Helen.

"Your mother," Helen spat, "was an interloper. What did she know about running a fine house? About being a good corporate wife? As soon as she married Mr. Julian she was quick enough to dump her own brat on me to raise."

Rachel recoiled as though she'd been struck. "I can't believe that's what you thought of us. All these years. I thought you . . . liked us. Loved us, even."

"Such is the servants' lot, dear." Rose adjusted her blouse once again and spoke in a loud clear voice, enunciating every word. I wondered if she thought Rachel was hard of hearing. "A proper servant must never express what they're thinking or feeling. That's the way it was in my day at any rate, and I'm happy to say things have changed since my mother and grandmother were in service. Helen could have simply quit after the first Mrs. Smithfield passed away, if she didn't want to work for the second wife. I'm going to speculate that she didn't do that because she'd become too attached to Mr. Smithfield. And him to her? That's what he led her to believe in any event. Am I right, dear?" Rose watched Helen. "The loyal housekeeper eternally hoping he'd finally do right by her. But he didn't. He remarried and made himself a new family."

Helen's eyes flashed with remembered pain. He'd noticed her all right. He'd made promises he never intended to fulfill. What a poisoned household young Rachel and her mother had walked into.

"Then, once he died, leaving you unmentioned in his will," I said, "it was too late for you to move on. You were too old to look for a new job, and too set in your ways in this household. So you bided your time, and waited. And you spun your web."

"Unmentioned. That's the word." Helen's face was tight with anger, her fists clenched. "Unremembered. All I did for him over the years. All he meant to me and all I thought I meant to him." She paused, breathed. No one said a word. "When he married her"—a poisonous look at Rachel—"that Rosemary, he explained to me that he had to do it. He needed the money she'd bring to the marriage to save the company."

"That was a lie," Rachel said. "My parents had no money. My father didn't even have life insurance when he died. My mother was barely keeping her head above water until she married Julian."

"So I found out, eventually. 'Never mind, Helen,' he always said, 'I'll take care of you. I'll always take care of you.' I nursed him when he was sick, I cared for him when he was dying. I . . . I was the one who loved him, when *she* was off at her fancy galas and parties."

"You mean when my mother sought escape from this house through her volunteer work," Rachel said. "My mother's marriage to Julian wasn't a good one. It was a disaster, and she was so terribly sad all the time. No wonder, if he was carrying on with the *housekeeper* under her nose. I wonder if she knew. Probably, she wasn't a fool."

She knew. I remembered Rachel telling me her mother

pretended not to notice a lot of things that went on in their house.

"I suspect Mom eventually didn't much care what he got up to," Rachel continued, "once she finally realized what sort of a man he was."

"Mr. Julian was a good man!" Helen protested. "She poisoned him against me in his final years."

"You keep telling yourself that, Helen. As for the here and now, you should just leave. Today. I'll pay you whatever severance you think you're owed, and then I don't ever want to see you again."

Helen walking out the door wasn't what I'd hoped to achieve by coming here. Rose spoke before I could. "You must have been shocked when he died, leaving you with nothing."

Helen turned on my grandmother. I braced myself to move if her anger turned physical. "He wanted to provide for me," she said. "He told me he would, but she ordered him to cut me out of the will."

This time Rachel's laugh was full of bitterness. "My mother never ordered him to do anything in all their years together. Better if she had."

Helen didn't seem to hear her. "What was there in this house for me after he was gone? Nothing, nothing at all, but where could I go? No money, too old to start over again. I never married, I never had a family of my own. He . . . he was my life, his family was my family. So I stayed. I worked for her. Her and her brats. Then she got sick. She was dying. My time had come at last. I couldn't have Mr. Julian, but I could finally have what I was entitled to as his wife in all but name. I told Stephen I'd see he was brought back into the will, and in exchange I wanted half. He was willing enough—he's a nice boy, but he's not terribly bright, and he never stood up for himself. He always did whatever I told him to. Yes, I managed to convince Rosemary to replace Kimberly's name with Stephen's, but she wouldn't agree to cut you out, Rachel,"

"Oh, Helen," Rachel said.

"You must have been devastated when the third will couldn't be found," I said. "All your plotting came to naught when Stephen sold the tea chest to an antique dealer. But then, lo and behold, it was located. Rachel, you called Helen and told her Kimberly had found it, didn't you?"

Rachel nodded.

"What was that, dear?" Rose bellowed. "I didn't hear."

"Lily's right," Rachel said. "I told Helen that Kimberly had located the will. I also told her Kimberly was staying at Victoria-on-Sea in North Augusta."

"In doing so you unwittingly signed your sister's death warrant." The sequence of events was falling into place for me now. "Helen went to Victoria-on-Sea to get the will before Kimberly could destroy it, but she left without it. What happened, Helen? What went wrong?"

"I didn't mean to kill her. I phoned her and told her I needed to talk to her. Some story about the house needing emergency funds for a new roof and I had papers for her to sign." She snorted. "What does Kimberly know about maintaining a grand house? She told me what room she was in, but I suggested we go for a walk instead. I told her I wanted the will, and I knew she had it. She said no. She said her mother changed her mind and that's why she hid the third will, because she didn't intend anyone to find it. Kimberly always was a stubborn brat."

Rachel choked on a sob and rested her face in her hands. Bernie's eyes were bright with interest, and Rose had edged so far forward on her chair I worried she'd fall off, although her hands still gripped her cane.

"I told her I wanted it," Helen continued. "She refused.

I . . . don't know what happened, but suddenly she was lying on the ground, not moving. I . . . I thought she was pretending. I left her there and went home."

"I doubt that," I said. "But we'll let the police sort the details out."

"The police?" Helen laughed. "You're going to tell the police that ridiculous story? Don't you know when someone's playing with you?" She looked around the room. At Rachel, sobbing softly. At Bernie, standing by the bookshelf. At Rose, sitting in a blue and yellow damask-covered wingback chair, back straight, hands folded over her cane. At me, watching and listening. "You wanted to hear a confession, so I gave you one. It's meaningless. Here's the truth—I went to the B & B that night, but I didn't speak to Kimberly. Instead, I saw you, Rachel, walking in the garden with Kimberly."

"I didn't—"

"You think you have an alibi? You'll soon find that won't hold up. The man who gave it to you? He needs funds for much-needed repairs to his boat or he's going to go out of business. That can be arranged. When your alibi collapses, and I'm questioned by the police, I'll reluctantly break down and tell them what I witnessed shortly before my darling Kimmy died. Such a tragedy, sisters falling out. Not my place to say, of course, but I always knew you were insanely jealous of Kimberly, her being Mr. Julian's daughter when you were nothing but a troubled outsider."

"You're very clever," Rose said.

"I can't have Stephen convicted of murdering Kimberly, so the next best is going have to be Rachel. Lily herself can be a witness; she saw us having such a lovely time at tea the other day. She can tell the police how fond Rachel and I always were of each other. So fond that nothing but my civic duty would force me to reveal what I saw that night."

"No one's going to buy that," Bernie said. "You'll never be able to pull it off."

"No? Years of deception and betrayal have taught me to pretend better than any acting school would have. You want me to leave, Rachel? I'm leaving. I won't be back. Until Stephen lets me move in, as I should have so many years ago."

I didn't know what to do next. I'd come here with the intention of confronting Helen with what I'd figured out. Had I expected her to collapse in a puddle of tears and confess all?

Yes, I can be naive sometimes.

Helen had told us what happened, filling in the details I'd missed, but when questioned she'd deny it. Would she be able to convince the police that Rachel killed her sister? She well might. "Why the fire in my garden shed?" I asked, stalling for time until I could come up with an idea of what to do next.

The edges of Helen's mouth turned up. All the sorrow and pain she'd showed when we were talking about her relationship with Julian Smithfield had disappeared, leaving only malice in its place. "Was there a fire? How unfortunate. If I'd wanted to warn you away from interfering in things that are none of your business, I might have set it, just because I could and because you've been annoying me. You're a stubborn little thing, aren't you? I might have to warn you again, if you persist with this nonsense of trying to be some sort of Nancy Drew, girl detective." She gave me a grin that had ice running down my spine. "You and your grandmother. Now, I'll be on my way. It would appear my employment in this house has been terminated. Without cause, I might add. You'll be hearing from my lawyers, Rachel. One way or another."

"Why don't we wait for the police to arrive," Rose said. Her voice was calm, her Yorkshire accent pronounced.

"They can find me if they need to speak to me," Helen said. "I wouldn't willingly go to them to tell them to arrest poor confused Rachel, would I?" She gave us all a grin that put me in mind of the shark tank at the New York Aquarium, where my grandparents had taken Bernie and me many times, and headed for the door.

She kept her eyes on me, clearly thinking I was the mastermind of our little group. That was a mistake. As she passed Rose's chair, Rose calmly shifted her cane and thrust it between Helen's ankles. The housekeeper screeched, lost her balance, toppled forward, and collapsed to the floor.

"Help! Help!" Rose tapped the center of her chest. "I need help in here."

Before I could so much as move, never mind gather my wits around me and do something clever, the front door crashed inward and police officers, led by Detective Amy Redmond, flooded into the room.

Faster than me, Helen rolled over and struggled to her feet. "Thank heavens you're here, Officer, that woman attacked me." She pointed to Rose. "And that one"—indicating me—"falsely accused me of murder. Arrest them both."

Redmond gave a jerk of her head to Officer LeBlanc, who grabbed Helen's arm.

"Did you get all that?" Rose asked.

"Loud and clear," Redmond replied.

"What are you taking about?" I asked. "How did you get here so fast?"

Rose rummaged around inside the front of her shirt and began pulling out wires. "Most uncomfortable, this. You need to come up with something that fits a lady's undergarments better."

"You were wired!" Bernie let out a bark of laughter. "You wily old dog."

Rose grinned at her.

"They tricked me," Helen yelled. "I spun them a ridiculous story because it's what they wanted to hear. There wasn't a word of truth in any of it. Rachel, tell them what this family means to me. What you mean to me. What you've always meant to me."

Tears streamed down Rachel's face. She said nothing.

Chapter 24

"Wired. Of all things."

Rose took a sip of her gin and tonic and grinned at Bernie, her face a picture of mischievous delight. Rose habitually enjoyed one G&T every evening before dinner. Today, she announced, was a two-G&T day, and she intended to start early.

Helen Chambers had been arrested for the murder of Kimberly Smithfield and for the arson at Victoria-on-Sea. Various other charges, she was informed, were pending. Bernie, Rose, and I had been allowed to come home, after being told the police would be in touch with us later to get our statements. Rose insisted Rachel not be allowed to stay alone in her house, and the shocked woman had been bundled out the door and into the back of my car.

Once we'd arrived at Victoria-on-Sea, Rose had taken Rachel into the drawing room and ordered me to prepare a G&T for her and a hefty serving of brandy for Rachel.

"I feel the need for a medicinal shot also." Bernie lifted the back of her hand to her forehead and did everything but collapse onto the fainting couch. "I've become quite light-headed all of a sudden."

I prepared the drinks, served the women, including a suddenly recovered and grinning Bernie, and took my leave.

By the time I finally arrived at Tea by the Sea, Marybeth and Cheryl had run out of most of the sandwiches and desserts and were offering only cream tea. I threw on my hairnet and apron, grabbed equipment and ingredients, and started to bake.

"Your presence is required, love."

"I figured it would be. I saw Redmond's car drive by a few moments ago. I have pastry in the oven. Tell her fifteen minutes."

"She's with Rachel now, and that should allow enough time for everyone else to arrive," Rose said. I put my phone away and checked on my tarts. The little shells were browning perfectly.

"Almost finished here." Simon put a batch of cooled currant scones into freezer containers. "What's next?"

"I've been summoned by the police to give my official statement." I finished the last of the curried egg salad sandwich filling and put it in the fridge.

Simon had burst through the back door of Tea by the Sea not long after I got in, his face creased with worry and concern. "Rose tells me you were in Chatham supervising the arrest of Helen Chambers for the murder. What on earth does that mean?"

"Supervising might not be the right word." I tied my apron behind me.

"Lily, how do you get yourself mixed up in these things?" Cheryl asked.

"Not by wanting to, believe me. We paid a call on Rachel and before I knew what was happening, Helen was telling us how justified she was in killing Kimberly, and Rose recorded it all. Although, I will admit I sort of egged Helen into confessing."

Cheryl shook her head and carried a pot of tea into the dining room.

"Need any help?" Simon asked, to which I'd replied, "Desperately."

Now, as I put my baking ingredients away, Simon washed his hands, and we left the tearoom together shortly after eight.

By the time Simon and I arrived at the house, a good-size gang had gathered in the drawing room of Victoria-on-Sea. Rose had earlier loaned Rachel her car so she could go to the North Augusta police station to be there when Stephen was released, and she'd brought him back here. Bernie had summoned Matt, as an interested party.

"Is this a social occasion?" I asked as we came in.

"You know Rose," Bernie said, "always the hostess."

"Those muffins are for tomorrow's breakfast."

Bernie, who couldn't cook, waved that triviality away. "You can make more."

I grumbled. As well as the muffins, Bernie had laid out tea and coffee, juices, a platter of cheese and crackers, and bowls overflowing with chips and nuts.

"Along with the snacks, I bought some beer and wine earlier," Bernie whispered to me as Simon went over to talk to Matt, "but Rose said this is an official police investigation, so maybe save those until they've left."

"I don't think Chuck Williams ever turns down an offer of a beer."

"You're probably right about that."

"I didn't expect a party." Detective Redmond stood by the windows, feet apart, hands on her hips. The curtains behind her were drawn.

"I'll take any chance I can get to come to a party," Matt said.

"I wasn't expecting to see you here, either, Mr. Goodwill. Or Mr. Badwell, as you're also known. I won't ask you to leave, but I will remind you that you cannot use anything you learn here, not until it's all been through the courts."

"I know the drill, Detective," Matt said. "Bernie, where's that beer?"

"I'll have one if you're offering," Chuck Williams said from the depths of the couch, where he was attempting to balance an enormous handful of chips in one hand and a cup of coffee in the other.

Bernie raised one eyebrow to me in a question.

"Might as well," I said.

Matt and Bernie slipped out. Stephen and Rachel sat close together on the second couch. Her face was white, framed by the long black hair, her eyes tired and drawn, her lips a thin, pale line. "I'll have one, too, thanks," Stephen said. He didn't seem any the worse for wear after a day spent in the police lockup. He drank coffee and munched on cheese and crackers. He gave me a slight smile when I came in, and I nodded in acknowledgment.

Bernie and Matt were soon back with beer and wine and glasses. Redmond shifted impatiently while drinks were offered, accepted, and served. "If . . ." she said at last, "we can get on with it. We don't have all day here."

"Another muffin, Inspector?" Rose said. "Some crisps, perhaps. Bernie, do get the good inspector a top up there."

"Don't mind if I do," he said.

Redmond gave Rose a furious glare. Robbie returned it from the depths of my grandmother's lap. Rose stroked the cat.

"I've always wanted to be able to tick police informant off my bucket list," she said. "At last, I can do so."

I rolled my eyes. There would be no living with her now. "I have one question," I said.

"Only one?" Redmond said.

"For now. Why didn't you ask me to wear the wire? Why involve Rose?"

Redmond sipped her orange juice. "You can't act, Lily. I'm sorry, but you would have broadcast loud and clear to everyone in that room that you were speaking for the record and hoping someone was listening."

"What about me?" Bernie said. "I can act."

Redmond stared at her. "Are you that un-self-aware? Never mind. It was Mrs. Campbell's idea."

"Gleaned from my years of reading murder mysteries," Rose said. "You can call me Rose, love. Sometimes it seems as though we're almost family."

"Perish the thought," Redmond muttered. "People regularly underestimate the mental acuteness of the elderly, usually to their detriment. If someone had to be wired, Rose was the one Helen would least suspect. Rose called me early this morning to say Lily and Bernie were up to something. She suspected that something had to do with going to Chatham and attempting to question the guilty party."

"You knew I hadn't done it." Stephen lifted his beer bottle in a toast. "Thanks."

Rose's look in return was frosty. "Your involvement, young man, is a matter still up for discussion."

Rachel put a protective hand on her brother's arm.

"As she intended to go along with Lily and Bernie," Redmond continued, "Rose asked if I wanted to listen in. I said I'd not only listen in, but I'd be close at hand in case assistance was needed. Which turned out to be the case. I have to point out, Lily, once again you've disregarded my orders and once again you've been lucky it worked out okay."

I said nothing. She was right.

"Has Helen been formally charged?" Matt asked.

"Yes," Redmond said.

"I had no idea," Rachel said. "All these years, Helen's been in our house, hating us."

"Helen didn't hate us," Stephen said. "She wanted a fair shake, that's all. Dad did promise her—"

"Don't say any more," Rachel warned.

"Is that what she told you?" Redmond asked him.

"It's okay, Rach," Stephen said to his sister. "Yeah, Detective. She told me Dad had intended her to inherit big-time from him, but Mom convinced him people would gossip. You can't favor a servant over your wife and children without a lot of talk."

"You were close to her? She confided in you?"

He drank his beer. "Sometimes, yeah. I didn't . . . have anyone else when I was a kid. My dad had no time for me. My mom was . . . distant. Rachel was in college and then she moved to New York, and Kimmy . . . well, Kimmy never worried about anything other than Kimmy."

"Tell us what happened concerning the third will," Redmond said.

"Pretty much what Lily figured out. Helen called me in LA not long before Mom died. She said Mom had suddenly decided to write a new will, realizing she'd been unfair to Rachel. Helen said she'd try to get Mom to recognize that I was doing okay now and I could be trusted with a full share of the estate. She said if she did that, it would be nice if I'd help her out. She didn't have much saved for her old age, after working for my family for so many years. I said, yeah sure." He shrugged. "I was happy to help Helen get something. I thought maybe a few thou. I had no intention of giving her half of my share of the whole shebang. Then Mom died, and the third will couldn't be found. Everyone was in a fit about that. Helen and Rachel trying to find it. Kimmy wanting to find it so she could get rid of it. I wasn't getting paid, as I was on a leave of absence from my job, and I needed some cash. So I sold some of Mom's things to the antique dealer for a few bucks."

"You shouldn't have done that," Rachel said.

"So you told me. More than once. I asked you for a loan, remember. You said you'd transfer me something, but you didn't. What else could I do?"

"I forgot, that's all. I had a lot on my mind. You could have reminded me."

"I know what my family thinks of me and money, Rach." He drank more beer. "Why bother?"

Simon caught my eye. He gave his head a small shake. Stephen wasn't making himself look good here. Bernie, Rose, and Matt were keeping quiet, letting the drama play out.

"When did you become aware that Helen Chambers had killed your sister?" Redmond asked in the same tone she might have used to ask if he wanted another beer.

"Don't answer that!" Rachel snapped.

Stephen paid her no attention. "I didn't know. I figured Kimmy's husband killed her. He married her awfully fast when he found out what our mom had left her. In the second will, anyway, and as far as he was concerned the third will was gone for good."

"You didn't report that speculation to the police when we questioned you about your sister's death."

"I'm not a rat," Stephen said. "What you do is your business."

"It doesn't work that way," Williams said.

Stephen shrugged, not much interested in how it worked. Rachel still had her hand on his arm, but her face was pinched in disapproval. She loved her brother. She carried a load of guilt about the way he'd turned out, but I doubted she liked him very much.

Amy Redmond watched Stephen carefully. She was trying to find a way of charging him with accessory after the fact. I had my doubts that she'd be successful. Helen Chambers had been like a mother to Stephen Smithfield, and he believed she was acting in his interests. He might have suspected she'd had something to do with Kimberly's death, but if so, he'd buried that suspicion very deep indeed.

"What's Helen saying?" Rose asked.

"She claims she came here that night to talk to Kimberly, and she saw Rachel arguing with her sister, so she left not wanting to come between them."

"That's not true!" Rachel said.

"I know. We've had another chat with the man you were talking to in that bar when Kimberly died. He's emphatic he was with you at the time in question. He later received a phone call from a woman who didn't give her name, but who suggested he might have been incorrect about the time. As an inducement to reconsider, a sizable sum of money was mentioned."

Rachel nodded. "I'm glad he was honest."

"Honest?" Redmond said. "Not at all. He agreed to take the money, and he made an appointment to see me at my office this afternoon. When he came in, in light of what Helen told you and Rose recorded, I asked him if he wanted to change his story. He rapidly reconsidered."

"She really was prepared to see me go to jail?" Rachel said.

"Oh, yes. Helen told me quite plainly that she doesn't believe you should be entitled to any portion of the family's estate. Julian Smithfield was not your father."

"Lucky me," Rachel said.

"Helen's not admitting anything," Williams said. "But we'll get her. She stopped at a gas station in Chatham Thursday night at around nine o'clock. She bought gas with her credit card. Big mistake that. On the gas station cameras she's recognizable and seen to be filling up her car. And after topping up her car, she filled a portable gas container."

"My shed!" Simon said.

"We found the empty container in the trunk of her car," Redmond said. "She tried to tell us the gas was for the lawnmower, but the gardener said he didn't need any, and Helen had never bought gas for him in any event. She lives in an apartment building, so she doesn't have a lawn that needs mowing."

"We'll get her for the arson," Williams said. "And it'll all flow from that. Any more beer there, young fellow?"

Matt passed him one.

"Any questions?" Redmond said. I opened my mouth, but she said, "No? Then we'll be on our way. Detective Williams?"

"What?"

"We're finished here. Let's go."

"Oh. Okay." He took a long slug of his beer and then reluctantly put the bottle down. He lumbered to his feet and grabbed a fistful of chips as he passed the coffee table.

Redmond stopped in front of Rachel and Stephen. She looked down at them. "We'll be in touch. If you think of anything further we might want to know, no matter how insignificant it seems to you, don't wait for us to contact you."

Rachel stood up. "I understand. I'll be staying at the house in Chatham for a while longer. My brother and I have a lot to talk about and some important decisions to make."

Headlights washed the drapes of the drawing room. I heard a car door slam and a moment later the front door opening and a man calling, "Hey! Anyone here?"

Wesley Schumann had returned.

Simon stuck his head into the hallway. "We're in here. What do you want?"

"Nothing to do with you, buddy." Wesley pushed his way into the drawing room. "I figured you'd be here," he said to Amy Redmond. "I went to the police station and they told me you were out. What's happening? I heard Helen Chambers has been arrested for killing Kimmy? Is it true?"

"It is," Redmond said.

"Can't say I'm surprised. I could tell the moment I met her she was a thoroughly unpleasant woman. Always watching. Always listening. Could barely manage to keep herself civil to Kimberly, who was, after all, her employer."

"You didn't think to inform the authorities of your impression?"

He shifted uncomfortably. "Well, I mean, it was nothing but my opinion, right? Don't you call that hearsay? Inadmissible?"

"Hearsay is inadmissible in a court of law," Williams said. "But it can give the police a new avenue of investigation to pursue. Meaning, pal, yeah, you had a responsibility to tell us about the relationships between these people. All of them."

I didn't have a lot of respect for Detective Williams, but the way he stared down the arrogant, full-of-himself Wesley Schumann changed my mind. Wesley dipped his head and muttered something that might have been, "Sorry."

But Williams wasn't finished. "You were specifically asked if you knew of anyone who had conflicts with your wife. You said no. Your words were 'everyone loved Kimmy.' "

"That's right," Redmond said. "As I recall, you added that the only person who might have wanted to harm Kimberly was Lily Roberts in a fit of jealously because you had married Kimberly, and not her. Don't leave town without letting us know where we can locate you, in case we need to pursue the matter further."

Wesley sputtered.

"Thank you for your time, Mrs. Campbell," Redmond said. "Everyone. We'll be in touch. Ms. Morrison, Mr. Smithfield, are you staying in town tonight?"

"No," Rachel said. "I'll call us a taxi to take my brother and me . . . home."

"Good night, then."

The police left.

Bernie got to her feet. "Don't let us keep you, Wessie. I'm sure you have places to go. Important people to see."

He looked at me. "Lily?"

I took a deep breath. "What Bernie said."

Simon put his beer on the table and took a step forward. Matt watched warily. Robert the Bruce leapt off Rose's lap and hissed at the new arrival.

"Okay. I get the picture. Rachel, why don't I give you and Stephen here a lift back to Chatham. We have business to discuss, might as well get to it now rather than later."

"Business?" Rachel fluttered her eyelashes. "Oh, dear, Wesley. Don't tell me you didn't hear that my mother's new will has been found." She looked at her brother. "How much did Mom leave Kimberly?"

"Two hundred thousand. Not even in a lump sum but in a trust fund," Stephen said.

Wesley turned all the colors of a sunset. His shoulders stiffened, his hands turned into clenched fists. A vein pulsed in his forehead. Simon and Matt tensed themselves. Robert the Bruce arched his back, and Bernie casually picked up an iron candlestick. Rose sipped her G&T and watched.

Wesley let out a long breath. "We'll see about that. Lily, I'm sorry you think I turned on you. It's just . . . can we talk in private?"

"No."

"Why don't I show you out, mate," Simon said.

"I'll go with you," Bernie added. "In case you get lost on the way to your car."

Wesley gave me one last long look. *What on earth*, I thought, *had I ever seen in him?*

He turned on his heels and left. Simon and Bernie followed him, and a few moments later we heard a car start up and peel down the driveway with the roar of the powerful engine.

"I hope no one's returning from dinner at the moment," Rose said. "The way that young man is driving, there might be a dreadful collision."

Chapter 25

The "party" broke up once Wesley had gone. Matt called a taxi for Rachel and Stephen, and she said they'd walk to the end of the driveway to wait for it. Bernie said she was absolutely bushed, all that bringing down criminals stuff could be tiring, and Matt said what was her rush, how about coming to his place for a nightcap. To which she agreed.

Rose declared that she'd prepare the breakfast instructions for tomorrow and then turn in. When she stood up, Robbie headed straight out the door.

Simon and I were left in the drawing room. We smiled at each other. I lifted the bottle of wine out of the cooler and checked the contents. No one had had any. "I could use a drink," I said. "How about you?"

He took the cooler out of my hands. "Sounds like a plan. Some of those crisps would be good, too." I picked up the bowl.

Rose was sitting at the reception desk, checking the notes in the registration book. The house was quiet.

"Okay if I head home?" I asked her.

"Certainly, love. I'm going to my room to watch some

telly for a while. I want to get caught up on the new season of *Death in Paradise*. See you in the morning. Oh, dear."

"Is something wrong?"

"A guest checked in earlier who is gluten-free, dairy-free, and nightshade-free."

Simon laughed. "What do they eat? Sawdust?"

"I'll come up with something for them," I said.

"You always do, love." Rose gave me a fond smile, and then she turned that smile on Simon and winked.

Simon and I took a detour through the rose garden. I carried the bowl of chips, and he had the ice bucket. The scent of the flowers on the still night air was intoxicating.

He cleared his throat. "Never a dull moment around here."

"To my occasional regret."

He stopped walking and turned to face me. I looked into his ocean-blue eyes. A lock of sandy hair flopped over his forehead. "Lily," he said.

I said nothing. I breathed.

Simon leaned over and put the wine on the ground. Then he took the bowl out of my hands and threw it to one side. As potato chips flew around us he gathered me into his arms, and once again he said, "Lily."

My heart leapt.

Gluten-Free Pancakes

Feeding people at a busy B & B means Lily has to be aware of dietary requirements. She's found that this recipe for gluten-free pancakes is quick and easy, and her guests enjoy them. She serves the pancakes with maple syrup and butter.

Makes about eight pancakes.

Put the following into a blender:

1 banana
2 eggs
2 tsp baking powder
2 cups oats
½ cup milk
1 tsp vanilla
Handful of chocolate chips (optional)

Blend until combined.

Pour individual servings into the center of a hot frying pan or griddle. (Melt about 1 tsp of butter in the pan first.) When the surface is covered with bubbles, flip and cook the second side one to two minutes until golden.

Blueberry Muffins

These muffins are a very popular item for the B & B breakfasts. Lily often makes an extra batch to freeze for emergencies. She always uses fresh (not frozen) blueberries. Tossing the blueberries with flour before adding to the batter helps the berries not sink to the bottom when baking.

Ingredients:
2 cups all-purpose flour
1½ tsp baking powder
½ tsp salt
2 cups fresh blueberries
½ cup unsalted butter, room temperature
1 cup sugar
2 large eggs
2 tsp pure vanilla extract
½ cup milk

For topping:
¼ cup sugar
¼ teaspoon nutmeg

Directions:

1. Preheat oven to 375 degrees. Prepare standard twelve-cup muffin pan.
2. In a medium bowl, whisk together flour, baking powder, and salt. Toss blueberries in a sieve with about 1½ teaspoons flour mixture to lightly coat.
3. Beat butter and 1 cup sugar on medium-high speed until light and fluffy, about three minutes. Add eggs, one at a time, beating until combined. Mix in vanilla.

4. At low speed, add flour mixture, beating until just combined, and then add milk, beating until just combined. Do not overmix. Fold in the blueberries. Divide batter evenly among the prepared muffin cups.

5. For topping, mix together ¼ cup sugar and nutmeg. Sprinkle sugar mixture on top of muffin batter.

6. Bake about thirty minutes.

Lemon Squares

These lemon squares are a popular addition to the sweets course of afternoon tea.

Makes about thirty squares.

Base:
2 cups butter, room temperature
½ cup confectioner's sugar
2 cups all-purpose flour
½ tsp salt

Topping:
4 eggs
2 cups granulated sugar
⅓ cup all-purpose flour
2 Tbsp grated lemon zest
1 Tbsp grated lime zest
3 Tbsp lemon juice
3 Tbsp lime juice
Icing sugar for dusting

1. Preheat oven to 350 degrees.
2. Mix together butter, confectioner's sugar, flour, and salt until well blended. The mixture will look like fine breadcrumbs.
3. Pat into a 9 × 13-inch greased pan. Prick surface with a fork. Bake for twenty minutes, until the pastry is golden.
4. Beat together eggs, granulated sugar, flour, zests, and juices. Pour the mixture over the cooked base.
5. Bake for fifteen to twenty minutes until set.
6. Cut into squares and liberally dust with icing sugar.

Read on for a special preview of the next Tea by the Sea mystery from nationally bestselling author Vicki Delany . . .

TROUBLE IS BREWING

At her Cape Cod tearoom, Tea by the Sea, Lily Roberts is feeling the strain, thanks to the Great Teacup Shortage—and a family fracas turned deadly . . .

Afternoon tea isn't just about flavorful brews and delicious treats. It's also about presentation—fine china teacups (never mugs!), with carefully coordinated saucers and plates. With her fragile stock running low, Lily visits an antiques fair where she snaps up a charming Peter Rabbit–themed tea set in a wicker basket, perfect for children's events. But a few days later, a woman named Kimberly marches into the tearoom, rudely demanding to buy it back—then later returns and removes an envelope hidden in the basket's lining.

An acquaintance of Lily's named Rachel is on the trail of the tea set too. Apparently, she and Kimberly are half-sisters, searching for their mother's final will. But it's more than a storm in a teacup when one of the sisters is found dead on the grounds of the B&B owned by Lily's grandmother, Rose. Is this a simple case of greed boiling over, or are there other suspects in the blend? It'll take some savvy sleuthing from Lily, Rose, and their allies to find the answers before a killer shatters more lives . . .

Chapter 1

I love my job. Like any job, like life, it has its ups and downs. It has its difficulties and problems, crises and disasters. Some days, I've been overwhelmed and wanted nothing more than to throw in the dish towel and walk away from Tea by the Sea, my tearoom.

But I never do. I take a deep breath, center myself, and ask what I should bake next.

Then there are days like this when everything comes smoothly together, and I do what I do best: make people happy.

And that makes me happy.

"When I get married, if ever I do," Bernadette Murphy said to me as she dumped a trayload of used dishes onto the counter next to the dishwasher, "you're going to cater it, Lily, and I'm going to have the reception here."

"You're going to have your wedding in my kitchen?" I grinned and looked around the small space. The Tea by the Sea kitchen is crowded when I'm the only one in it.

Today I was not the only one in it: as well as my two regular assistants, the mother-daughter duo of Cheryl and Marybeth, my friend Bernie had pitched in to help.

Bernie didn't bother to reply.

"I hope," I said, "I'll be outside at your wedding, drinking tea and nibbling on scones, wearing a gorgeous dress and a fabulous hat, making polite conversation with interesting people, not stuck in here, working." I leaned back against the butcher block in the center of the room, rotating my shoulders to give them a long, luxurious, welcome stretch.

"I might let you have a few minutes off," Bernie said, "as long as you don't take advantage."

"Anything in particular making you think of your own wedding, Bernie?" Marybeth reached around my friend to get at the row of tea canisters on a top shelf, and Bernie ducked.

"Don't we all think of weddings when we see other people being happy at theirs?" she said.

"I don't," Marybeth said. "I think, sometimes, I might have been too hasty rushing to the altar, never mind having the kids so soon."

"Marybeth—" I said.

"Ooops." She let out a choked laugh. "Did I say that out loud? Don't let my mom hear; she'll launch into a round of I told you so's."

"Don't let me hear what, and why am I going to say, 'I told you so'?" Cheryl asked. She also carried a tray piled high with used dishes and empty teapots.

"Nothing!" Marybeth said.

"While you're getting the tea, honey, can I have another pot of Darjeeling, please."

"What's happening out there?" I asked. "Are they almost finished?"

"They are. The food's mostly gone, for now. Several tables have asked for another round of tea and some want top-ups of the wine. The bride's about to open her gifts, and her mother sent me in to ask if you'd be so kind as to come out so she can thank you."

"Me?"

"Yes, you, Lily. Simon's already taken his bows as the provider of the floral arrangements, and he's showing some of the guests around the gardens."

"What about me?" Bernie said, "Do they want to thank me for putting the scones and sandwiches on the stands in such an organized fashion?"

"No," Cheryl said.

I untied my apron, pulled off my hairnet, and adjusted my ponytail. I never tire of being thanked. It doesn't happen often enough in the restaurant business.

My name is Lily Roberts, and I am the proud owner and head baker of Tea by the Sea, a traditional afternoon tearoom located in the Outer Cape region of Cape Cod. I'm a culinary school-trained pastry chef, and I worked for many years in some of the best bakeries and restaurants in Manhattan before taking a deep breath and making the plunge to open my own place. This is our first summer and so far the venture has been a roaring success. My restaurant serves afternoon tea only, and I have some worries if that's going to be enough to see us through the long winter when the gardens are bare and the tourists scarce. But I can adjust on the fly, and I'll make additions to the menu, or even branch out into catering, if I have to.

Never mind that: today was all about enjoying the day and helping a young bride enjoy hers. Tea by the Sea had been taken over for a wedding shower. Twenty women were gathered on the patio to enjoy the best of my offerings and to celebrate love. In case of rain, the group booked the interior of the restaurant as well. Fortunately, that indoor refuge proved to be unnecessary.

They'd paid handsomely for the privilege of taking over

my place, and I'd gone all out with the food and the table settings. Our gardener, Simon, spared no effort in assembling individual floral arrangements for the tables and ensuring the plants on the pots scattered around the low stone walls and the flagstone paths were in their best shape.

Cheryl and I left the kitchen, followed by Bernie and Marybeth. The main room of the restaurant was empty, lights turned low, tables laid for tomorrow.

"Was it the bride's mother who asked for me," I said to Cheryl, "or the groom's?"

"I don't know. I didn't catch any names. Early sixties, silver pantsuit, tons of jewelry?"

"Sounds like Mrs. Reynolds. She's the groom's mother. She's the one who paid for it all. The bride's mother was part of the Zoom call when we made the arrangements, but she didn't have much input." In fact, she had pretty much no input at all. Every time she hesitantly tried to get a word in edgewise, Mrs. Reynolds laughed lightly and carried on talking.

"The guests are a mismatched lot," Marybeth whispered behind me.

I knew what she meant. I'd been outside when the mothers arrived, wanting to greet them and ensure everything was in order. Sophia Reynolds, mother of the groom, pretty much screamed money, with her Boston Brahman accent, slightest hint of Chanel No. 5, silver designer suit sized in the low single digits, rows of pearls, Jimmy Choo stilettos, perfectly cut and dyed blond hair, equally perfect makeup and manicure. Whereas Jenny Hill, mother of the bride, wore a perfectly nice off-the-rack pink dress with a black belt cinched too tightly around her ample middle, pantyhose that bunched around her ankles, and solid black flats with laces. She, or someone else, had made an attempt with her makeup, but her eyebrows were overgrown, her lips cracked and dry. Her brittle brown hair, streaked with gray, was pulled behind her head and fastened into a tortoiseshell clip.

The smile Jenny gave me was warm and genuine, whereas Sophia Reynolds peered down her long nose at me and the edges of her lips turned up, ever so slightly.

"Thank you so much, Lily." Jenny twisted her hands in front of her. "Everything's been marvelous and Hannah is thrilled."

"It's all been perfectly satisfactory," Sophia said. "Dear Jenny wasn't sure about having a tea for this precious day, but I told her it would be absolutely perfect. Didn't I, dear?"

Jenny let out a slightly embarrassed giggle. "And you were right, Sophia. As you usually are. I've never had high tea before, and I didn't know what to expect."

"Afternoon tea, dear," Sophia said. "Not high tea. I told you, they're totally different, isn't that so, Lily?"

Jenny flushed. Behind me, I heard Bernie, never one to fail to express her opinion, mutter, "How kind of you to point that out."

I spoke quickly. "My customers use the words interchangeably as do many Americans these days. Although, yes, afternoon tea is the correct term."

Sophia waved her left hand. The diamond caught the sunlight. If the international space station had been passing at that moment, the astronauts might have seen the resulting beam.

"People are *soooo* uncultured here in the colonies." Bernie stepped forward. "Bernadette Murphy. Of the Lower East Side Murphies. So pleased to meet you." She shoved out her right hand. "I don't actually work here. I'm a novelist by profession, but I offer Lily a hand now and again when she needs it."

Sophia blinked and cautiously accepted Bernie's hand.

Bernie shook it as though she were trying to get a ball out of a dog's mouth.

I stifled a groan. Bernie was not only not from the Lower East Side, she wasn't a novelist. Not yet anyway, having not completed her first book. But Bernie, always one to make instant judgments, had instantly decided she didn't like Sophia Reynolds.

I didn't like her much either, but she was paying me a lot to entertain her guests, and after years spent in the restaurant business I know being nice to the customers is part of the price.

Bernie, before taking time off to write her book, had been a forensic accountant at a major Manhattan criminal law firm. Being nice to the clients had never been in her job description.

"That lady's waving her glass at us, Bernie," I said, indicating a woman in her early eighties, overdressed, overhatted, and overjeweled. "Why don't you get her a refill?" Marybeth and Cheryl were busy refreshing teacups and clearing tables.

"Okay," Bernie sauntered off.

I turned to the mothers and caught the tightness in Sophia's lips and the shadow behind her eyes. She blinked and focused on me again. "That lady is Mrs. Regina Reynolds. My mother-in-law. She does enjoy a tipple in the afternoon now and again."

Jenny raised her eyebrows at me but said nothing.

It was a spectacular Cape Cod summer's day, warm but not too hot, a handful of fluffy white clouds slowly crossing the brilliant blue sky. All the tables on the patio were taken and the air was full of the scent of baking, salt from the sea, and the lush English-style country garden beyond the low stone wall. Mismatched and cracked teacups hanging from the branches of the massive oak tree in the center of the patio tinkled cheerily in the soft breeze coming off Cape Cod Bay. Women cradled their fine china teacups or flutes of sparkling wine, leaned back in their chairs and chatted. A few of the guests had gone for a stroll in the gardens or down to the bluffs to admire the view over the bay. The first round of food, scones with butter, jam, and clotted cream and delicate tea sandwiches had been consumed. In contrast to the usual way of presenting afternoon tea, I'd been asked to bring the desserts out later, after the bride opened her presents. As well as an assortment of teas, we served guests Prosecco. Bottles of excellent Champagne were cooling in the fridge, to accompany the sweets course and to toast the happy couple.

At Sophia's request, we'd dragged a wing-back chair out of my grandmother's drawing room to serve as the bride's throne, and Bernie and Marybeth had draped the chair with yards of shimmering white-and-gold cloth. Jenny had brought an enormous bunch of cheerful balloons in primary colors and tied it to the back of the chair. The table beside the chair was buried in gaily wrapped presents.

The tea guests were all women. The groom and some other men would join us later for desserts and Champagne toasts. They wouldn't have far to travel. The groom's family and his best man were staying at Victoria-on-Sea, my grandmother's B&B. Tea by the Sea sits at the end of the long B&B driveway, close to the road.

"I don't believe you've met my daughter," Jenny said to me. "Our guest of honor. Hannah!"

I didn't need to have the bride pointed out to me. As she walked from table to table, chatting to her guests, exchanging some air kisses and some genuine hugs, she simply glowed. So much so I thought she might also be able to be seen from space. Hannah Hill wasn't a beautiful woman, but she was lovely, in the way all young, healthy, happy women are. She was on the short side, as was her mother, at about five foot four; not overweight and not too thin.

Her hair was almost jet black and fell in gentle waves to the center of her back. Most of the hair was held back by two pins glistening in the sunlight, but a few soft tendrils framed her lightly tanned face. She heard her mother's call and turned to us with a sparkle in her warm dark eyes.

Jenny's own eyes glowed with adoration as she watched her daughter cross the patio toward us. I glanced at Sophia and saw something very different there. Her face was tight and her jaw set. Her eyes narrowed with what might have been anger.

Then the young woman reached us, and Sophia wrapped an arm around her shoulders. "My son's bride, Hannah. I suggested the ladies dress formally for afternoon tea, but dear Hannah always prefers to go her own way, don't you, my darling."

"It's a summer afternoon in Cape Cod, Sophia," Hannah said with a smile as she shrugged the arm off. "I don't have a suitable tea dress."

In my opinion, Hannah was dressed perfectly for the day in a simple yellow sundress with a thin black belt and low-heeled black sandals. Gold studs were in her ears, a plain gold chain around her neck. The diamond in the ring on the third finger of her left hand was small and discreet, but the ring was beautifully designed.

"My congratulations," I said. "I'm Lily, the cook here, and I hope you enjoyed everything."

"It truly was marvelous, thank you. You couldn't possibly have arranged a better day, weather-wise. Can you make sure we have the same on Saturday?"

"Lily's a miracle worker," Bernie said. "But even she can't do everything. Congratulations."

"Thank you," Hannah said.

"I'll try my best," I said. "But I suspect you don't need any luck from me. You're having your reception at the yacht club, I hear. It's a beautiful setting, and they know how to accommodate whatever weather comes their way."

"It is lovely there. I'd never even been to Cape Cod until I met Greg. His family loves it so much, Sophia persuaded us to have our wedding here."

"My family had a vacation home not far from Provincetown for many years," Sophia said. "A long time ago. To my intense disappointment, my parents sold the property shortly before my own marriage. They said they didn't get enough use of it. Ralph and I have often discussed buying a similar place for our family. But the time never seemed right. I don't suppose it will ever come. Not now that the children are grown and with the constant pressure of the family business. You know how it is."

"I so do," Bernie said. "My own real estate ambitions are being held back until I can get that leaky roof fixed."

Sophia threw Bernie a look, suspecting she was being insulted. Which she was.

Another young woman joined us. She was about the same age as Hannah, with the same gym-toned body and flawless skin of Sophia. She'd dressed for afternoon tea in a calf-length beige dress with three-quarter-length sleeves trimmed with white lace. A fascinator in the same shade as her dress, topped with three blue feathers, was arranged in her sleek golden hair. She was the same height as Hannah and her mother, but today she towered over them in her four-inch heels. "Are we ever going to get this show on the road, Mom? Jack keeps texting me to ask if I'm finished yet."

"Well pardon me if Jack's getting inpatient," Hannah snapped. "I told you you could invite him to join us when Greg and the rest do."

"Well, pardon me if Jack doesn't want to hang around with this lot any more than necessary." Her tone and accent were exactly the same as Sophia's, and it was obvious they were closely related. "Tea and gardens aren't exactly his thing."

Hannah raised her eyebrows at her own mother and Jenny shrugged.

"Not exactly mine either," the newcomer muttered.

Sophia clapped her hands lightly. "As rudely as McKenzie might have put it, it is time we got on with the party. I told Greg and his father to be here at five, and we never want to keep the gentlemen waiting, now do we?"

"Good heavens no," Bernie exclaimed. "That would never do."

I threw her a furious glare. Bernie mouthed, *sorry*.

Sophia issued instructions. "Jenny, dear, you may escort Hannah to the bride's chair. McKenzie and the other bridesmaid, whatever is her name again? Never mind, they can hand Hannah her presents and clear up the wrapping and other trash. Do remember to keep the cards with the gifts. Hannah will have to send thank-you notes and she needs to keep them straight." Without waiting for anyone to reply, she clapped her hands, loudly this time. "Ladies, ladies. Your attention please. Darling Hannah, our blushing bride, would like to open her gifts now."

"Alice isn't here!" Sophia's mother-in-law yelled.

"That is not my problem, is it?" Sophia muttered under her breath.

"Bernie," I said. "Would you go and round up the guests who're visiting the gardens, please. I noticed a few heading to the back of the house to see the view."

Bernie had donned a knee-length black skirt and plain white blouse as her waitress uniform. She picked up the hems of her skirt in both hands and gave me a little curtsey. "Yes, m'lady."

"Might I have read anything your friend has written?"

Sophia said as Bernie scurried away on her errand, and Hannah, Jenny, and a scowling McKenzie headed for the bride's chair. "I'm on the library board of our town, where my husband's family has always been generous patrons."

"Bernadette Murphy," I said. "Remember the name. You will be hearing it someday." *If she ever gets the blasted book finished.*

"I hope she's not writing any of that genre stuff. I mean fantasy and murder mysteries and the like. So common." Sophia sniffed and followed her future daughter-in-law.

BOOK
CLUB
BETWEEN THE CHAPTERS